Donald F. Averill

THE KIDNAPPING OF
MEGAN ISAACS

INK START MEDIA
5710 W Gate City Blvd Ste K #284
Greensboro, NC 27407

PROLOGUE

"Hey, Drum! Hows yer feet?"

"Damn near froze, William. We gotta get out of this weather. Snows damn near three foot deep in the open."

"Winds pickin' up some, too, William."

"Yeah, I can feel it, Barney. We'll stop in that clump of trees yonder an shelter thar. I'm not seein' too good in this cussed blindin' snow."

"This here's shit, William, We shoulda stayed at Polaris 'nuther week. Had shelter an vittles."

William yelled back from the lead position, "Had no sign of storm like this, Edward. We gotta ride it out under them trees. My feet gettin' wet—not good!"

Drum said, "Years ahead I'm gonna recollect this blizzard of eighteen and seventy-four. Hope I can keep my toes."

William yelled puffs of vapor into the wind, "Come on, boys! Twenty more yards to them trees." The snow beneath the branches in the cluster of trees was less than a foot in depth, and William Flade and Flint Drum began clearing an area for a tarp to be spread out. All four men dropped their packs between two closely growing trees to form a wall against the wind.

Drum yelled out, "Gather firewood! We're gonna freeze without some heat."

Virgil Naff and Barney Wigner trudged through the foot-deep snow to the western edge of trees, gathering fallen branches and pine needles. Barney turned back toward William and Drum, and had taken only three steps before Virgil yelled out, "Will ya look at that! Come here, Barney!"

Barney dropped his load of firewood and joined Virgil, "What?"

Virgil pointed, "Am I seein' things? Ain't that a cabin?"

"Damn, if it ain't. I'll get the others. Go see if anybody's home."

The cabin was deserted and the four men moved in, boarded up an open window, and had a fire blazing away after a half-hour of labor. Drum made coffee on a potbellied stove.

"Who belongs to this cabin?" said Drum.

"Them letters above the door—J-W," Virgil observed. "S'pose he's dead?"

William said, "No doubt, if he's outside."

Virgil commented as he looked around the cabin's interior, "Covered with dust. No one been here in long time—place been deserted, J-W ain't comin' back—I can damn guarantee it."

The four men sat out the storm for another twenty-four hours before the sun came out and the snow began to melt. A chinook wind disposed of the majority of the snow and the miners/trappers decided to stay for the summer and in the fall would consider moving on. In the meantime, the men built cabins, declaring the J-W cabin to be used for business purposes only.

Business was conducted on the first day of the month and during the third meeting, William said, "We've got the start of a town here. What should we call it?" No one had a name to offer, so he said, "Think on it, an we'll talk again next month. In the meantime, I think we should send back east for some womenfolk. We need ourselves some wives."

Barney stated, "They won't know where to come, William. We got to have a name. We can pick um up in Polaris and bring um here."

"I got a name. What about Sudden?"

"That's not a name, Drum. That's how we found this cabin—all of a sudden," said Virgil.

William offered, "What do ya think about Suddenly?"

Drum laughed, "I suddenly think that's a good name—Suddenly is the name of our little town."

All four men agreed on the name, and the next day, Virgil headed east to find four wives.

CHAPTER 1

Julie Drum was the only ranger responsible for the forested area within a twenty mile radius of her small town, Suddenly, Montana, in the Bitterroot Range where her husband, Tom, had died in a forest fire four years previously in 2014; not directly from the flames of a fire, but from falling timber from exploding trees during the conflagration. She had been left with raising two boys, eight year old Danny, and twelve year old David. She had not expected the task was going to strain her mental and physical abilities to any great degree, so she had accepted the ranger job without reservations. The choices for employment for a young widow were limited in the little mountain town and she didn't want to pull up roots and start a new career somewhere else foreign to her family. Her boys had been under enough strain in the last four years.

The 2018 spring weather was finally making an appearance in the far western Montana area. Winter always seemed to hang on forever in the Bitterroot Forest and only begrudgingly surrendered to a few days of warm sunny weather nudging the fifty degree mark. Cooler temperatures, back down to the high thirties and low forties, would undoubtedly return in a few days, but the reappearance of the chill should last no longer than a couple weeks, maybe three at the most, before spring would burst forth with the appearance of early wildflowers, song birds, and a week of school vacation.

The mountains had forever influenced the arrival of spring, warm days only began to reveal themselves for an extended period during the first week of June and lasted until September. Then the first hints of fall would be signaled with changing leaf colors and cool evening temperatures.

According to the most recent census, the meadow containing of the original miners' cabins and corrals had expanded from a village into a town of 1,847 residents. Tourism, camping, and hunting were the chief activities of the nearly isolated community. There was only one paved road into the area, but several dirt and partially graveled roads were scattered through the surrounding forests most leading to fire observation towers.

Sixteen year old David Mitchel Drum, and his twelve year old brother, Danny Mills, retrieved the Christmas present, a drone kit, from the younger boy's closet, and were going to assemble the four-motor flying camera. It was spring break—warm enough to go outside with only a sweater and maybe a light jacket. The first warm Saturday without precipitation had greeted the mountain community after six months of unfriendly weather. Danny was carrying the box, about the size of three shoe boxes, and David, carrying a handful of small tools, led the way to the backyard deck.

"Hi, David!"

David had just placed the hand tools on the backyard picnic table and was startled by the feminine voice. Megan's salutation was recognized immediately as from the next-door neighbor, but she hadn't spoken directly to him in months. She was going steady with the captain of the football team, Rick Hadley, a senior who thought he was God's gift to all the girls in Forest Hills High. The other high school boys knew better than to mess with Rick's girl. She suffered shunning by the boys and the girls, formerly even some of her closest friends, gossiped incessantly. Megan had learned to accept the quarantine from the boys and the envy of the girls. She had been chosen to be the girl of the most popular and handsomest boy in the school. She had given little thought to what would happen when Rick went off to college.

David turned slowly toward the voice and focused on his pretty brunette neighbor. Megan's birthday was only a week later in February than David's. They had passed the driver's

test a day apart. Megan had been first and she teased David about the fact that she was the more experienced driver.

"Hi, Meg. Where's Rick? Is he sick?" David rhymed Rick with everything he could think of at every opportunity. David and Megan had always carried on a battle of words, ever since they were old enough to talk. Their word sparring was accepted as good natured fun by their parents and it rarely resulted in any bad feelings, and those lasted only a day or two.

"Funny, David. No, he's not sick. He's working with his father today. I need a ride."

"Sorry, Mom's got the truck. No wheels."

"We can borrow Dad's jeep, but I can't drive a stick shift. Would you please take me down to the drug store? I need to pick up my allergy medicine. I'm completely out."

"Ah—I don't think so. You know, you should have gotten your pills yesterday. I don't want to get the crap beat out of me because I drove you around town. Little Ricky wouldn't like me in a car with you. What would people think?"

Megan stood there mulling things over, grimaced, turned, and started back towards her house. After taking about five steps she spun around, ran to the fence, and said, "What if we take your brother with us?"

"You'd better ask him if he wants to go, Megan. I can't make him come along with us."

Megan motioned to Danny to come over to the fence. Danny put the lid back on the drone box and joined Megan and David.

"Will you please go with David and me in my father's jeep so I can get my allergy meds?"

Danny smiled, knowing he had Megan at a disadvantage. "What are you gunna do for me?"

"Could you just do me a favor, Danny? I'll be eternally grateful." Megan gestured toward Danny but he stood far enough away so she couldn't reach him. Danny knew what happened to a guy if Megan got her hot little hands on him. He would melt. All his friends fantasized about going on a date with Megan, but he kept his thoughts to himself, Megan was his next door neighbor. He had known her his entire life—mostly as his sitter. She was more like a sister than a sex object. But...

"I'll go with you if you give me something." Danny felt a surge of power.

Megan's eyebrows rose in expectation, "What do you want?"

"You have to kiss me on the lips—a real kiss, not just a little peck."

Megan's eyes searched over the backyard as she considered Danny's demand. She looked at David, rolled her eyes back, and said, "Oh, all right. Come here—and keep your tongue in your mouth."

Danny moved toward Megan and puckered his lips, but kept his eyes open. When he felt Megan's lips touch his, he jerked back at first contact and then leaned forward for more.

"That's it, buster. I did my part of the bargain. If you say anything to anyone about this, I'll deny it and make you look like an idiot. Is that straight?"

Danny was speechless and just nodded. His power was gone. He had wasted a lip lock.

"Okay, let's go." Megan tossed the keys to David. "The jeep's out front." Megan went through the house, locking both front and back doors, David started for the jeep and Danny secured their house.

David swung into the jeep and motioned for Danny to get in beside him. He didn't want anyone to see Megan sitting in contact; they might get the wrong idea and it would undoubtedly get back to Rick. Danny climbed in and snapped his seatbelt. As Megan climbed in, Danny stretched out his right arm on the top of the seat behind her.

Megan leaned back to get comfortable and latched her belt. She leaned forward and stared at Danny, "Hey! We're not going steady, Danny. You got a kiss—that was all. Keep your hands to yourself!"

David scowled at Danny as the key was turned and the engine fired into life. "Come on, Danny, behave yourself. You got what you wanted." Danny smiled.

Danny intertwined his fingers in his lap and leaned back into the bench seat. He resolved that next time he would be better prepared for a kiss. He had to remember to lean into it.

The mile to the drug store was uneventful. No one uttered a single word, not even at stop signs. Danny studied Megan's face furtively. If only Rick weren't around, but that wouldn't happen for another year. Then he might have a chance. Why does my next-door neighbor have to be so pretty? Her mom and dad aren't especially good looking. He smiled as he considered that Megan had visited a plastic surgeon. David turned on the Main Street, pulled into one of the diagonal parking spots in front of the drug store, and shut off the engine.

Megan opened her door and looked at David, "You guys can wait here if you want, or come in with me. It will probably take some time—I'm guessing about fifteen minutes." She released her belt, hopped out of the jeep, crossed the sidewalk, and went through the automatic front door.

David glanced at Danny, "Let's go in. I want to look at a .22 with a scope. Dad's hunting rifle is too powerful for squirrels and rabbits and the ammo costs too much."

When the two boys got inside, they could see Megan talking to the pharmacist in the back of the store. Mr. and Mrs. Zeller had run the store for David's entire life. They were known by everyone in Suddenly and they knew everybody in town. Once in a while Mr. Zeller, Bert, would forget the name of a child, but Mrs. Zeller, Sharon, would remember, especially the names of babies. She knew all the youngsters in town.

As David moved toward the sporting goods section and Danny hurried to the aisle of toys, David heard Megan say, "About ten minutes? Okay, I'll talk with Mrs. Zeller in cosmetics. I'll be back." She looked at her phone to check the time and walked down the aisle where Sharon was rearranging a display of lipsticks, scrambled by customers.

Danny was sitting on the floor checking out the dart guns. He read the warning that the guns could be mistaken for a real gun and possession might lead to unforeseen trouble from police. As he admired the brightly colored plastic Tommy guns in the sealed packages, he heard a male voice, "Show the druggist the knife and I'll get the drugs." Danny looked up and down the aisle, but couldn't see anyone; the voice had come from the adjoining aisle. He put the package down so not to make a sound and listened.

"Got the list?"

"Yeah! You hold the drug man away with the knife. Make sure he doesn't move to press any alarms."

"Don't worry, he won't move or I'll cut him good."

"Make sure you don't kill 'im."

"Yeah, yeah. Don't worry. Let's do it!"

Danny heard footsteps move down the aisle toward the pharmacy counter in the back of the store. He darted over to the sporting goods and grabbed David.

"Those two guys are going to rob Mr. Dowd! I heard them talking! One has a knife. What are we going to do?"

David reacted quickly. "Go tell Mrs. Zeller and Megan to hide or go next door and call Sheriff Howell. I'll get Mr. Zeller and a baseball bat." Danny was frozen in place. He just stared at his brother. "Go, Danny!" David pushed Danny to get him moving. Danny ran to the front of the store not looking back.

David stepped away from the rifles, which were tied down, and grabbed an aluminum baseball bat. He looked over the aisle and saw Mr. Zeller on one knee arranging magazines. David darted over to the books and periodical section, knelt, and whispered, "There are two guys trying to steal drugs from Mr. Dowd. My brother overheard them talking. What should we do? One guy has a knife. Danny's telling Mrs. Zeller and Megan to leave the store."

Mr. Zeller reached under his apron and extracted a small handgun a little larger than a carpenter's measuring tape. "Let's get closer so we can see what's going on. James will let them take whatever they want. We'll nab them after they start toward the door. James will be safe then."

David looked at Mr. Zeller for instructions. "What should I do?"

"I'll shoot the one with the knife in the leg and you blast the other one in the knee with that bat. That should put them both down. Bonnie should be calling the sheriff by now if Danny told her what was going on."

The two men were behind the counter. The guy with the knife was holding James, the pharmacist, by the white jacket with the knife at his throat. Mr. Zeller and David were watching as the other thief was tossing bottles of pills into a pillowcase.

"Hurry up, Tom, we've gotta get out of here."

"Hold your water, Stan, I'm moving as fast as I can. The drug names look all alike when there's so many bottles side by side."

"Come on, let's take what you have and go. Step on it!"

"One more minute, I see a couple of other bottles in a box." Tom tossed another bottle in the pillowcase, stood up and said, "That's it. Let's get the hell out of here."

Stan shoved Mr. Dowd to the floor and said, "Stay there, old man or you'll bleed all over the floor!"

The two hoodlums vaulted over the drug counter and started down the nearest aisle but stopped suddenly when Mr. Zeller appeared about ten feet in front of them. They didn't see Zeller's gun and Stan said, "Out of the way you old fool!"

Mr. Zeller shot Stan in the right thigh and was aiming at the other leg. Stan fell to the floor yelling, "Goddamn! He shot me! Help me up, Tom!"

Tom reached down to grab his brother's hand but didn't even touch him before David swung the bat and crushed Tom's left knee. The crunch of breaking bone was louder than the pop the gun had made. Tom fell to the floor, dropping the pillowcase, screaming like a stuck pig. "Son of a bitch! My leg's broke!"

David, Mr. Zeller, and Mr. Dowd were standing over the men on the floor when Megan appeared and squirted the robbers with pepper spray.

"Hey! Don't do that, Megan!" David grabbed Megan's hand that held the unit so she couldn't use the spray again. "Why did you do that? Those guys were out of it already."

Megan stepped back and put the spray in her purse. She looked at David and said, "I've never used it before so I thought this would be a good time to try it."

CHAPTER 2

The two disabled robbers were yelling for something to alleviate the pain in their eyes. The damage to their legs had become secondary. Mrs. Zeller went to the pharmacy in the back of the store and brought eyewash kits to the two men. Sharon and Mr. Dowd began to help the men clear the painful pepper spray from their eyes.

Megan stood there realizing the trouble she had caused and knelt beside Sharon.

"I'm sorry, Mrs. Zeller, I seem to have caused more trouble than it was worth, but I was mad at them for trying to rob your store. They could have hurt someone."

Mrs. Zeller looked up, smiled, and said, "Don't worry, dear. The eyewashes are pretty cheap; we get them wholesale, you know."

Mr. Zeller stood over the two men with his gun alternately pointing at one and then the other as the three customers in the store drifted to the windows and went outside to watch the sheriff and the ambulance arrive, sirens blaring at different frequencies. Danny placed his hands over his ears trying to mute the noises. When the cars stopped the sirens quieted.

Sheriff Howell entered the store with his gun drawn and the ambulance crew followed at a safe distance, shielded by the sheriff's more than generous body.

"What's going on here, Bert? You can put your gun away, I've got this." The sheriff had his .45 six-gun pointing at the men on the floor. "Wha'd they do?"

Bert Zeller slid the gun into his pocket underneath his apron and said, "These two held up Brian in the back. They put the pills they were stealing in that bag." He pointed at the bag of drugs that spilled on the floor when David smashed the robber's knee.

"So you shot that one. What's wrong with the other guy—next to the bag?"

"Davy Drum blew out his knee with a baseball bat. That one had a knife. He's going to need some surgery. The other one just needs a .22 slug removed. He'll be fine—just a bit sore for a week or so. On second thought, maybe we should leave the lead slug in him so he'll get poisoning—teach him a lesson."

"Well, I'd better cuff 'em and get 'em over to the hospital." He looked at the Cardiff brothers, the ambulance crew, and said, "You boys can go. I'll take 'em in the squad car." Sheriff Howell turned and saw Danny and asked, "What's your name, son?"

Danny looked up at the enormous man in front of him and said quietly, "Danny, sir."

"Fantastic! Do you know how to put handcuffs on a thief?"

"I think so; I've seen it done in the movies and on TV."

"Okay." The sheriff tossed two pairs of handcuffs to Danny and said, "Cuff 'em, Dano."

Everyone watched as Danny began putting the two men in handcuffs. The Zellers and Mr. Dowd laughed and Sheriff Howell said, "I've always wanted to say that!" He smiled as he holstered his six-gun and adjusted his belt. Sheriff Howell dropped to one knee and picked up the bag of drugs. He almost toppled over when he stood up, but grabbed the wristwatch display to steady himself.

Danny thought the sheriff had been eating too many doughnuts and burgers. Everyone said Sheriff Howell practically lived in his squad car. Few of the public ever saw him walking around town. He even drove the two blocks to the courthouse for trials.

"I'll have to take these drugs as evidence. I'll have Ginny send you an inventory before the day is out. I imagine you'll have to order some more from Butte."

Mr. Dowd's smile turned to a frown and he asked, "Do you have to take all of those, Sheriff? I might get a prescription for one of those before I can get some replacements."

"I'll have Ginny call you after she's got them inventoried. We'll photograph the bottles and you can come over and pick them up—probly in an hour. I have to get these idiots to Dr. Tritt's office at the hospital first."

"Okay. Do you want all of us to give statements?" Mrs. Zeller asked.

"Only those of you that took part in corralling these boys. I'd like to see those of you in my office tomorrow at 9:00 a.m. Please be prompt. I've got things to do." The sheriff grabbed the two robbers, hoisted them to their feet, and dragged them to his patrol car.

Danny followed out to the edge of the sidewalk and watched the sheriff shove the two injured men into the back of his car and drive away. When he went back into Zeller's, Megan was talking to Mr. Dowd.

"Are you calm enough to get my prescription ready, Mr. Dowd? I can wait a little longer."

"It will take me a few minutes longer, Megan. Why don't you and the boys get some ice cream? The Dairy Queen is open, you know."

Megan was enthusiastic. "Oh! That's a good idea. It's going to be a hot day."

She didn't have to ask the boys to take her to the soft ice cream palace, they had heard what Mr. Dowd had said. They started toward the jeep and Megan ran to catch up. David got in the driver's seat and leaned forward to extract his wallet from his left rear pocket. His billfold inspection netted only two dollars. He was under a little stress, a small cone was $1.89. He could only afford one cone—for Megan. David grabbed Danny and whispered, "Do you have any cash on you?"

"No, my wallet's at home. What do I need any money for?"

"I want to buy cones for all of us, but I've only got two bucks."

"Tell them you'll do their dishes tonight. They have to clean up and I bet you can get lots of ice cream—free."

"Yeah, sure. That won't do me any good now."

"What are you guys talking about?" Megan was climbing in the jeep. She clicked the safety belt and said, "I'm buying; let's go to the DQ!"

Danny poked David's right thigh and smiled. The four blocks to the edge of town were covered in about twenty seconds. The main drag speed limit was fifteen miles per hour. As they entered the restaurant, one of the girls working behind the counter waved to David. He recognized Jenny Drake and waved back. There was only one customer in front of them so they didn't wait long for Jenny to wait on them.

"Three large vanilla cones, please." Megan looked at the boys for their approval and they both nodded. Megan stepped forward and as the cones were given out, she gave Jenny a twenty.

"Here, David, hold mine for a sec." Megan handed her cone to David while she received change for the twenty. She stuffed the coins and bills in her jean's pocket and reached for her cone. As she licked her ice cream, she motioned towards a booth and they all sat down, Danny on one side and David on the other. Megan slid in beside Danny. Danny looked at his brother, smiling, and raising his eyebrows.

Megan looked at David, "Are you going to work this summer at one of the lookout stations? You're old enough now, right?"

David had his mouth full and swallowed the cold glob before he answered. He wiped his mouth with the back of his hand and replied, "If Mom wants us to man a station, we'll do it, but if they're all rented out, I guess not. What are you going to do?"

"Daddy wants me to start working at the bank, but I'm not allowed to handle money. I'd probably do some office work— simple stuff, I guess." She looked a little disappointed.

"That's better than sitting around the house doing nothing. Are you still interested in becoming an artist? What about photography?"

Danny had almost finished his cone when he stepped on something under the table. He could see it was a plastic fork partially stuck under the bench. He tried to reach it, but the table didn't allow him much freedom so he leaned back a slid under the table.

"What are you doing, Dan?" David inquired.

"There's something under my feet, I'm trying to get it." Danny was on his hands and knees and could see a plastic fork stuck under the bench where he had been sitting with Megan. He tugged on it and it came loose. He started up from under the table when he heard David.

"There's your boyfriend, Megan, sicko Ricko. Looks like he sees us. I just might be in some trouble. Danny's under the table and not visible. Stay under there, Danny, let's see what Ricko has to say."

"Don't call him that, David. You don't know him."

"That's right—and I think I don't want to."

Rick was walking towards the booth where he could see David and Megan. He was frowning. As he got closer, he said, "What's going on, Drum bum? What are you doing with my girl?" Rick slid into the booth pushing Megan over with his hand on her hip.

"David drove me to the pharmacy to get my prescription allergy meds. We're waiting for Mr. Dowd to get my meds ready. There was an attempted holdup and Mr. Dowd got shook up a little. He told us to get some ice cream and then I could pick up my pills."

Danny hadn't made a peep and was watching the six legs. He saw Rick's hand move over onto Megan's left thigh and begin to move upward. Megan swatted his hand away, but it resumed its previous position and started squeezing. Danny looked at the fork and decided to react. The fork was in his hand with only the tines sticking out. Danny took aim and jammed the fork into the back of Rick's hand. Blood started dripping as soon as he hit skin and bone.

"Son of a bitch! Why'd you do that, Megan? I'm bleeding."

Rick had jumped up from beside Megan and was standing in the aisle holding his right hand with his left, towering over diminutive Megan, scowling.

"I didn't do anything. And don't you cuss around me! I didn't ask you to join us and put your dirty hand all over me!"

Danny climbed out from under the table to his former position beside Megan. "You got your blood on my nice clean fork, Rick. Now I'll have to get another one." He looked at David and smiled.

"You little shit! Wait 'til the season starts, I'll bury your scrawny brother. You can't get away with crap like that."

"Shut up, Rick. You're making a scene out of a few scratches. David had nothing to do with it. If you take it out on him, we're done. I'm thinking about that anyway. Going with you is beginning to be more trouble than it's worth, so straighten up. Go back to work."

Rick turned and stormed out of the restaurant, motioned to a friend in a pickup, got in and slammed the door. They drove off, wheels screeching, headed out of town.

Megan got out of the booth and watched Danny climb out. She put her hand on Danny's shoulder and said, "Thank you, Danny. You did the right thing."

Danny, an inch shorter than Megan, replied, "I saw you push his hand off your leg and when he put it back, I figured you might want some help, so I jabbed the fork into his hand. I hope it hurt more than he said."

"Good job, Danny. I just hope he doesn't mess with us anymore. He's too big and strong for us to fight him."

"Thanks, David. Shall we get Megan's pills and go back home? I want to get the drone flying."

"You guys have a drone? How cool is that? I want to learn to fly it. Has it got a camera?"

As the three got in the jeep, David said, "Thanks for the treat, Megan, and the drone does have a camera."

"Yeah, and thanks for the fun. That was the first time I ever jabbed anybody with a fork and drew blood. That was a wonderful adventure."

David was laughing as he backed the jeep out of the parking spot and drove back to the drug store. Megan went in, got her pills, and in a few minutes, they pulled into the Isaacs' driveway. Megan, Danny, and David sat in the jeep for a few moments before Megan sighed and said, "Thank you for the exciting morning, double D's."

David replied, "You're welcome, Miss Isaacs. We're going back to work on the drone. If you want to come over, we'll be in the backyard. Thanks again for the ice cream—and Rick's hand." They all laughed as David dropped the car keys into Megan's outstretched palm.

CHAPTER 3

As Danny and David walked to the backyard table to resume assembly of the drone, Danny said, "I hope I didn't make trouble for you."

"You did the right thing, Danny. I would have said something if I had known Rick was feeling Megan under the table. You were in the position to react and you had the guts to do something. If Rick comes after me, he'll get in major trouble at the school, with the cops, and with Mom. I pity him if Mom gets ahold of him; he'll be in deep shit."

"Thanks, bro. Let's get back to work on the drone. Are you hoping Megan comes over?"

"Yeah! It would be more fun to have her around, but I don't know if she could help us assemble the drone." David picked up a set of tiny screwdrivers and opened the case.

Danny lifted the top off the drone box and exposed several plastic bags of parts. "She can follow directions, can't she? I'll bet she can follow a recipe. Think she can cook?"

"I remember Megan made brownies for school one time in the sixth grade, but she probably had help from her mom. They put nuts in them and she had to take the brownies home. Some kids were allergic to the nuts, but I got to eat some of them. She brought them over to the house. Well, let's get busy; open that instruction manual."

A half-hour later, the drone was taking shape; two of the four motors had been installed and wires to the batteries had been attached to the motors.

Danny commented, "I don't think Megan's coming over. I bet she's on the phone with lover boy."

"Yeah. She's probably apologizing, but he should be doing that." David looked at Danny and said, "Forget about Megan, what's the next step?"

Before Danny had a chance to answer, Megan appeared at the fence again. "David, could you take me to the hospital?"

David dropped his screwdriver and walked towards Megan, "Something wrong? You need a doctor?"

"No, nothing like that. I have an appointment to see Mrs. Shannon. She wants to talk to me about being a candy striper."

"Oh, that's cool. Volunteer work at the hospital can be rewarding—Mom told me it's a good thing to have on your résumé. I've never wanted to empty bedpans though." He grinned, "You wanna go *now*?"

"Not right now, but later, if it's not a problem. We don't need to take Danny—just you and me. The interview is at one o'clock; after lunch."

"Why don't you want Danny to go along?"

"He can go if he wants, but I don't care what Rick thinks. If he does anything to you or Danny, he'll be in deep poo-poo—and he knows it." She smiled and concluded, "Will you drive me to the hospital after lunch?"

"Sure. Do you want to help us with the drone?"

"Well, I'm not very good at putting things together. I'll let you guys do that, but after you get it finished, I want you to show me how to fly it."

"Okay, but that will be awhile. I'll come over at 1:00 p.m."

"Promise?"

David laughed, "Yeah, I promise."

The boys watched Megan walk back to the patio of her house and disappear through the slider.

Danny looked at David and raised his eyebrows, "She has a nice walk, doesn't she?"

David continued watching the back of the Isaacs' house where Megan had vanished. "Better keep your eyes on the drone, little brother. You have plenty of time before you have a girlfriend."

"*Girlfriends*, David."

"You'd better develop some more muscle, Danny boy. The girls don't want a pile of bones for a boyfriend. When Mom gets home tonight, we'll talk about getting a set of weights. We can both use them. I'd like to bulk up for football and you can start putting on some real muscle. It won't be very long until you're as tall as I am."

For some time, Danny had been thinking of doing more exercise to put on some weight and develop his muscles. He liked to run but when his mother was away from town, he had to stay close to home or with David. "We could cut firewood, David. Mom could show us some places and it would save Mom the cost of buying us weights. Maybe we could sell the firewood and buy the weights ourselves."

"Hey! Good thinking, little man. I should have thought of that. We can use Dad's old chainsaw—but Mom might say that it's too dangerous."

Danny was thinking, not working on the drone. "We could have her take us out to a place that needs clearing and we could show her that we know how to use the saw."

"Yeah, let's talk with her about it after dinner when she's relaxing."

Danny smiled, "After we tell her about the holdup and the fork attack?"

David said, "We'd better talk to her about those things as soon as she gets home. We don't want someone else to tell her about the holdup attempt and the Dairy Queen incident."

"Do you think the sheriff will have already told her about the holdup?"

"Maybe, Danny. We'll know as soon as she sees us after work."

After lunch, the boys continued the assembly procedures until 12:55, when David left to drive Megan to the hospital. Danny reread the directions for the drone construction and realized they didn't have the correct battery. He called Rob's Hobby Garage and found he didn't have enough money to buy the battery. He would have to wait for David to return. They could ride their bikes to the hobby shop, it was only about a mile from home.

When David and Megan arrived at the hospital, Megan said, "You can come in with me, David, I don't know how long the interview will last. You don't want to sit out here in the jeep, do you?" Megan had gotten out of the jeep and started toward the hospital entrance. She had stopped at the door, turned, spoken to David, and then entered the building.

David pulled the key out of the ignition, stuck it in his pocket, and followed Megan into the air-conditioned building. He caught up to Megan as she walked down the right-hand corridor to room 125, the office of Mrs. Geneva Wallen, Hospital Social Representative.

"You can come in with me, but they'll probably ask you to leave. Some of the questions might be personal."

"No problem. I just want to be sure you're talking to the right person. I've seen Mrs. Wallen before."

"When was that? Recently?"

"No. She talked to us when Dad was killed in that fire."

"I remember that. I was so sorry you lost your father in that terrible fire. I remember I cried when you felt so bad."

"Well, I think you'll like Mrs. Wallen. Let's go in." David tapped on the door and heard, "Come in." He opened the door and ushered Megan into the office.

The attractive woman, perhaps approaching fifty years old, graying blonde, dressed in a light-blue suit, stood and said, "You must be Megan, and I remember your boyfriend, David Drum." She walked around the desk and extended her hand to Megan. "I'm Geneva Wallen, Social Director." Mrs. Wallen and Megan were nearly identical in height, but the director was wearing heels; Megan wore pink and white athletic shoes.

Smiling, Megan shook her hand and said, "He's not my boyfriend, Mrs. Wallen. David drove me here for the interview. He's my next-door neighbor."

The director glanced at David, smiled, and said, "Nice to see you again, David. How are your mother and brother doing?"

"They're fine, Mrs. Wallen. How's your dog?"

Mrs. Wallen laughed and replied, "I have two little guys now. I got another Chihuahua so Ernie would have some company. My new border is Max; he's really cute. They chase each other around the house. My husband wants to take them out in the woods and leave them, but he's just joking. If he did that," she smiled, "he'd end up in the emergency room."

Megan asked, "What does your husband do, Mrs. Wallen?"

"He's the city engineer—busy all the time approving plans for sewers, new buildings, and such. I think it's kind of boring, but he enjoys it. He's always telling me the city will be named Wallenville before long."

David felt like he was holding up the interview, so he said, "I'll step out and wait for you Megan."

Mrs. Wallen commented, "The interview should only take ten to fifteen minutes, David."

"Okay. I'll wander the halls for a few minutes."

David exited the office and began walking down the long linoleum tiled hallway. He could see a red exit sign pointing to his right and an emergency sign designating the opposite direction. He turned left and followed the red stripe on the floor to the emergency rooms. He was curious to find out if the two robbers were still being treated.

As he approached the first room, he could hear someone speaking, "Do you have insurance?"

"Insurance! You kiddin' me? I ain't had work in damn near a year. Where would I get insurance?"

A doctor replied, but David didn't recognize the voice; it didn't sound like Dr. Anderson. "If you don't have your knee reconstructed, you will limp for the rest of your life. Limb and joint reconstruction are expensive processes. You should have it done soon. You'll need insurance."

"Just patch me up, doc. I'll sue that little bastard that broke my knee."

David recognized the next voice; it was the sheriff. "You don't have the money to sue anybody, Jess, and besides, you'd lose and have to pay a lawyer hundreds of dollars. Lawyers don't come cheap."

"Yeah, yeah. How much for a lawyer?"

"About $300 an hour."

"Jesus Christ! I should have been a lawyer. They're bigger thieves than me."

"Maybe so, but they're legal. Let me give you one piece of advice. If you do anything to that young man that hit you, you will never walk again. Is that plain enough for you?"

The emergency room was quiet. The only thing David could hear was his own breathing.

The sheriff suddenly boomed, "Do you understand me?"

"Yes sir."

The sheriff's pager caught his attention and he stepped outside on the ambulance entry area to make a call. The doctor said, "I have to get you a knee brace from another room, I'll be right back."

David sat down in a chair beside the emergency room just before the doctor exited into the hall and strode to a door three rooms away, entered a code, and went in the room. David could hear the robbers talking.

One of the men began by saying, "Damn cuffs. We can't get out 'a here."

"How's that wound, Cliff?"

"Hell, I don't know. It feels dead. That doc gave me a shot so it wouldn't hurt when he dug out the bullet."

"He musta give me the same thing. My knee don't hurt anymore. I'd like to get ahold of that little bitch that peppered us. If she's a virgin, she won't be after I'm finished with her."

"Didn't you hear what that sheriff said, Jess? We'd better not come back here after we get out 'a jail. If you get sent up on rape, you'll be gone a long time."

"He won't remember us after a year or so. I'll come back all right."

David heard the back door open and the sheriff reenter the room. "I'm going to have one of my deputies pick you boys up and give you an escort to jail at the courthouse—soon as the doctor is finished with you. You fellas mind your manners. You try to escape and my deputy will shoot. He's a damned fine shot. You understand?"

David didn't hear any reply, but the two injured must have nodded. The sheriff pushed aside the curtains to the emergency room and stepped into the hall. He noticed David. "You been here long, son?"

"Yes sir. I'll walk with you to your car."

"Come along then, I've got to get back to my office." The sheriff motioned for David to join him and they walked down the hallway toward the admissions desk. David felt tiny beside the sheriff—probably outweighed by a hundred pounds. Sheriff Howell was known to have lunch in his squad car. Burgers and soft ice cream for two was his usual order, but that was just hearsay.

"I heard those two guys talking when you and the doctor left the room for a few minutes. I thought I'd better tell you what I heard." David related what he had heard to the sheriff.

"Their mouths are going to get them in trouble. They don't know when to shut up. Neither of those guys is worth the skin they're in. If they think I'll forget them, they're very wrong. I review everyone I arrest every so often so I don't forget. I can't be sure someone might try to shoot me, so I'm very diligent about reviewing faces. My faces file is not too big. Suddenly is a pretty quiet place. Thanks for telling me what you heard, David. Maybe you'll be a deputy some time?"

"I don't think so, sir, but I'll keep that in mind. I'd better find out if Megan is finished with her appointment with Mrs. Wallen. See you tomorrow at the interview."

CHAPTER 4

Sheriff Howell shook hands with David and exited the hospital. David watched as the sheriff climbed in his patrol car. The car's suspension sagged noticeably with the extra weight added to the driver's side. David grinned and turned around to see Megan walking toward him, smiling.

"So what happened, Meg?"

"Mrs. Wallen said I could start next Monday afternoon. I don't want to have to ask you to drive me here all the time, David, it's not fair to you; I have to be able to drive Dad's jeep."

"I don't mind driving you."

"I want you to teach me to drive a stick shift. That's final."

"Um, okay. When do you want your first lesson?"

"Well, you can give me some pointers when you drive me home. We'll have to arrange a time—maybe tomorrow?"

David grinned, "Okay, but it will have to be in the evening. I should be home with Danny right now. Mom told me to be with him during the day. I didn't think we'd be gone this long. We can use the parking lot at the fairgrounds or the football stadium for lessons. You can't run into anything out there."

Megan sat back and buckled her safety belt. "Okay, about 7:00 p.m.? It's light until after eight. Come over at seven and we'll take the jeep—unless Dad wants to go somewhere. He might want to go to the firing range; he bought a new gun."

"That's all right, we can drop him off and pick him up afterwards—if the jeep still runs."

"Thanks a lot, David. You're a real friend." Megan pouted and crossed her arms at her waist.

David smiled and pushed his fist gently against Megan's left shoulder. "Come on, Meg. You know I'm just kidding. Can't you take a joke?"

"Got you!" Megan laughed and hit David's right bicep with her fist. "Take me home, James!"

David smiled, "So now I'm your personal chauffeur?"

"Just my teacher for a day or two while I learn how to drive a stick-shift. Then you're fired!"

As David started the jeep, he began telling Megan what he was doing with the shift lever and the foot pedals. Megan frowned as too much information was flooding into her brain at once. She listened to David as they drove home. David took a long route so he would have to stop at red lights and explain what Megan would have to know.

When the jeep pulled into the Isaacs' driveway, Danny met David to relay a message from their mother. He waved and waited for the engine to die before he spoke.

"Mom called and said to take the hamburger out of the freezer and let it thaw. She wants us to get some buns and cheese, and check on the mayo to see if we've got enough. Oh, yeah, pickles, too."

"Is that all, Danny?"

Danny thought for a few seconds and then replied, "Oh! She'll be home around six." He watched Megan climb out of the jeep. "Hi, Megan. Are you going to work at the hospital?"

"Uh huh, I start next Monday. I'll help set your broken bones if you have an accident."

Mrs. Isaacs came out the front door, put her arm around Megan's shoulders, and turned towards Danny and David. "I'm glad I caught you boys before you disappeared. Mr. Isaacs called from the bank a few minutes ago and wants you and your mother to have dinner with us tonight. We're going to have a guest for dinner and Dennis wants all the Drums to meet him. Can you get in touch with your mother? I hope you don't have anything planned."

David glanced at Danny, decided to accept the invitation, and replied, "Thanks, Mrs. Isaacs, we don't have anything planned. Mom said she'd be home around six o'clock, but she'll want to get cleaned up."

"All right then, we'll have dinner at 7:00 p.m. We'll see you then."

On the way to the backyard, Danny said, "What about the stuff Mom asked us to get?"

"Don't even think about it, bro, we're going to have a free dinner. Mom won't care and we'll get that stuff tomorrow. Put the hamburger back in the freezer. Think about it, Danny, we'll be having dinner with Megan."

"I wonder who Mr. Isaacs is bringing home. Maybe some new girls?"

"I doubt it. Probably some old codger around his age—maybe an old college buddy."

"Think Mr. Isaacs is older than Dad would be?"

"About five years, about forty or so, maybe even forty-five."

"Jeez, David. Is Mrs. Isaacs that old? She doesn't look that old."

"No, she's about Mom's age—thirty-five or thirty-six. Why all the interest in their ages?"

"Just curious. Let's get to work on the drone."

Megan entered the house with her mother and asked, "Who's coming to dinner?"

"All your father told me was his name, Scott something. I didn't catch the last name."

"Is he an old guy? Is he married?"

Sarah chuckled, "I don't know, Megan. You'll find out when he gets here. Would you please vacuum the living room?"

"Okay. What's for dinner, anything special?"

"Venison steaks—the ones Mr. Ashmore gave us. I have to thaw them out, they're in the freezer. Please do the vacuuming, then you can make the salad."

While Danny checked for the make of the battery they needed, David called their mother and informed her of the new plans for dinner. She said she would try to get home a little earlier than six o'clock so they would have plenty of time to get ready. The boys were supposed to wear clean school clothes since the dinner was not a formal affair. She was curious about Scott, apparently a newcomer to Suddenly, and she had heard about the attempted holdup from Sheriff Howell who had radioed her while he downed two cheeseburgers. She wanted to hear all about the unsuccessful robbery from the boys.

The boys rode to the Hobby Garage and bought the battery for the drone, returned home and installed it. A few minutes after five o'clock, they put the aircraft away, changed clothes, and finished reading through the operating manual.

Julie returned home at 4:56, worn out from spending all day scouting hiking trails, removing obstructions caused by fallen trees, and repairing direction signs. She hoped her work would help prevent hikers from getting lost or hurt. She parked her gray-green pickup truck in the driveway, slid out of the cab and slowly made her way to the front door as she glanced up and down Beaver Lane watching for anything unusual in the neighborhood. Spring was the time for new arrivals to appear in the community and she had begun to watch for drifters and visitors she had not seen before. She had become more wary of newcomers ever since her husband had died in a fire that had been started by an ill-informed tourist during the fire season four years ago.

"Boys! I'm home." She shoved the front door closed and tossed her keys and cell phone on the little table near the entrance..

"We're in here, Mom." Danny's voice came from the kitchen.

"Okay. I'm going to shower and change clothes. Are you guys ready to go next door?"

David answered, "We're ready. Should we tell Mrs. Isaacs that you'll be about an hour late?"

"Funny, David. You know, you're not too old for me to give you a paddling. I'll be ready in about twenty minutes—we'll go over to the Isaacs' together."

Twenty-three minutes later, Julie Drum appeared in a summer dress and sweater. She had tried on a pair of heels but decided to wear flats instead, she was a bit unsteady in heels and she didn't want to look unwieldly in the presence of a man she had never met. She certainly wasn't going to wear her hiking boots to meet a newcomer. The first impression might be important. It had been a long time since she had gotten dressed for dinner, even though it was a last minute invitation from the next door neighbors'.

Danny was the first to react. "Wow, Mom, you look great!"

David added, "More like awesome, Danny."

Julie pirouetted and said, "Thank you, boys." She knew she looked good, but it was nice to have a second opinion. The boys didn't realize Julie was tired of mourning and had finally decided it was time to move on; the boys needed more of a male influence in their lives, other than their next door neighbor who was rarely contributing to decisions for his own family. Bruce Isaacs' work at the bank had become all consuming.

Megan had mentioned to David that her mother, Sarah, had begun to argue over trivial things with her husband, and had expressed her displeasure with his lack of interest in family matters. Sarah knew Bruce wasn't seeing another woman, the town was too small to keep an extramarital affair a secret for more than a day.

Julie was resolved to investigate any new men that had come to visit Suddenly and perhaps were here to stay. This was going to be her initial opportunity since she had formulated her new approach on the first of January, but she had a checklist of attributes her second husband must possess, no exceptions.

"You both look handsome in clean clothes, hair combed, and hands washed. Are you guys ready?"

David checked his watch, "We'll be twenty minutes early, Mom."

Julie grinned. She had a good rejoinder. "That's all right, I'll help Sarah in the kitchen. You can talk with Megan—I know you'll like that."

They left through the front door and started over to the Isaacs'. Just as they arrived at the entranceway, before they rang the doorbell, Megan opened the door and welcomed them into the family room.

"Mrs. Drum, Mom wants you to come to the patio, she needs some help. I'll talk to David and Danny." Megan motioned for the boys to sit on the sofa and she escorted Julie past the kitchen to the rear of the house. She came back to the family room, knelt in front of David, and began to talk in a whisper, "I've got something planned—it's very funny. Do you want to help me?"

David and Danny grinned and leaned toward Megan. They were used to Megan's pranks, which were usually harmless, but they had to find out what she had in mind before they agreed to assist.

It only took a minute to relate her idea and when she was telling them what to do, her father and dinner guest came in the front door. She quickly finished and said, "Use your imagination if you can't remember what I told you." The boys nodded and stood up when Mr. Isaacs introduced the newcomer.

"Scott, I'd like you to meet my two neighbor boys, David and Danny Drum, and my daughter, Megan. Kids, this is Scott Loebner, he's looking for a temporary place to rent."

Following the initial pleasantries, Sarah and Julie appeared and another round of introductions took place. Mr. Loebner was over six feet tall, dressed in a plaid shirt with sleeves rolled up, jeans and cowboy boots. David guessed he worked outdoors, maybe he was a rancher: his ruddy cheeks and blond hair resembled that of a lifeguard—spending many hours in the sun. He was handsome, appeared to be about the same age as his mother, and David noticed when Scott shook hands with his mom, the two seemed to hold hands for a much longer time than others did during the other introductions.

While the group moved outdoors to the patio and barbeque area, Danny remarked to David, "Did you see his hearing aid? Maybe he's married and his wife has been yelling at him for a long time." Danny snickered and punched his brother on the shoulder.

"You sure, Dan? I didn't see a hearing aid. Which ear?"

"Behind his left ear. It's small and flesh colored. Old Mr. Peterson has one like it but a little bigger. He's constantly looking for batteries."

Chapter 5

The Isaacs' backyard concrete patio, surrounded by arborvitae, had a large picnic table, a barbecue, where Mr. Isaacs was cooking steaks, and a refrigeration unit for beer and pop. Mr. Loebner was standing a few feet away from Mr. Isaacs holding a beer and talking with Mrs. Isaacs and Mrs. Drum. Both ladies were smiling and then they started to laugh when Scott held his can of beer up toward the sky.

Megan and the boys were talking in spurts, slightly above whispers, as Megan and David were bringing plates and other table settings out to the patio from the kitchen. Danny sat in a lounge chair watching his mother and Scott as they continued their conversation after Mrs. Isaacs darted into the house. Danny suddenly wondered if Mr. Loebner was going to be his next father—he wasn't sure how he felt about that. Sarah Isaacs was absent only for only a minute or two before returning with a table-cloth. Danny reviewed what he was supposed to say.

"Megan, you and the boys come here and hold things while I spread the table-cover."

As soon as the table top was covered, Mrs. Isaacs and the kids set the table. Everything was ready except for the steaks. Sarah drifted over to the fire to check on the steaks.

"Steaks are ready! Bring your plates!" Mr. Isaacs was waving the barbecue fork like he was conducting an orchestra, motioning for more volume from the brass. Megan and the two boys were first in line to get their venison steaks, then Scott and the rest of the adults followed, Mr. Isaacs last. When the young people had their venison and were moving back to the table, Megan raised her eyebrows and said, "Wait until everyone has had a bite of meat before we start our routine, okay?"

David grinned, "We've got it. Don't worry, Meg, Danny and I know what to say."

The boys glanced up from their plates occasionally while the adults were eating and Danny was the first to notice the signal for David to ask the question. He poked his brother, nodded, and whispered, "Now, David."

"Mr. Isaacs, where did you get the venison?"

"Mr. Wigram gave it to me last fall, David, ten pounds in all."

"Dad, isn't Mr. Wigram the undertaker?"

"Yes, Megan."

Danny said, "That's about the time old Mr. Russell passed away, wasn't it?"

Julie Drum replied, "Mr. Russell died last October. I remember his son was here to make arrangements. Bernie Russell was a nice old man, about eighty-nine when he passed."

David added, "He was a heavy smoker, too."

Danny commented, "I thought my meat tasted a little smoky, David."

There was dead silence for a moment and then Mr. Loebner started laughing. "When did you three put that together? That was very clever. You boys even got your mother involved."

"Megan? Did you come up with that? You ought to be ashamed of yourself—and when we have a guest for dinner! I should ground you."

Megan said plaintively, "No, Mom, please don't ground me. David is going to teach me how to drive a stick shift so I can drive myself to the hospital. I start work next Monday after school for two hours on Mondays and Thursdays."

"Well, that's the first I've heard of that. When were you going to tell me?"

"At dinner tonight. I didn't know we were having company. I didn't want to bother you while you were getting ready for company."

"David, you and Danny are co-conspirators. How did you get involved?"

"Mom, you're making a big deal out of it. I'll bet Mr. Loebner thought it was funny." David smiled and looked at Mr. Loebner.

"I have to admit that I saw it coming as soon as it was mentioned that the meat was from the undertaker. If I were the kids' age, I probably would have pulled the same stunt. I wouldn't be too hard on the kids."

Megan said, "Thank you, Mr. Loebner. I'm curious—what do you do for a living?"

Loebner took a drink of beer, leaned forward, turned his head to the side to see Megan more clearly, and replied, "I'm a tracker."

Danny's interest had been piqued. "We've got black bears, mountain lions, moose, and elk in the Bitterroot that hunters follow. What do you usually go after? Do you work with big game hunters?"

Scott glanced across the table at Danny, reached behind his left ear, removed the apparatus Danny had seen and put it in his left breast pocket before answering. Everyone was waiting for his answer.

"I track two-legged animals, Danny. I work for the criminal division of West-Com. I chase signals from scammers—primarily from India and Nigeria. They pretend to be computer technicians and tell you they're getting signals from your computer that means it needs to be fixed. If you let them on your computer they search your files for information such as bank account and credit card numbers, passwords, and any other vital statistics that would allow them to steal your identity or your money."

Julie asked, "Why are you in Suddenly, Mr. Loebner? Have you traced signals from the Bitterroot?"

"Not from the Bitterroot, but from Butte, Boise, and Spokane. I'm stationed inside the triangle connecting those three cities so I can move quickly to each location."

Danny was listening intently and had a question, "How do you travel, Mr. Loebner, a super-fast car?"

"Helicopter, Danny."

"You fly a chopper?"

"Uh-huh. It's out at the football stadium. I figured it would be okay to land there since there's no football until September. What do you think?"

"I guess that's all right." Danny looked at David and said, "You think that's okay?"

"Next week there will be a soccer game on the field and there's going to be some PE classes that will be using the field. You'll have to park it somewhere else then. How long will you be in Suddenly, Mr. Loebner?"

"I'm not sure, but it could be for several months or longer, maybe a year." Scott looked at Julie and the Isaacs and asked, "Do you know of a place I could rent for a while?"

Sarah Isaacs looked at Julie and replied enthusiastically, "What about the apartment above your garage, Julie? Could you rent it to Mr. Loebner?"

Julie didn't hesitate, "Sure. We haven't used it in several years, though. It's probably a little dusty. Some of Tom's firefighter friends used to stay there when they were fighting nearby fires. There's room enough for three if someone sleeps on the floor. There should be an air mattress up there. Do you have someone else with you?"

"Nope. I have to be able to fly at a moment's notice so I work alone and bring law enforcement agencies in when I need them for backup or transporting prisoners."

'When we're finished with dinner, I'll show you the apartment. If you want to stay, the boys and I will help you clean the place; it will need some dusting and vacuuming. The water has been shut off for some time, so we'll have to get a few valves turned on. You can decide on the rent—an amount that will suit your budget."

"I'm sure that the accommodations will be more than satisfactory, Mrs. Drum, certainly better than sleeping in the chopper."

Megan stood up, grabbed David's hand, and they approached her father. "Dad, can David and I take the jeep for a half-hour? He'd going to teach me how to drive a stick shift."

"Ah, it's all right with me, but check with your mother."

"Thanks, Daddy." She pulled on David's arm and said, "Let's go, David."

David hesitated, "Aren't you going to ask your mom?"

"I already did. She said it's okay with her. Come on, it's going to be dark soon. Let's go!"

They drove to the parking lot adjacent to the football stadium where Megan took the driver's seat. David explained the positions of the shift lever and then had Megan start the jeep.

She had a little trouble with the gas and the clutch, but after a few tries, David recommended that she give the engine a little gas before she let out the clutch and shifted. After about ten minutes of trials and errors, she began to catch on and was able to drive around the periphery of the parking lot with only minor problems. David didn't want her to give up after her first lesson and complemented Megan for her initial success; he wanted to take a look at the helicopter parked on the stadium grass.

"Okay, Megan. Let's stop for this evening and we'll continue tomorrow. I want you to practice moving your feet like this." He showed her the foot technique and then commented, "Let's take a look at Mr. Loebner's chopper. I want to see what he pilots."

David was surprised when he saw the Bell helicopter. He had assumed it would be similar to a chopper that he had seen on reruns of the television show MASH; a two seater and skids for a landing gear. He was amazed at what he saw and had to get up close to peek inside.

Megan didn't know much about helicopters, but she was fascinated by what she saw. It was big, painted all black, and with its sleek lines, looked powerful. She ran her hands over the fuselage as she looked into the cabin and said, "How fast do you think it will go, David?"

"I don't know, but it's kind of scary—don't you think? I wonder what those blinking lights mean."

"Oh, I didn't see those. Let's get out of here. This thing freaks me out." She turned away from the chopper and ran back to the jeep, climbed in the passenger seat, and waited for David to return and get in the driver's seat.

"Hurry up David! I'm getting cold."

David walked the last few steps to the jeep and reached into his pocket for the keys. "You want to drive?"

"You take the wheel, I'm not good enough to drive on city streets."

As David started the engine, he saw a pickup approaching when he glanced in the rear-view mirror. "Let's get out of here, someone's coming."

Megan swiveled her head around and looked at the approaching vehicle. "I think that's your mom's pickup. Think she's looking for you?"

"Nope, she'd be beeping the horn if she wanted to talk to me. She must be giving Scott a ride to the chopper. Should we stick around?"

"No. I'm getting cold. I want to get home and have some dessert. I didn't eat much for dinner—I don't like venison."

"All right, we'll go past the school; that's the shortest way home. I'll talk with Mom when she gets back home with Scott. Danny's probably waiting for me to help him clean Scott's room."

"I'll help you guys with the cleaning—I like to vacuum." She scooted over closer to David and rubbed her arms to remove the goosebumps. "Do you like Scott? He's kind of sexy and I think he likes your mom."

David had driven away from the football field and was passing in front of the school when he remarked, "Yah, I think he's cool, and I noticed Mom paying close attention to him. She was full of smiles and Scott noticed she looked great. I'm wondering what will happen if he's living above our garage."

"Would you like to ride in his helicopter? I'm curious to see what that would be like."

"If he asks me to take a ride, I'll ask if you can go to, Megan."

"Awesome! That gives me something to look forward to besides working at the hospital."

"That was your son and Megan, wasn't it?"

"Uh-huh. I'll bet they were looking at your helicopter. Where is it?" She laughed, "Do you have it cloaked?"

"You can't see it from here, it's on the other side of the bleachers, about on the fifty-yard line. I'll show you. Park over there." Scott pointed at the far end of the bleachers, about thirty yards from the position of the slow moving pickup.

Julie parked the state vehicle and walked around to the passenger side where Scott stood fumbling with his left hand in his pants pocket.

Julie smiled, "Lose your keys?" She watched as Scott reached up and placed something behind his ear. "I didn't know you were hard of hearing. Do you read lips?"

"I can, but not when it's getting dark. It's not a hearing aid. I'll show you." Scott reached out and took Julie's right hand with his left and began walking toward the grassy field.

As they came around the bleachers and Julie saw the helicopter, she uttered, "Oh, shit."

She stopped, glanced at Scott, and said, "I'm sorry, I don't usually talk that way, but that thing looks almost like it's from another planet."

Scott laughed and said, "I want it to look alarming—especially to criminals. Once a guy gave up when he saw me approaching in the ship. When the wheels are up and the chopper is homing in, it can be scary, I guess—but that's a good thing. Come on, I'll show you the inside and I'll get my bags."

CHAPTER 6

They walked twenty yards to the chopper and stopped about a yard from the side near the leading edge of the cabin. Scott looked down at Julie and said, "Okay, try to get in."

Julie scanned the outside of the fuselage looking for a handle on the door to the cabin, but none was in sight. The composite had no indentations or indications of any type of handles or locks. She smiled, stepped back about a foot, and knocked on the cabin door. Nothing happened so she laughed and looked at Scott. "I give up. How do you get in?"

Scott smiled and replied, "Like this." He moved to the other side of Julie and pointed at the small apparatus behind his left ear then wiggled his ears. Julie jumped away from the cabin when the door popped open and the interior light illuminated the instrument-packed interior.

"Oh! Jesus, that scared me. Who designed that whatchamacallit? I'll bet you came up with that, didn't you? That is very clever. I don't think I could ever get in—I can't wiggle my ears."

"Well, there is a more conventional way of opening the cabin." Scott peeled the appendage from behind his ear, slammed the cabin door and gave the little apparatus to Julie. She turned it over in her hands, and after close inspection, tried to give it back to Scott, but he put his hands behind his back and said, "Speak clearly, but softly into the device and say open cabin."

Julie followed Scott's directions and the cabin door popped open.

"I like the more conventional approach, Scott." She smiled and returned the soft plastic device to Scott, who stuck it in his breast pocket, climbed into the cabin and grabbed two suit-cases, one medium sized and the other small, but larger than a shaving kit.

"Want to get in and look around?"

Julie shook her head and said, "Maybe some other time. We need to get back and get your apartment cleaned—it's prob-ably a bit unsanitary. Are you allergic to dust and spider webs?"

"No to dust, but I don't appreciate spiders or their webs much. Is there a microwave available?"

"Yep, and a small refrigerator, flat screen TV, phone, and a bathroom—it needs to be updated, maybe you could spruce it up a bit, if you have the time, of course. My husband had planned on doing that."

Scott dropped to the ground with his two bags and spoke into his shirt pocket, "Lock."

They walked back to the truck and started back to the Drums' home.

"Do you have any ideas where I might park my chopper where it won't interfere with the school or any other town functions?"

Julie thought for a moment before replying. I can think of a couple of places; I'll show you on a map of the town boundaries and the adjacent areas when we get home."

"Great. I'd like to see who owns land on the outskirts of Suddenly—sometime I might have to land where I hadn't prepared. It's good to know who I have to deal with if there is any damage."

"Does that happen often?"

"No, but once I had to put down in the middle of a cattle herd. One of the animals broke its leg running away and I had to buy the critter." Scott chuckled, "But there was a good side to it; I had steaks for six months."

Julie laughed, "Well, I have a similar situation—with downed trees. I can cut them up and use them for firewood, but I rarely have the time. I'd like David and Danny to learn how to use my husband's chainsaw, but I'm a little wary of their safety. I can't watch over them when I'm working."

As they pulled into the driveway, Scott said, "Maybe I can find the time to take the boys out and cut some wood for your fireplace. It would be dry for use next fall."

"That would be nice and the boys would enjoy being with a man for a change. Thank you for the offer."

"Are David and Megan dating?"

"No, but David has loved Megan since they were little kids. Megan is impulsive and David is more of a thinker so they have differences of opinion—quite often actually, but David likes the competition. He is very protective of Megan and doesn't like her being taken advantage of by her current boyfriend."

"And who is that?"

"Rick Hadley, a senior football player. He'll probably get an athletic scholarship to Montana State, the U. of Idaho, or maybe even Washington State. He's pretty good. His father owns some of the land on the outskirts of Suddenly."

"Hmm. I might have to talk to his father about renting some space to park Delilah."

Julie cut the engine and laughed. "Delilah? You're kidding. Why would you call your chopper Delilah?"

"When the thieves see her coming, they lose their strength and surrender. I'd like to keep that between us, if you don't mind."

Julie opened her door and said, "My lips are sealed. Let's see if the boys have made any progress with the cleanup in the apartment."

Scott, carrying his two bags, followed Julie through the house and out to the garage in the back of the lot. The apartment lights were on and they could hear the sounds of a vacuum cleaner and music. When they reached the landing at the top of the stairs, Julie stopped and looked through the door window. She motioned for Scott to take a look inside. The boys were moving their dust cloths in time with the music, and Megan was dancing with the vacuum cleaner as she raked the appliance over the large rug that nearly covered the hardwood floor.

"Looks like they're having fun, Julie. I hate to interrupt them, but I've had a long day and need to get some sleep."

"Yeah, me too, and I've got another long day tomorrow. I've got to go with the kids to the sheriff's office. They have to answer some questions about the attempted robbery today."

"I heard about that, but they did a good job helping the drug store owner. I wouldn't worry about them answering a few questions, they acted appropriately. Megan might get a scolding for use of pepper spray."

"Let's get you settled. We can talk more in the morning." Julie entered the apartment and Danny turned off the radio so he could hear what his mother was saying.

"Have you finished the clean up?" Julie looked around the cabin, ran her finger over the kitchen counter, and looked for traces of dust, but found none. The boys had done a good job. Megan turned off the vacuum cleaner and said, "I'm finished Mrs. Drum—I vacuumed the entire living area and the bathroom. The shower needs to be wiped down—I ran some water in it."

Scott tossed his bags on the bed and said, "I'll do that, I need a shower anyway. Thanks for cleaning up, guys. I'll see you all tomorrow." He moved toward Julie, said, "Good night and thanks for everything. I'll see you in the a.m."

As the kids left the apartment, Julie gathered the cleaning equipment, said, "Good night, Scott," and followed Danny down the stairs.

Scott was up and showering at 7:00 a.m. He quickly shaved, put on clean clothes, and had just started some coffee when there was a knock on his door. He heard Julie's voice inviting him to come down for breakfast.

"I'll be right there. Give me a minute." He turned off the coffee maker and combed his hair with his fingers, glanced in the mirror to make sure he was presentable, and started down the outside stairs. He had descended two steps before stopping and returned to lock his door. There were things in his luggage that were private—he had no idea what the boys might want to investigate, but he wasn't completely confident that they would mind their own business—he didn't know them well enough to make that determination.

Everyone was up by 7:30 and discussing plans for the day while they were eating breakfast when Scott joined the Drums. As he ate toast, eggs, and bacon, he listened to the boy's plans to meet with the sheriff. When there was a lull in the conversation, he volunteered to accompany Megan, David, and Danny to the sheriff's office at nine o'clock.

Julie questioned, "You're sure you can afford the time? Don't you have things to do for your work?"

"Nothing urgent. You have more important things to do than I do right now."

"I doubt that, but thank you for the offer."

The phone rang and Julie answered, "Hello, Drum residence. This is Julie." She listened for a few seconds and replied, "A lawyer? Why would the kids need a lawyer, Ginny?" She listened again for a short time and said, "I'll see if the Isaacs have a lawyer to represent all the kids—thanks, Ginny. Bye."

Julie put the phone on the wall cradle, frowned, and sank into the chair beneath the phone.

David stood up and walked toward his mother. "What's wrong, Mom? Why would we need a lawyer?"

"I'm not sure, Davidy. I'm going to check with Mr. Isaacs. Ginny said she had just called the Isaacs because of Megan being involved."

Scott said, "I'm sure it doesn't amount to much. From what your boys have said, they have nothing to worry about. I think your sheriff is just making sure everyone is represented. If you want, I'll represent Danny and David; I've been in many trials and know the ropes."

Julie replied, "But you're not a lawyer. Ginny said I should get the boys a lawyer."

Scott raised his arm with a finger extended to get Julie's attention, "Can we talk in private for a moment?"

Julie was biting her lower lip and frowned, "Sure. Let's step outside for a moment."

She followed Scott outside onto the patio and asked, "What is it?"

"I didn't want anyone to know about this, but I think I can trust you to remain tightlipped. I'm an FBI special agent; I have a degree in criminal law."

Julie was both mildly surprised and amused. She smiled, "I had a feeling that there was more to you than you were letting on at dinner yesterday, but you are a good actor; I believed everything you said.

"I hope you don't hold it against me. I'm beginning to like you and your boys."

Julie didn't want to be too forward, but thought she had little to risk. "My first impression of you was very favorable, Scott. I hope to get to know you much better. How long will you be staying in town?"

"I can't tell you, Julie—not that it's a secret; I just don't know. There are too many variables at play in my present investigation."

"Well, I appreciate your confiding in me. I'll tell the boys you can represent them at the meeting with Sheriff Howell."

Megan came over to the Drums at 8:45 and Scott and the kids squeezed into the jeep for the ride to the sheriff's office. Julie had gone to work knowing that the kids were in good hands; she was confident that Scott would manage any legal problems, even though she couldn't imagine anything arising that might put the boys or Megan in jeopardy.

There was a lawyer representing the two thieves at the meeting. David and Megan were both shocked that, due to extenuating circumstances, the criminals would be out of jail in only two months. David had not told Megan about overhearing what the two men had said about her in the hospital, but he was going to tell Scott about it as soon as he and Scott were alone.

At the conclusion of the meeting, as Scott and the kids were on the way to the jeep, they heard a siren coming from the direction of the hospital. Sheriff Howell came hurriedly from his office and spoke to Megan, "Megan, Rick Hadley has been in a terrible accident and is just arriving at the hospital. Do you want to go with me to see him?"

Scott stepped toward the sheriff and said, "We'll all go, Sheriff Howell. I'll drive the jeep." Megan sat between Scott and David as they sped to the hospital. David grasped Megan's right hand and said, "I'm sure he'll be all right, Meg. Doc Anderson is a really good doctor, especially for broken bones."

"You think he's got broken bones?" asked Danny, who was sitting in the back hanging onto the roll bar. "Maybe he just has a broken nose."

Megan gave Danny a dirty look and replied, "A broken nose wouldn't be a terrible accident, Danny; it has to be something else. Let's wait and see what the doctor says."

When they arrived at the hospital, Megan commented, "That's Rick's mom's car—she'll know what happened." There was late model red Buick situated at an angle across two parking spaces, as if the driver had been in a hurry and had paid no attention to the painted markings on the asphalt.

Megan was the first of the group to enter the medical facility front door and she saw Rick's mom talking to a nurse. "Mrs. Hadley, what happened to Rick?"

CHAPTER 7

Vivian looked at Megan, hesitated for a moment and then rushed to her, arms outstretched. The two women hugged and everyone could hear Vivian's voice, "Rick's legs were both broken and mangled so badly, he might never walk again. He'll never play football!"

"But what happened?"

"They were logging near Randolph's Peak and a cable broke when they were pulling a tree up the mountain side. The wires in the cable were old and when they snapped, the cable was like a whip and Rick couldn't get out of the way. It was like a lawn mower cutting a blade of grass. Adam said there was blood everywhere. They called 911 immediately and the ambulance arrived in seven minutes. Adam and the others applied tourniquets to both legs. Fortunately, Rick was knocked unconscious. Adam feels terrible; Rick is his only son."

Scott and the boys were listening to Mrs. Hadley's explanation and saw Doctor Anderson approaching the two women. He whispered something to Vivian and began to usher her to a chair by the front window adjacent to the admission kiosk. He turned toward Megan and said, "You'd better wait here. I need to talk to Vivian privately."

Megan joined the men and they watched Mrs. Hadley talk to the doctor for about fifteen seconds before Rick's mother said, "Oh, no, you can't do that!"

Dr. Anderson replied, "But Vivian, if we don't amputate both legs soon, he will die of gangrenous poisoning. He has only a few hours if we don't take both legs pretty soon."

"Can you take him by ambulance to Butte?"

"Not Butte, they don't handle cases like this. It would have to be Spokane or Boise, but they're both too far away—it would take too long by ambulance."

Megan had heard everything the doctor and Vivian had said, as had Scott and the boys. David and Megan looked at each other and said, "The helicopter!" They turned to Scott and he said, "You don't need to ask, I'll fly him to Boise, it's closest. Let me talk with the doctor."

Scott quickly joined Mrs. Hadley and the doctor and said, "I can fly your son to Boise, Mrs. Hadley; it will take just over an hour. What do you think, Doctor?"

"Who are you?" Dr. Anderson seemed a bit suspicious of the stranger and Mrs. Hadley asked, "You have an airplane here in Suddenly? We don't have an airport."

Scott introduced himself and showed the doctor his fake identification papers from West-Com. "I have a helicopter parked on the football field. Megan and David have seen it—so has Mrs. Drum. You can have David call his mother for verification if you want to check."

Vivian called to Megan, "Does this man have a helicopter on the football field?"

"Yes, Mrs. Hadley—and it's fast and kind of scary looking."

Vivian glanced at Dr. Anderson and he nodded agreement for the chopper to take Rick to Boise. Dr. Anderson said, "I'll call ahead so they'll be waiting for him. There's a landing pad on the roof of the hospital."

"I'll get the bird. It will take me about ten minutes; be ready to load him on the chopper as soon as I land in the front parking lot. We'd better take a nurse, too."

"I'm going, too." Mrs. Hadley couldn't be dissuaded—everyone knew that. She was going along to be with her son and to give permission for any special medical treatment for Rick.

Dr. Anderson said, "All right, let's get going. There's no time to waste."

"Can I go, too?" asked Megan at the last minute.

Scott quickly fired back, "There's no time to get permission from your parents, Megan. Come with me and the boys, we've got to get the chopper and you and the boys will have to go home—and stay there until one of your parents knows what is going on. Let's go!"

Scott tossed the jeep keys to David and they piled in. David spun the wheels on the blacktop and squealed down the street toward the football field. David passed through one red light and skidded through a sharp right-hand turn, accelerated, and ten seconds later skidded to a stop behind the stadium bleachers. Scott ran for the chopper and in less than ten more seconds was in the pilot's seat starting the engine. By the time Megan and the boys were able to see the helicopter, the rotor was turning so fast the individual blades were invisible.

David grabbed Megan and Danny so they wouldn't get too close to the chopper and get blasted with dirt and grass from the field as the bird took off. The kids squinted and put their hands up to protect their faces from the gust of air generated by the main rotor blades.

Megan grabbed David and Danny in a hug and said, "Isn't this exciting—I've got goosebumps all over my body."

Danny couldn't resist, "Show me."

Megan pushed Danny and said, "You little fart—aren't you excited, too?"

"Sure, but when you hugged me, I got even more excited, like when a big rocket takes off. That was better than the kiss." Danny smiled and asked David, "Didn't you get excited when Megan hugged us?"

"Well, little brother, it's always nice to get a hug from a pretty girl, but Meg and I have known each other all our lives and we've had plenty of hugs, but I can't remember any kisses."

"You don't remember kissing under the mistletoe when we were ten?"

"Oh, yeah, but that was when everybody was watching and we were expected to kiss. That wasn't a girlfriend-boyfriend kiss. I'll bet you and Rick have had some real scorchers."

Megan grinned and said, "I'll never tell. Danny, you weren't supposed to ever say anything about kissing me in the backyard. Remember?"

"Don't worry, Megan, I can keep a secret—unless someone offers me a large amount of money."

"Just remember, Danny, if you break your promise, you will be mud—in addition to being a little fart."

Megan pulled at David's arm and said, "Let's go back to the hospital and watch the chopper take off again. It's awesome to feel the wind and power from the helicopter, besides, I'd like to see Rick before he goes to Boise."

Danny added, "And I'd like to watch for those goosebumps, Megan."

"Oh, shut up, Danny. David, please tell your brother to be quiet. I'm worried about Rick."

"I understand that, Meg. I've been thinking; what if he loses both legs and is going to spend the rest of his life in a wheel chair? Would you want to marry him? He won't be playing any football in the future, that's for sure. Is he still going to go to college and get a degree?"

"Stop, David! Rick hasn't even said he loved me. He's been thinking about college, scholarships, and that kind of stuff. He said if he doesn't get a scholarship, he'll just stay home and work for his father. That's all I know. Come on, let's go. We'll miss the takeoff."

They did miss the chopper taking off and heading southwest. When they arrived at the hospital, they could see a black speck in the sky over the forest and could barely hear the sound of the helicopter in the distance.

"Nuts! We missed it. I hope Mrs. Hadley doesn't get airsick; she told me once that she doesn't like to fly." Megan climbed down from the jeep and said, "Please wait for me, I need to talk to Mrs. Wallen about something."

"Okay, Meg. We'll be right here, but don't take too long."

Megan appeared from the main entrance after spending approximately five minutes in the concrete and brick building.

David had seen the look on her face before—she was very disappointed. She didn't say anything as she got back into the jeep; she just sat there looking straight ahead with her fingers intertwined in her lap. David knew better than to say anything; he started the engine, backed away from the curb, shifted into first, pulled onto the street, and drove home in silence.

Danny had also noticed the lack of Megan's usual joyful, animated behavior and he instinctively kept his mouth shut; he would find out more when he talked with David at home. He devoted his thoughts to Scott and what the inside of the helicopter was like with Rick strapped to a gurney. He imagined Rick was lying unconscious, his mother and the hospital nurse keeping close attention to his vital signs. Danny wondered if Mrs. Hadley had any medical training. He knew very little about her, having only seen her a couple of times before at football games, when his mother pointed out Rick's father and mother. Mrs. Hadley didn't smile much.

When they pulled into the Isaacs' driveway, Megan slid from the jeep quickly and went in the house. While David and Danny sat there thinking about what their next move was, Megan reappeared.

"Can I have the keys?" was all she said.

David got out of the vehicle and said, "Go on home Danny, I'll be there in a minute. We'll work on the drone." He then walked over to Megan, gave her the keys, and said, "Are you all right?"

"Yes." Megan's eyes looked steely, her face without expression, "Go home David."

They turned away from each other without another word being spoken. David had taken four steps when he heard the Isaacs' door slam shut. He went to the backyard, expecting Danny to have the drone on the picnic table, but Danny and the drone weren't there.

David heard the slider open and Danny called out, "Hey, David, Mr. Loebner is on the phone; he wants to talk to you."

"Scott? How could he be on the phone? He's flying to Boise."

"I don't know, but he wants to talk to you." Danny held out the phone to David.

"Hello, this is David."

"We're just passing over Clayton—about halfway to Boise. I've contacted the hospital and they're waiting for us. They have several bone and limb reconstruction specialists ready to work on Rick. Tell Megan I'll have Mrs. Hadley call her as soon as she knows anything from the doctors. I imagine she will call in a few hours, but it could be tomorrow morning." There was a pause, and then, "Are you and Danny all right?"

"We're okay. We're going to work on the drone. We might have some questions for you when you get back. I think you know about drones, right?"

"I'll do what I can to help. I'll be back this evening with the nurse; she has family to take care of. Say hi to your mother for me. Take care, David."

"Bye, Mr. Loebner."

Danny and David had some lunch and set to work on the drone, which was nearly complete as far a construction was concerned. The next step was to test fly the small craft, but Danny wanted to make sure they didn't lose it by flying too high, a slight wind had developed in the early afternoon.

"Wait a minute, David, let's tether it to the fence. I'll get some of my kite string."

"Okay, I won't start the motors until we attach a line to it."

Danny disappeared into the house and David read the takeoff instructions one more time. He pictured the drone at first then he imagined he was sitting in the pilot's seat of Scott's helicopter. A voice interrupted his daydreaming.

Chapter 8

"David, I'm sorry I treated you badly. I was in a foul mood." She didn't explain any further, but appeared to be ashamed of her actions after leaving the hospital.

"Don't worry about it. I figured as much, so I kept quiet; so did Danny. We've had some experience with women; well, at least one."

He smiled and moved closer to Megan so he didn't have to shout across the backyard. "I do have something to tell you. We had a call from Scott and he told me to tell you Mrs. Hadley would call you when she knew more about Rick's condition, but it might not be until tomorrow. Scott said he would be coming back to Suddenly this evening. The nurse had to come back home to care for her family."

"Oh, that's right. Mrs. Berg has two small children and she doesn't trust her husband very much with the little kids; they take advantage of him and get him to let them do things she doesn't allow. They'd be eating pizza and ice cream for every meal if she weren't home."

"So do you want to tell me what the problem was?"

At first, Megan seemed reluctant, but then smiled, "No, but I'll tell you anyway—you know you are my best friend, and I don't want you to be irritated with me—until after we're through with the driving lessons. I need you to help me figure out the clutch and shifting into reverse. I really need to know how to back up."

"Well, I'm glad you consider me to be your best friend. So what was the problem?"

"When I went into the hospital, I asked about Rick's condition and the nurses said they couldn't tell me anything, so I saw Mrs. Shannon. I was sure she would give me some information, but she said she could only give out medical information if I was family—so she said her hands were tied; she couldn't help me. That kind of pissed me off since I was going to start working at the hospital next Monday—what difference did a few days make?"

David nodded and said, "I understand your frustration, but they're just following protocol, aren't they?"

"Yeah—I guess so." She sidestepped so she could see the drone behind David and asked, "Have you flown that thing yet?"

"Not yet. We're just about to for the first time."

"What's Danny doing with the string?"

David turned around to see what Megan was seeing. "We're putting the drone on a tether so we don't lose it while learning how to use the controls. Danny was more afraid we'd lose it than I was. I figured we'd take off and land a few times from low altitude before we go above the house or the trees."

"Makes sense to me. Can I try to fly it after you guys practice a little?"

David smiled, "I guess so. Crashing it wouldn't be as bad as wrecking your dad's jeep."

"Oh, come on. You think I'm clumsy with toys?"

David grinned, "I remember you broke some of my things when we were little."

"There was a reason for that, David. You were playing too roughly and I tried to get you to stop by throwing things at you and then running home."

"Yeah, I guess you're right." David turned around and said, "Ready, Danny?"

"Yes, Captain. Ready for takeoff—up to seventy-five feet maximum altitude."

David and Megan both laughed at Danny calling David 'Captain.'

"Your brother is really getting into this, isn't he? I have to see this."

David moved over to the control box, flipped the power switch and the propellers began to rotate.

"Okay, Megan, you're going to get the drone into the air—slide this switch to the right—very slowly until the drone is hovering above the table." David pointed to the slide switch and Megan began moving the black plastic knob. When the drone began to lift from the table, Megan said, "Oh!" stepped back, and dropped her hands to her sides. She appeared to be startled at what she had done.

David took the controls and maneuvered the drone around the backyard and then returned it to its original position and shut off the engines.

"Something wrong, David?"

"Nope, little brother. I just thought you'd like to go through the entire routine and fly it around by yourself. You were watching everything I did so you can try it now." He set the control pad on the table and moved over beside Megan. "Besides, Danny, the battery will have to be recharged before long, so use your flight time wisely."

David and Megan watched as Danny guided the drone as high as it would go with the string pulled taut, then the younger Drum lowered the aircraft to about ten feet, circled the backyard, and landed it on the table top.

Danny smiled and looked at Megan, "You're next, Megan. I think the battery is running low, so don't try to go too high—we don't want a crash on the first day of flying."

"Thanks for the warning, Danny boy. You're a real charmer."

Before Megan had a chance to start the little motors, she heard her mother yell from next door.

"Megan! You have a call—it's Mrs. Hadley!"

"All right, Mom, I'm coming!" Megan turned toward her house and started to dart towards home but suddenly put on the brakes when the five foot high fence was in her way. She quickly made it through the gate, almost stumbling, and broke into a run. "Sorry, guys, I've got to take this call. Be right back."

Danny and David had watched Megan in her flight through her backyard and Danny said, "She even runs pretty, David."

"Yeah, I was thinking the same thing. Take away the boobs and long hair and she would look like a boy running. But then..."

Danny started laughing, "Then we wouldn't have a pretty neighbor."

"You got that right. Let's take the battery out of the drone and start recharging it. It should be at one hundred percent by tomorrow. If Scott isn't busy in the morning, we can ask him some questions about flying—I've got a bunch."

"Sounds good. I've got some, too."

Megan was gone for nearly ten minutes before the boys saw her coming back across her yard toward the gate in the fence. When she got closer, she asked, "What happened to the drone?"

David explained, "We had to recharge the battery; there wasn't enough juice left for you to fly it. You can do it tomorrow. What did Mrs. Hadley tell you—any news about Rick?"

"Rick's left leg is going to be in a cast and should heal all right, but his right leg was such a mess they're going to substitute an artificial bone in his thigh. Some of the muscle tissue will have to be removed, but they think they will be able to fix the artery and he won't lose the leg. He's still in surgery, so the doctors couldn't make any promises."

David said, "Geez, that doesn't sound very good. I guess he'll miss graduation this year."

"I think he has enough credits to graduate, but he'll probably have to be in a wheelchair. I guess I could push him around if his mom would allow me."

Danny was listening and asked, "Did Mrs. Hadley say when Scott was coming back?"

"He'll be in the air in about thirty minutes and should be back in about an hour and forty-five minutes. Mrs. Berg has to be back home for dinner so he'll fly her to the hospital where her car is. Mrs. Hadley told Mr. Loebner to park his helicopter south of Roosevelt Road beside Cowpiddle Pond. He wants someone to pick him up."

"Hey, Megan, we can do that. You need to practice your clutch work and we can drive around down there on those dirt roads. Driving on those old trails into the woods requires lots of shifting. What about it?"

Megan thought for a minute and replied, "Dad told me to make sure I had enough gas and a good spare if we drove around out there. I've never changed a tire before, have you?"

"No, but I've seen it done. My dad had to change one of Mom's truck tires once and I watched."

"Yeah, but that was at least four years ago, David. Do you still remember?"

"Come on, Meg, a guy doesn't forget how to change a tire. I'd better call Mom and tell her where we're going, and Danny has to come with us."

"That's all right with me—you'll have more hands to change a tire. I'll bet he can tell you how to do it." Megan's eyes sparkled as her neutral facial expression morphed into a big grin. "I'll tell Mom where we're goin'. Meet you out front." She tossed the keys to David and hurried back into her house.

Julie Drum was driving from Forest Meadows toward Hidden Lakes on a dirt and gravel road that hadn't been travelled since before winter had arrived the previous fall. The old single lane road was surprisingly free of clutter from broken limbs and downed trees caused by the heavier than normal snowfall that January and February had brought. She suddenly hit the brakes when she noticed what appeared to be a rusty piece of metal in the center of the trail waiting to puncture a tire or damage the undercarriage of a vehicle.

Investigation of the object yielded a somewhat surprising result; the object was an old bear trap that was so rusted it couldn't possibly function in its present condition. With some effort, she tossed the antiquated trap in the back of her truck and continued on toward the three small lakes concealed from ground view but easily noticed from an aircraft. She made a mental note to ask Scott to fly her over the area at low altitude so she could observe the condition of the relatively small bodies of water. For her to do a ground level inspection would require a full day of hiking, maybe with the boys in June—after school was out for the summer.

She continued through the densely forested region to the turnaround and headed back toward Forest Meadows, approximately 500 feet below the Meadow Peak lookout tower number 19. She had to investigate if there was any foul weather damage to the fifty-foot structure. A Mr. and Mrs. Ormond had rented the tower for the summer, and would arrive on or about the first of June. Julie hoped the couple would have taken the course of instruction for reporting fires, otherwise a couple of hours would have to be devoted to directions and explaining their responsibilities when reporting fires. She always hoped the newcomers would realize how important their proper function as firewatchers was to the preservation of the forest.

As she climbed upward along the zigzag pathways and concrete steps ascending rock outcroppings, her mind drifted to wondering what Scott was doing. He hadn't had time to explain what the FBI's presence in Suddenly was all about. Julie began to question if Scott Loebner was even his real name; he was probably using an alias when he was doing field work.

Had he lied about being an FBI agent? She was going to be very cautious about the information she divulged to this intriguing helicopter pilot.

She was out of breath when she reached the observation deck and living quarters at the sixty-foot level of the tower. As she looked around the deserted motel-sized top floor, it suddenly occurred to her that Danny and David were becoming friends with Scott. She was going to have a talk with her boys; did they think Scott was sincere? David's opinion of Scott would be the more dependable, Danny was too young to be suspicious of the new comer.

CHAPTER 9

The return trip from Boise was going to be somewhat faster now that the ship was about 400 pounds lighter, but probably only five to ten minutes shorter than the flight time to Boise from Suddenly's hospital.

Scott was thinking about the Drum family as he ferried Mrs. Berg back to Memorial Hospital. Julie Drum was intelligent, had two smart handsome boys, and was a really good looking brunette, about five-eight and from his eyes, in great physical shape. He couldn't think of anything not to like about the entire family. He was assuming Julie was in her middle thirties and had taken good care of herself, in spite of the burdensome days of raising two active boys.

Scott hadn't noticed or heard of Julie being involved with any of the men in Suddenly, but he had only been in contact with a half dozen of the town's citizens, half women and half men. In those brief conversations, Julie Drum hadn't been mentioned. He would have to keep his eyes and ears open to find out more about Julie, but he couldn't believe that she didn't have guys falling over themselves trying to hook up with her.

As he scanned the horizon and glanced at Mrs. Berg to see that she was all right, he decided to make a determined attempt to make friends with Julie's two boys—the best sources of personal information about their attractive mother. He had a perfect way to get on their good side. When in Boise, he had purchased a miniature TV camera and transmitter suitable for the boy's drone, but his original plan was to have the boys help him do some tracking with their small aircraft. Inadvertently, he had stumbled onto another use of the gift.

Mrs. Berg poked Scott on the shoulder and said something, but he couldn't make any sense out her lip movements; the motor was too noisy, he was wearing headphones, and he had never expended much effort to read lips. Scott shook his head and pointed at the receiver covering his ears. She nodded her understanding, shook her head, and waved her hands—it wasn't important. He'd ask her what she had tried to say after they land. He grinned when he thought maybe she'll forget.

Scott turned and announced to Mrs. Berg, "We'll be back at the hospital in about fifteen minutes."

She replied with a thumbs up, leaned back in her seat, and looked out the window toward the ground; the sky was perfectly clear, the sun behind them. Scott looked down and could see the shadow of the helicopter racing across the ground slightly ahead of them.

It only took Julie a couple of minutes to survey the observation tower accommodations and directional equipment before she began the descent to ground level. She always enjoyed looking over the forest from the top of ridges, and the views from tower 19 were no exception, until she had almost reached the rocky ground level. She tripped on the third step and twisted her right ankle—severely. She knew she should have been watching where her feet were being placed where the steps were angled to avoid a large boulder. She dropped to the offending step and sat down hard. She thought, "Damn! I would have to hurt myself at the top of the ridge. The climb down to the truck is going to be a bear—every step will be a pain. I'd better not loosen my boot, my ankle will swell up like a balloon."

Julie looked around the timbers supporting the tower and spied a weathered piece of 2x4 about four feet long. It would have to do for a crutch of sorts; at least she would be able to support some of her weight as she hobbled downhill to her truck. As she began moving down the relatively steep slope, she began to wonder how she was going to drive with her right foot in such pain, but she had no choice, she was alone on the ridge. Her thoughts were directed to the short-wave radio in the dash. It will come in handy, if she needed to contact the sheriff for support. She'd see how things were going when she got to her vehicle.

Julie began to think of crossing a desert and having run out of water when she was halfway to her truck, but what she was desiring was not water, but the soft seat in her pickup.

It seemed like sweat was pouring from her entire body when she reached her truck, threw her crutch to the side, and climbed in the cab. She began to scold herself—the cab had been closed and sitting in the sun; the seat was so hot she couldn't sit down. "Why hadn't I cracked the windows?"

"Oh! The blanket behind the seat!" She got on her knees and reached behind the backrest and extracted one of the blankets she had stashed for winter conditions if she was ever marooned in the cold weather. Doubled up, the wool blanket kept the heat from penetrating through her trousers to her backside. With the engine running, she felt the trip home was going to be painful, but she thought she could tolerate the discomfort for the hour's drive, but Julie hadn't counted on the jostling over the crude roadways. She drove for about ten minutes and had to stop; the pain was becoming unbearable.

"I've got to call Sheriff Howell, he'll come and get me; I'll lock up the truck and get it when my ankle feels better, or after I've gotten some pain killers."

"Sheriff's Office, Ginny speaking. How may I help you?"

"Hi, Ginny. This is Julie Drum. I've hurt my leg and can't drive any further; I'm ten minutes from lookout tower nineteen coming towards Suddenly. Could the sheriff or deputy Doureline come pick me up?"

"I'm sorry, Julie, but the sheriff had to go to Butte, and the deputy's cruiser is being repaired—he hit a cow on Road 131 last night. What about Scott Loebner? He's on his way back from Boise and should arrive at the hospital in the next ten minutes"

"Scott was in Boise?"

"Yes. He flew Rick Hadley, Mrs. Hadley, and Nurse Berg to Boise about three hours ago;

Rick had a terrible accident. I'll call the hospital and they'll give Scott your approximate position."

"Tell Scott to pick up my boys—they'll know where I am."

"Okay, Julie. Hang in there. Help of some kind will arrive in the next half-hour."

"Thanks, Ginny."

Julie left the truck doors open to get some air circulation and lay down on the bench seat to wait for some help, hopefully Scott and her boys. The solitude didn't bother her; she closed her eyes and listened to the calls of birds and the sough from the occasional puffs of afternoon air through the nearby trees.

Megan had driven through the hilly dirt roads three times after David had taken the jeep through the course once and she was tired of constantly shifting of gears. She braked, shut off the engine, and slumped over the steering wheel. "I can't do this any longer, David—I'm sick of it."

"Congratulations, Meg. I was just going to tell you that you have passed the test with a nine out of ten. The last pass was almost perfect. Let's go home and we can all take showers to rinse off the dust."

Danny added, "I'm all for that; my guts are scrambled. Take me home, Megan, before I have to go to the doctor."

Megan gave a questioning look to David and he shook his head; Danny was just jerking her chain. She started the engine, shifted into first and started back home. The five minute drive was made without any problems and Megan smiled when they pulled into the Isaacs' driveway. Mrs. Isaacs was standing outside the front door and she rushed to the jeep.

"David, you and Danny are supposed to meet Mr. Loebner at the hospital; your mom sprained her ankle and can't drive. She wants you boys to show Scott where your mother is. The hospital will tell you where to look for her. Megan, you need to take the boys to the hospital and come right back; I don't want you driving your dad's jeep any more than necessary."

"Oh, all right, but I wanted to pick up some of my friends and drive to Boise to see Rick in the hospital."

Her mother was surprised at first and then said, "Oh, you're joking with me. For a second, I thought you were serious. You can fill up the tank on the way back—have you enough money?"

Megan looked at David and shrugged her shoulders, she didn't know how much gas the jeep tank would hold.

"About thirty bucks should do it, Meg."

She restarted the jeep, backed into the street, waved at her mom and took David and Danny to the hospital. Scott was leaning against the fuselage and stepped away from the craft as the jeep approached. He waved and climbed into the cabin before the jeep had come to a stop. The boys hopped out of the jeep, thanked Megan and clambered into the helicopter. Scott pointed to the safety belts and started the engine, looked at David and asked, "You know where tower nineteen is located? Your mom is about ten miles this side of the lookout."

The engine noise was almost loud enough to prevent hearing, but David yelled, "I know where she is, let's go!"

When the chopper lifted off, the boys glanced down at Megan and saw her wave as they went straight up and began moving away from the hospital. After ten seconds into the flight, David realized they were going in the wrong direction. He tapped Scott on the shoulder and yelled, "That way, Mr. Loebner, and pointed to the left."

Scott removed his headphone and responded, "Okay, David. I was going to ask you for directions as soon as we got away from the hospital—I know the noise is not appreciated by patients and doctors." Scott moved the ship in the direction David had pointed and looked back at David for further instructions. He said, "We're moving much faster than ground traffic, so watch closely for landmarks—things appear differently from above."

"Keep going to the water tower and then follow the road on the east side; that will take us to lookout tower 19. We should see Mom's truck on the road. She'll be happy to see us."

Five minutes later, Danny yelled, "I see Mom's truck—over there." He pointed about two hundred yards ahead to a spot almost devoid of trees where there was a place to set down the chopper not forty yards from the Forest Service truck, which looked deserted.

Scott slowed the chopper and gradually began dropping in altitude. The draft from the helicopter stirred up a cloud of dust and pine needles making it difficult to see the ground, but Scott sat the craft down with only a slight bump and idled the engine, the blades beginning to slow their rotation. Scott released his seat belt and turned toward the boys behind him, "Let's check out your mom, boys."

Danny and David charged toward the canopy door, forcing Scott to deplane a little more quickly than normal, but he followed the kids at a walk as they ran to the truck. David was first to arrive at the vehicle and he called out, "Mom! Where are you?" Danny was quick to comment after he looked in the truck bed, "She's not here, David."

"Boys! I'm in the cab lying on the seat. Thank God you're here—my leg hurts like crazy."

David swung the driver's door wide open and saw Julie reaching toward him, struggling to sit up.

"She's here, Danny. Help me pull her out of the cab."

"Wait, boys. Let me lift her out and sit her down. We don't want her to put weight on her leg; she might injure it some more."

David and Danny moved aside and Scott leaned in the truck and said, "Put your arms around my neck and I'll pull you out so I can carry you to the chopper, okay?"

Julie was happy to see her boys and proud of them for trying to help, but when she was in Scott's muscular arms, she realized how strong he was and how pleasant it felt to be carried by a powerful man to his helicopter.

When the four arrived at the craft, Julie wondered how Scott was going to lift her into the cabin, it was more than four feet from the ground and there wasn't a step.

Scott summoned the boys and had them form a chair with their arms so they could boost their mother up three feet and Scott could lift Julie the final distance from inside the cabin. When she was safely buckled in one of the rear passenger seats, Scott said, "David, can you take Danny and drive the truck back home?"

"No problem. I just need the keys—Mom?"

"I shouldn't let you drive a state car, but hell, it won't hurt this one time. Just be damn careful." With that admonition, she tossed David the keys and said, "Remember, no hot-rodding," and laughed, and then winced when she felt a stabbing pain in her leg.

"Geez, Mom, I know I can't drive as fast as the chopper can fly; it wouldn't even be close." David looked at Scott, "Mr. Loebner, are you going to take Mom to the hospital?"

"I think so, her ankle might be broken—she's in too much pain for the injury to be just a sprain. One of us will call you from the medical center and let you know." Scott whispered, "Better drive to the emergency ward and find out about her ankle. I believe she'll be wearing a cast and I'll need to be picked up when I park the chopper. We can all get home together if you have the pickup."

David nodded, smiled, and said, "Okay. See you at the hospital."

CHAPTER 10

Julie was sitting on a gurney when the boys arrived at the hospital emergency room. Doctor Rennick, the youngest physician at the medical center, was applying a cast to Julie's ankle and foot, her boot and dirty sock were on the floor beside Scott who occupied a chair at the side of the room and was reading a magazine as the physician worked.

David asked, "What's the verdict, nurse?"

"She's a doctor, David. I broke my ankle."

David was embarrassed about addressing the emergency room doctor as a nurse, but he had never met a female doctor before; he had assumed all the doctors in Suddenly were men.

"I'm sorry, doctor. Is it a bad break?"

"Well, that question can be taken two ways. The fracture is clean and should repair quite nicely, but it's a bad break for your mother, she won't be able to work for at least a week. I'll give her a walking cast then and she can continue her normal duties. The new cast will have to be worn for a couple of months, then she'll have to rebuild some muscle due to atrophy."

The disgust was evident in Julie's facial expression. She had so many duties to perform before fire season was in full swing: checking the nine remaining towers in her area, removing obstacles from forest roads, and contacting and training tower renters were some of the most important responsibilities of her job. How was she going to get through the next nine weeks with a cast on her leg? At least managing the boys would not be difficult because they would be in school and when at home, they were reasonably independent.

When Scott and the Drums were all back at the house, Scott volunteered to cook dinner, but the boys would have to help while Julie sat on the sofa and rested her leg.

She reached for the remote but sudden thought to ask, "Scott, do you know how to cook? Maybe we should order some pizza."

"You just relax, Julie, the boys and I are going to prepare a sumptuous meal. I found a bottle of wine in your cupboard—want a glass?"

"Oh! That's been in there for years—it might have spoiled, but let's try it; we can always pour it in the sink if it's bad."

Scott gave Danny some instructions and in a few minutes, the youngest Drum came into the living room with a serving tray, a wine glass, and the freshly opened bottle. He poured about an ounce of the red liquid into the glass, handed it to Julie, and stepped back to observe.

Julie took a sip and exclaimed, "It's good, Scott! What a great idea!" Danny took the glass, filled it halfway and returned it to Julie. "Thank you, Danny."

"Well done, Danny. You might get a job at the country club in a few years if you don't want to attend college. Now, come back in the kitchen and help your brother and me." Scott had been watching as Danny served the wine.

Danny began setting the table and as he was placing the utensils beside each plate, the doorbell rang. "I'll get it." He dropped the knives on the table in a pile and rushed to the door.

He was greeted by Mrs. Isaacs and Megan.

Mrs. Isaacs smiled, "Hi Danny. How is your mother?"

Julie answered the question from the sofa. "I feel fine, Sarah. Come in."

Danny stepped aside and winked at Megan as she squeezed by him. She shook her head and gave Danny a dirty look.

When Sarah saw Julie on the sofa drinking wine, she glanced into the kitchen area and saw Scott and David occupied with something on the counter top near the stove. She looked back toward Julie and said, "I knew you hurt your leg so I wanted to invite you over for dinner; Bruce has something important to finish at the bank, so he's coming home late. He told me to go ahead with dinner, he'd grab a burger on the way home, but I haven't started cooking yet. It looks like you already have something going in the kitchen." Sarah winked at Julie and was quickly acknowledged, "I need to talk to you later, neighbor. How would you and Megan like to join us for dinner?

Julie called out, "Scott, two more for dinner; Megan and Sarah are going to eat with us. Do you have enough of everything?"

"No problem—we're having ham and waffles; wine for the adults and milk, pop, or water for those underage. It's almost ready, better wash up."

"Megan, please hand me those crutches." Julie pointed to the crutches in the corner by the front door.

The three women moved down the hallway to the first floor bathroom and a few minutes later, met with the men at the dining room table where there was a platter full of waffles and serving plate of ham. Scott served Julie and the others stabbed slices of ham, quarters of waffles and sat where they wanted. The boys sat on either side of Megan.

During dinner, Julie explained how she injured her leg and the events that led to the men coming after her in the helicopter. "I was so happy to see my boys and Scott; the cab was getting so hot, even with the doors open, and there was a fly I wanted to hunt down and squish, but every move was so painful, I had to tolerate that pesky bug for almost an hour."

After dinner when the Isaacs were getting ready to depart, Sarah had an opportunity to talk with Julie alone. "Julie, I think Scott is a keeper. If I weren't happily married, I'd be in competition with you. Don't you think he's dreamy?"

"He's very attractive and He seems to like the boys, but there's something about him—I can't explain it—it's just a feeling."

Sarah smiled, "I know the feeling."

"Sarah! Not that. He's just too smooth. I'm going to do a little investigating—see what I come up with."

"Well, thanks for dinner and keep me informed. I promise I won't say anything."

"Yeah, right. Good evening, Sarah."

"Bye, Julie. Take care of that leg. Have the boys help you more than normally. Come on, Megan. Your father will be home before long and he'll wonder where we are. Then he'll probably call the sheriff, before he checks with the neighbors. You know how he gets when he's tired."

Scott and the boys had cleaned up the kitchen with some assistance from Megan and they were finding places in front of the TV when Sarah and Megan left for home. Julie left the crutches by the front door, hopped to the sofa, and plopped down beside Danny.

"You all right, Mom? You're breathing awfully hard."

"I'm okay. I haven't hopped like that since junior high school—I'm out of practice." She glanced at Scott when he stood and said, "I'm headed for bed. I've got to fly to Dillon and Butte tomorrow, but I should be back in the late afternoon or early evening. Don't expect me for dinner."

Julie said, "Thank you for the tasty dinner, Scott. It was nice of you to take over and crack open that bottle of wine. It was like we were celebrating my broken ankle." She laughed and said, "When will you be leaving tomorrow?"

"As soon as the sun's up—I'll see you later in the day. Take care of that ankle. Good night, boys, Julie."

The Drums said, "Good night." David followed Scott to the door and said, "Good night, Mr. Loebner." Scott gave David a slight wave and disappeared around the side of the house.

"Okay, guys, off to bed with you. You're going to go with me to check out fire towers tomorrow. I think we can finish that job by the end of the week and then you can have the weekend to fly your drone before school starts on Monday. Thank you getting me back home and helping Scott with dinner."

"You're welcome, Mom. You want me to drive your truck in the morning?"

"Not only that, but you and Danny will have to climb the towers and check out the accommodations and the Osborne Fire-Finders. I'll give you a list to follow to make sure everything is ready for the occupants."

Danny gave Julie a hug and said, "Good night," and took the stairs two at a time to his upstairs bedroom. David said, "Go on to bed, Mom. I'll lock the doors and get the lights."

Julie woke up early in the morning hearing footsteps on the stairs from the garage. A glimpse of her alarm clock indicated Scott had actually gotten up before the sun rising above the horizon had lightened the surroundings; it was 5:45—too early for her to get up. She turned her damaged leg under the covers, but winced at the pain; the blankets offered too much resistance to free motion. She had to keep her legs in positions so the pain was minimized , which meant sleeping on her right side; those pain pills were going to be used today. She drifted off and slept until 7:30.

Julie forced herself to get up and get dressed after procrastinating for a few minutes past 7:30 a.m. Her alarm had announced the coming of a day of pain and frustration; she would have to sit and watch the boys climb the fire towers and inspect the cabins. She hated taking pills to deaden and control pain, but this time she had no choice. Julie tried to get a clean pair of trousers on but had to give up when the pants were just too tight, so she put on a pair of her husband's pants and turned up the cuff about three inches. She couldn't wear a pair of boots, so she put on a pair of house slippers—they would have to do.

"Boys! Get up and have something to eat; we've got to get out of here and get something accomplished. Wear boots today." She hobbled into the kitchen, cooked enough hot cereal for at least three people, scrambled six eggs, and started packing a cooler with enough food for six boys, although she had only two, she knew how much David and Danny could eat on an active day. She tossed in a package of frozen vegetables to keep everything cool, and six bottles of water.

She didn't have to prod the boys, they had dressed and attacked breakfast in what Julie considered record time. It seemed to Julie they never got ready so quickly on school days. The first tower to be inspected was nearly the farthest from Suddenly at a little over eight miles away on a hill that overlooked a beautiful valley and the southern leg of the lesser Mosquito Bend River. Neither of her boys had been there before, and the road to the three story tower, was unimproved, better suited to an off-road vehicle, but the pickup was up to the task. Julie was surprised and impressed how well David negotiated the difficult terrain with the small truck.

From the outside, it appeared that tower seventeen had withstood the winter months without damage, but Julie reviewed the list of items she wanted the boys to check, especially the fire-finder or the alidade. David was in charge of aligning the Osborne instrument and Danny made sure there was no damage from rodents, presence of bird nests, or bee hives.

David spent about ten minutes completing a thorough inspection of the fire-finder and the boys finished their duties almost simultaneously. Danny looked down from above and yelled to Julie, "Everything is okay, Mom. We're coming down."

Julie chuckled and shouted back, "Don't twist your ankle on the steps!" When she was watching Danny on the tower deck, she noticed several contrails high above which made her wonder what Scott was doing. He hadn't said why he was going to Dillon and Butte, but she concluded it was none of her business; he would tell her if he could.

Four miles to the east, tower twelve was the tallest of the ten structures Julie had to monitor. At twice the height of number seventeen, the sixty-foot structure was prone to wind damage and was built almost entirely from steel beams and girders. In the past some of the windows had been blown out and rain water had damaged the cabin interior. Julie hated to repair the glass windows and usually had just reported the breakage; another crew would be sent out from Butte to fix the problem. Following the twenty minute trip to the monolith, the Drums took time for lunch. Julie felt the boys needed something to eat before the climb to the top, but she wasn't particularly hungry and only drank water.

As they ate and shooed away flies, David asked, "Where's the next one, Mom?"

"Five point three miles due north at the rim of Shadow Valley. It's on a ridge overlooking the depression between Broken Ridge and the Rutland hills. We'll have to ford three small streams to get there, so we might have to skip tower twenty and come back early and hike from Indian Lodge mesa. It will take all day to do that one without travelling on wheels."

"But, Mom, you can't hike with that cast." Danny reminded Julie of her injury.

"That's right—we'll go as far as we can in the pickup and reevaluate the distance. If we can't get there today, we'll go home."

"I vote for that; I'm tired of driving over rocks and bumps. I think my butt is going to need a pillow tonight." David rubbed his right buttock.

CHAPTER 11

The Drum family was unable to get to tower twenty without an off-road vehicle so Julie decided she would come back another time when she was able to hike in, but she was fairly sure that wouldn't happen for at least nine weeks. By then, school would be out, and if no one had rented or otherwise manned that station for the fire season, the boys could hike in and stay several weeks, if not all summer—but she wondered if they could do it unsupervised. She didn't want to reinjure her ankle before it had sufficient time to mend and she didn't want the boys to risk injury hiking in by themselves. She thought that perhaps Scott could fly them in when he wasn't busy hunting criminals.

Scott had flown to Butte to meet with a captain Lloyd Obertti concerning a report that had come from Dillon. Someone, apparently from the vicinity of Suddenly, had asked some less than reputable individuals in Barry's Bar and Grill if they could carry out a kidnapping. The bar's owner met with Dillon police, who had contacted the FBI after the locals heard about the plan, afraid the perpetrators would take an individual across state lines or into Canada; both federal crimes and beyond the jurisdiction of the Dillon police.

When at the Butte airport, following his meeting, Scott filled the chopper's tank with 100LL AvGas and landed a half-mile from the outskirts of Dillon in a forested area hidden from the main drag. He donned clothes to add authenticity to his disguise as an out of work trucker, and walked into Dillon to Barry's place.

As Scott entered the bar area, he felt like he had time travelled to the 1950's, the bluish haze of smoke almost made him gag; he had never smoked—never had any desire to. Three young men were playing pool, cigarettes hanging from their lips, and betting on every shot. A patron had his back to the door and was talking with a middle-aged woman two stools to his right. As Scott approached the bar, the man swiveled his stool and scanned Scott from head to toe, as did the woman.

The woman offered her hand and said, "I'm Sally. Newcomer?"

Scott nodded, shook Sally's hand and sat down between the two patrons, "Scott."

"What'll you have?" asked the barkeep.

"Coors—can, not draft."

The man to Scott's left said, "Jay-jay," and extended his left hand, holding his half-filled mug of beer in his right, a spot of suds clinging to his beard below his lower lip. He appeared to have been at the bar for some time.

Scott replied, "SL. How yah doin'?" Scott filled his mouth, swirled the fluid and swallowed.

"Thirsty, ain't you?" Sally observed, then she asked, "What are you driving, a semi?"

"Was, until I got to Butte. CTN fired me—picked up a hitch hiker—a vet needed a lift, but pickin up hitchers is against company policy. Pissed me off; the guy needed a ride."

"So how'd you get to Dillon?"

"Flew in."

Sally laughed, "I'm wondering where you put your wings— you an angel or somethin'?" She smiled and twisted some of her blonde curls around her black finger nails.

Scott noticed her tattooed wristband of tiny daggers. "Yeah—you got that right," Scott chuckled; Sally had no clue how close she was to being correct. He decided to forge ahead and find who hires for odd jobs, "Are there any jobs for a helicopter pilot around here?"

Jay-jay said, "You fly a chopper? That how you got here?"

"That's right; it's parked about a half mile out in a meadow."

"Ah, that's why we didn't hear it. Why'd ya land so far out?"

"I don't like people messing around my chopper; it attracts all kinds. If something gets screwed up, it could kill me."

"Want another beer?"

"No thanks, Jay-jay. I've got to fly to Suddenly for dinner. Got to have my wits about me when I'm flying."

"No shit? You goin' to Suddenly? My brother needs a hand; his son got hurt and can't help with loggin' anymore. How much can your chopper lift?"

"Three-quarters ton if I strip it down to bare necessities. What's your brother's name; maybe I can haul some timber for him."

"It's Hadley, Adam Hadley. His son is Rick Hadley. He's a star football player—or was. Adam said Rick might not walk again."

"That's tough luck. Got your brother's number?"

Jay-jay grabbed a napkin, borrowed a pen from Sally, and scribbled a number on the soft paper he had pulled from the dispenser between the salt and pepper shakers. He gave the napkin to Scott and said, "You make damn sure you call him, he's shorthanded. And tell him I sent ya. You'll make some good money and he might have another important job."

"Well, I'd better get goin' if I'm to make my dinner date. Nice meeting you and Sally and thanks for the tip about getting some work. The truck company cut me off without my last pay-check—punishment for ferrying a soldier to Butte. I don't think that was legal but what was I to do, hire a high priced lawyer?"

"Good luck to ya, Scott. Say hello to my brother and his wife for me."

Scott had walked a mile, spent thirty minutes at a bar, had a beer, and had gotten some important information—all in less than an hour. In about fifteen minutes he would be back over Suddenly, another fifteen and he would be back at the Drums'. If he was too late for dinner with Julie and the boys, he would toss something in the microwave, eat, hatch a plan for working for Adam Hadley, and go to bed early; it had been a long day. He wondered what Julie and the boys had accomplished with their investigations of the fire lookout towers.

When Scott landed on the outskirts of Suddenly, he was surprised to see Julie's truck, but when the dust and needles quit swirling around, he saw David and Danny standing outside the truck waving. He sealed the cabin and walked toward the waiting reception committee.

"Hi, boys. How long have you been here?"

David said, "Just a few minutes. We drove out to pick you up when we heard you fly over town. We were under those trees where the ground was firmer, but I decided to move closer when you were landing; the ground is fairly hard where it has been exposed to the sun. How was your day?"

"I met an interesting person in Dillon. If you haven't eaten dinner yet, I'll tell you about my meeting while we eat; your mother will be interested."

"Come on, Mr. Loebner, tell us about it," Danny didn't like to wait for anything intriguing, and the way Scott was talking, the information was going to be good, maybe very good. Danny realized he was going to have to wait, but his imagination was going full blast.

He thought to himself, "Why would Mom be interested? Did whatever it was have to do with her job? Was another ranger moving to Suddenly to help with overseeing the forest in the Suddenly district? Was Mom going to be transferred to a different area? Oh, well, I guess I'll just have to wait and find out what Mr. Loebner tells Mom."

Mom had cooked hamburgers and made a green salad by the time Scott and the boys arrived back at the house. They were all eating, but Danny couldn't stand not knowing what the news was, so he said, "Who did you meet in Dillon, Mr. Loebner? Was it a man or a woman?"

Scott chuckled, "It was Jay-jay Hadley, Adam Hadley's younger brother. He wants me to see his brother about a job—hauling timber. Since Rick was hurt, Adam needs another worker, and he thinks I can help by moving cut tree sections to the loader.

I've never done that before, so I'll have to talk with Mr. Hadley and decide whether I want to try it. I think it could be pretty dangerous lifting logs. I'll meet with him tomorrow and see it it's something I want to do."

Danny was disappointed, having imagined something entirely different than Scott had revealed, he had found no excitement generated from Scott's meeting with Mr. Hadley's younger brother, but he hadn't the vaguest knowledge of what Scott was working on, and didn't foresee any turmoil in Suddenly until summer arrived and another year of school was over. It was Danny's experience that fire season usually coincided with the start of summer vacation. He pictured flying the drone over a fire and warning the fighters of impending disaster, perhaps being able to save lives in the process.

Julie knew nothing of the reason Scott had flown to Butte, only about what had taken place in Dillon, about potentially flying for Mr. Hadley, but she was a little worried when Scott admitted never before having ferried logs with his helicopter. She knew that job could be very risky, especially on windy days. She had heard of cables giving way and logs being dropped from the sky striking the forested area like bombs, occasionally killing workers on the ground.

"What did you do in Butte, Scott?"

Scott had expected Julie to ask that question. "Filled my tank with AvGas—I was down to fumes. Last time I got fuel was in Boise—they don't carry one hundred octane low lead aviation gas in small towns. In a pinch I can use high octane gasoline for cars." Scott didn't mention his meeting with Lloyd Obertti. Although he trusted Julie, he didn't want anyone to know what his assignment was; an agent had to keep secrets, or perhaps lose his life.

Scott changed the subject, "Have you been flying the drone, boys?"

David answered, "We've been too busy to do much more than take off and land a few times. Danny and I have both flown a little. This weekend we'll get more experience—unless Mom wants us to defuse some nuclear bombs." He looked at his mom and smiled.

"Very funny, David. You know that I don't have paid sick leave. You'll have the entire weekend to fly the drone; I promised."

"Geez, Mom, I was just joking around. Danny and I have been having fun climbing those towers. Oh, yeah, I forgot to tell you, after I thought about it, I think the window in the tower was shot out, not blown out by wind."

"When did you come up with that?"

"It was something Danny said after we got back home. He asked me if a twenty-two bullet would break the glass in the tower. I told him maybe if shot from fairly close. Then I remembered seeing two partial circular holes on fragments of the glass as I cleaned it up. At first, I thought when the glass fell into the cabin, it might have hit something and made those rough edges when it hit the floor."

Scott said, "How big were the holes?"

David thought for a moment and said, "About a half inch. But that's just a guess, but bigger than a pencil."

"Sounds like a hunting rifle to me." Scott remarked and glanced at Julie.

Julie nodded and replied, "That happens almost every year to one of the towers in my area. A hunter can't track down a game animal and gets frustrated, decides to take it out on a glass window on a fire lookout tower. I recommended to the department that the windows should be replaced with some sort of plastic, but nothing has been done about it yet; it's an expensive job and the towers are losing their importance now—monitoring by air and the use of GPS are taking over the lookout's jobs."

Scott commented, "So the people renting the towers really aren't very important for reporting fires anymore?"

"We want them to think they are helping, and they are, but not like in the before modern technology days. The renters like to think they are protecting the forests—a good response to our advertising for their assistance, but they only confirm what we have pinpointed from the air. They pay rent and the forest service benefits—helps pay my salary anyway."

CHAPTER 12

The Drums kept busy the next two days checking the fire towers and didn't see Scott until close to noon Saturday morning. He had gotten back from working for Mr. Hadley after midnight Friday and quietly showered and went to bed. He had slept for nearly ten hours before he heard the Drum boy's voices in the backyard.

Scott looked out the apartment window overseeing the backyard and saw the boys flying their drone, still tethered. Megan sat at the table with her head tossed back, looking at the drone circling overhead. As he observed the young people, he considered what it might be like having a daughter as pretty as Megan. Would he be so strict with her to investigate every young man she dated? Probably, but keeping her on a short leash might cause a severe strain on their relationship. He would have to be cautious, but bow to the knowledge that he had raised her with good moral values. Scott knew that Megan was dating Rick Hadley, and Mr. Hadley was definitely no gem, but Mrs. Hadley seemed genuine and very concerned with Rick's well-being.

He looked at David and imagined him as a potential son-in-law. David was a handsome sixteen year old, still developing physically, intelligent and thoughtful. Scott wondered what David would major in at a university; his grades were probably good enough to get scholarship money, lessening the pressure on his mother. He wasn't as gregarious as his brother, Danny.

Danny was a spur-of-the-moment kid and loved to joke with everyone. He was nearly as tall as his brother, but probably thirty to forty pounds lighter. He was very clever at solving problems, both mental and physical. Being the second son, Danny had learned much from watching his older brother.

His mind wandered to the boy's mother. Julie was a really attractive woman, smart, and possessed a great sense of humor, and in addition, had a high threshold of pain—she was taking the broken ankle in stride and continuing her responsibilities as if little had taken place. She certainly wasn't a whiner.

Scott dressed quickly, grabbed a small, gift wrapped box he had brought from Boise, and joined the backyard group. Megan was the first to see Scott approaching from the garage.

"Hey, guys, there's Mr. Loebner. He must have gotten back from the Hadleys' last night."

Danny was flying the drone and couldn't look away, but he said, "Hi," nearly simultaneously with David. David noticed the box, pointed at it, and said, "Something for Mom?"

Scott gave the box to David and commented, "No," he smiled, "something for your drone."

"Here, Megan, you open it. Pretend it's a birthday present."

Megan turned away from the others, tore off the wrapping and said, "Wow! David, it's a TV camera for the drone." The ad on the box cover was easy reading.

"Geez, Megan, let us see it."

She turned around and held out the box, "It says it'll work on any drone of the type D4; is your drone that kind?"

Scott said, "It better be; the guy I talked to knew just about every type of drone ever made—in his opinion."

Danny stated, "It's a D4, David. It says so on the instruction manual."

"Bring the drone back in, Danny. Let's see how this is gonna work." David opened the box and read the small instruction pamphlet for a few seconds. "We need a CRT and rabbit ears."

Megan glanced at the instructions, looked David, and said, "What's a CRT?"

"It's an old television—a cathode ray tube—before flat screens like we have now." David was thinking about what was in the coat closet next to the living room. "We've got rabbit ears in our hall closet with the light bulbs and Christmas wrapping paper, but we don't have an old TV."

"We've got one. It's in a plastic bag in our garage on a shelf. Dad was going to give it to the Salvation Army, but they said they didn't want it. I think it has a fifteen inch screen, but it's an old black and white set, and it's heavy."

"Do you think your dad would let us use it?"

"Sure, David. He'd give it to you just to get it out of the garage."

"Awesome, let's get it. I'll carry it."

While Megan and David retrieved the old television set, Scott and Danny took apart the drone, removed the video memory card, and the original camera. Following the installation procedure, they inserted the TV camera, lithium hydride battery, and tiny integrated circuit transmitter tuned to channel 3. Danny rummaged through the hall closet, found the rabbit ears, and returned to the backyard with the old antenna and a screwdriver.

David and Megan arrived with the TV and an extension cord as Scott was talking to Danny about the adjustable nature of the antenna. David unwound the cord, plugged into the CRT and walked toward the house where the outdoor electrical box resided. When David had the cord connected he yelled back, "Turn on the TV, Meg!"

The set lit up and nothing but snow could be seen, just what Scott had expected. "Okay, Danny, pilot the drone up about twenty feet and press the 'On' button twice." Everyone watched the aircraft rise to twice the height of the house and an image appeared on the CRT.

David poked Megan and said, "Wave at the drone Megan."

Danny yelled, "It works, Mr. Loebner; that's awesome! Look, Megan, you're on TV!"

Scott said, "We're all on TV, Danny. Give us a scenic tour of the backyard."

The drone started slowly circling the yard, starting near the backdoor and moving from tree to shrub to fence and on to hovering over the garage roof momentarily before moving on, completing a full loop of the yard.

"Time for lunch! Everyone come inside, get warm, and get ready for your noses to drip. I've got homemade minestrone, cheese and crackers, and sweet potato pie. Boys, you'd better put the drone away, there's a storm front coming through and we'll probably in for some lightning and heavy rain."

Danny brought the drone in for a perfect landing, turned off the motors, and the TV screen went blank. With the drone and the controller in his grasp, Danny headed for the garage to stow the aircraft. Scott was coiling up the extension cord and Megan was carrying the TV set toward the open garage door. David was following Megan toward the garage and said, "What about it, Megan—do you want to stay and eat with us? We'd like to have you stay, unless your mom has something planned."

Julie was listening to David from the slider, rubbing her arms because of the chilly outdoor air infiltrating through the screen door. She said, "You're invited, too, Scott."

Megan set the CRT inside the garage on the floor and turned around to face David.

She grinned, "Do you have plenty of napkins or Kleenex for me to wipe my runny nose?"

David laughed, "I don't know about napkins or Kleenex, but I'll get you a roll of toilet paper—if that will do."

Danny grinned and added, "You can use my handkerchief, Megan. I only used it once for a sneeze a couple of days ago. You can shake out the dried boogers."

"You know what, Danny? You're disgusting." She began walking back toward the gate to her back yard, but changed her mind and ran to catch up with David and Scott, who were just about to enter into the kitchen through the slider. They stepped aside, opened the panel for Megan, and followed her into the house.

Danny was jabbering to Julie when Scott, Megan, and David returned from washing in the bathroom.

"No, Mom, Scott got us a real TV camera for the drone. We just got it checked out and it's awesome. Now we'll all be on TV—I'm going to write a play and we'll record it for posterity."

David laughed and said, "Posterity? You mean to keep it and show it to your kids? By that time the type of recording devices we have now will be obsolete and you'll have to go to a museum to play back the recording. But, first we need to get a battery operated TV so we can use the drone and camera away from the house, maybe out in the forest. If we can do that, I'll help you with your production; I'll even do a commercial for you."

Megan commented, "I'll be the heroine, Danny; you and David can rescue me from some scums—like those two guys that tried to rob the pharmacy."

Danny was serious about his intentions. "What kind of commercial?"

"I don't know, maybe a pill that will prevent you from brain injury, or plastic windows that are bullet proof."

"Okay boys, come get a bowl and help yourselves to some soup. Megan, you and Scott are first, while my boys get back to the real world." Julie looked up at the ceiling when a clap of thunder shook the windows announcing the arrival of a storm.

When everyone had started eating, the rain was coming down in torrents, seemingly trying to wash the shingles off the top of the house. The water striking the composition roofing made a low frequency rumble like sixteen kettledrums, the sound of the cavalry charge in an opera.

Julie got up and went to the kitchen window to see the downpour. "God, this is going to make a mess of all the roads to the lookout towers, and I've still got to check out the Shadow Valley observation post."

David said, "That's tower twenty, Mr. Loebner; we had to skip it. It's really hard to get to; you have to ford three streams— takes a four wheeler to get in there."

Scott replied, "I could fly you in, Julie. That would get it out of mind so you could concentrate on other things. How is that ankle doing? I could climb the tower for you and check out the cabin."

"My ankle is feeling pretty good, thanks. Don't you have other things to do for your job? I can't have you flying me around so I can do my job, but thanks for volunteering. By the way, did my boys thank you for the camera?"

"I forgot, Mom. I'm sorry," Danny said.

"Yeah, me too. Thank you Mr. Loebner. Mom, I forgot, too. I think it was because of all the excitement."

Julie shook her head, "I'm surprised at both of you for not having any manners. I think you need a refresher course. Okay, no fooling around with the drone for the next week."

"You mean until next Sunday?"

"Yes, Danny, until next Sunday, and if I discover that you've violated my conditions, the drone will go in the fireplace and the camera will be returned to Mr. Loebner. I'm serious."

"I'm sorry, Mom. We won't fly the drone." David couldn't look at Megan; he was too embarrassed and couldn't think of anything else to say.

There was a few seconds of silence, a crack of thunder made everyone flinch, and a loud explosion, not far from the neighborhood because of the deafening noise caused Megan to cry out, "What was that, Mrs. Drum!" Megan grabbed David's arm and hung on tightly.

"Lightning must have hit a tree; we'll take a look when the rain stops and the storm passes." Julie looked at Scott and said, "We have a little excitement like this once or twice a year."

Scott reacted, "Sounded like a stick of dynamite to me."

Everyone was sitting down in the living room and talking about the storm when the phone rang.

Julie answered, "Hi, Sarah. What did you say?" She looked at Megan and said, "It's your mother, Megan. She says not to worry; they're all right. Lightning hit the chimney on your house—it gave them a terrible scare. They were glad you were over here." Julie listened for a few seconds, grinned, and said, "Okay. Good bye, Sarah."

"Megan, your mom said to stay here until the rain stops and then you can go home."

"Thanks, Mrs. Drum, but I think I'll go now. Mom probably needs some support."

"I'll go with you, Meg. We'll cover up with my dad's raincoat." David was pulling a large, yellow, vinyl coat from the hall closet.

Scott glanced at Julie and she nodded; it was okay with her; the rain had lessened considerably. Julie said, "Come right back, David."

David and Megan stepped out on the front porch and watched the rain for a few seconds before David said, "Let's put the coat over our heads; you hold with your right and I'll hold with my left." He extended his right hand and touched Megan's left. "Here, grab my hand and don't run too fast, you'll beat me to your front door," he grinned and they took position.

"Ready? Let's go!" It took about four seconds for them to get to Megan's front door where they dropped the coat, but were still holding hands.

Megan said, "I've forgotten to say thank you before, David. I wouldn't worry about it. Thanks for bringing me home." She pulled David's head down to hers and kissed him.

David was a little surprised, but said, "Thanks, Megan." He smiled and hurried home with the raincoat over his head.

CHAPTER 13

Ms. Sidwicke's Biology class met at ten o'clock Monday morning. Students were seated in alphabetical order and Megan was directly behind David; they had not talked since Saturday's venture into the rain and that interesting interaction on the Isaacs' front porch. The talking between students faded with the sound of the bell starting class.

The lecture began, "I have decided, after having a discussion with Principal Personette, to venture into something we have never before studied except for briefly mentioning it when we talked about recessive and dominant alleles or traits." She scanned the twenty-two students and saw that she had their more than usual attention.

"I need two volunteers, one male and one female; they cannot be related, in other words, no brother and sister combination." She looked around, as did the students, to see who would volunteer for this obvious sex-related pairing. There were no volunteers.

David turned so he could make eye contact with Megan and pointed to her and then himself. Megan frowned and then smiled, nodding her acceptance and inclusion as a volunteer. David raised his hand and said, "Megan and I will volunteer, but first we need more information about the experiment." A murmur spread throughout the class; the others had not heard of Rick's accident and knew that David was in for trouble by pairing up with Megan.

"Thank you, David, I was going to give some more explanation after I got some volunteers. I wanted to see if all of you followed the adage 'don't ever volunteer.' I'm happy to see that some of you do not follow the crowd." Everyone except David and Megan seemed to be fidgeting as the teacher scanned the class letting them know she was disappointed with them.

"Here's the deal: I want you each to get samples from your family members so that we can observe DNA sequences that exhibit family relationships. In your case David, you can select some adult male to represent your father. His genetic fingerprint will show that he cannot be your father. However, you must inform each individual what you are doing and must have their permission. I will include consent forms with the sampling containers; make sure you get them signed and dated, otherwise we cannot use their specimen. Please see me at the end of class for the sample containers and authorization sheets."

Megan went to Spanish IV after biology and David had PE so the neighbors didn't talk about their DNA assignment until lunch hour.

"Do you think your Mom and Dad will object to the swabbing of their cheeks for the DNA testing?"

"I don't think so; I can't imagine why they would. They know they're my folks. What will your Mom say?"

David laughed, "She'll probably want to collect the samples. I think she's done some DNA stuff before on animals. I'm going to ask Mr. Loebner for a sample—there's no way on earth he could be my father."

Megan grinned and poked a fork with a cube of lime Jell-O on it at David, "Are you sure about that?"

"Yeah—one hundred percent sure. The pictures of my dad when he was a teenager look just like me." It was time to tease Megan, "But you, Megan, are so pretty—you don't look that much like either of your parents; could you be adopted?"

Megan looked down at her tray at the vibrating Jell-O, her leg was bouncing up and down slightly shaking the table. She had suddenly turned very serious and frowned, "Geez, David, I never thought of that. You might have ruined my day. Now I wonder."

"Oh, come on, Meg. I was teasing. Suddenly is such a small town everyone would know if you were adopted, and besides, who would care? I sure wouldn't mind at all. Put it out of your mind; don't you have to work at the hospital today? Maybe you'll find out some more about Rick."

"I go to Memorial right after sixth period so I won't see you in study hall. I'll talk to you tonight and tell you about my first day as a candy striper. I think that uniform is God awful—if you want my opinion."

"You'll look awesome, Meg, but watch out for the male patients—don't get to close to them—you'll have pinch marks."

"Oh, shut up! You're almost as nutty as your brother."

Julie had given in to Scott and had him fly her to the Shadow Valley fire lookout tower to check the conditions of the cabin and the fire finder apparatus. Julie borrowed two walkie-talkies from Sheriff Howell so she and Scott could communicate when Scott reached the top of the observation post. Julie remained in the chopper at the only landing area close to the tower and Scott hiked a quarter mile to the structure. Five minutes after arriving at the cabin, he called Julie.

"Hey, Julie, it smells a little musty in here and the place needs some dusting, but the Osborne works fine; I sighted it in as you instructed. I don't see any breakage in the cabin, but a few of the wooden steps need some work—looks like a little dry rot."

Julie sighed, "Well, that's good news. Please measure the treads that need to be repaired and I'll get some replacements. The boys can help me fix them before anyone rents the cabin for the summer."

"I can help you with that, Julie."

"Thanks, Scott, but you must have your own work to do—unless you haven't been honest with me."

"Suspicious, huh? I've been honest with you about my job but I can't tell you what I'm working on right now. Hopefully, my current assignment will be over before July gets here."

"And then you'll be moving on?"

"That's too far in the future to know what I'll be doing. I must admit I'm getting pretty tired of moving around the country, staying in one place for a few weeks or months before having to move on."

"No current girlfriend or wife involved?" There was a moment of silence. "Sorry if I'm getting too nosey."

"That's all right. I've been running around the country for so long I haven't formed any close relationships—with people, that is."

"Oh! You have a pet. I bet it's a dog."

"You're right. It's a dog. He's in a kennel in Spokane; I miss him but it's only been a week since we parted company. His name is Spectrum—he's some of everything, but looks mostly like a German Shepard." Scott laughed, "He likes beer."

"Aha! You have a drinking buddy. So are you finished up there? I'd like to go back home and get warm, my cast is cold and uncomfortable. Let's get back in the air and you can turn on the heater."

Scott had been descending the tower while they were talking and had already hiked about halfway back to the helicopter. In only a few minutes he was back and surprised Julie who was sitting with her eyes closed, thinking she would be waiting another half hour for Scott to return. He knocked on the canopy and she flinched, opened her eyes, and saw Scott smiling, looking at her like he had caught a thief stealing Christmas presents.

The cockpit door swung open and he said, "Sorry I scared you; I was almost back when we quit talking. Anything else to do out here?"

Julie answered quickly, "Nope! My toes are so cold; let's get out of Shadow Valley. I don't know if you had heard this but Big Foot has been sighted around here before. It gets kind of creepy in the late afternoon shadows. There's a story about a log-ging truck that was found on its side not far from here."

Scott began laughing as he climbed in the chopper beside Julie. "Do you believe those Paul Bunyan tales?"

"I used to think those things were figments of imagination, but over the years I've seen some strange things. Did I tell you I found a bear trap in the roadway last week? One of the old timers said it was from the 1880s. I can't figure out how it got in the middle of the access road."

"Huh. That does sound a bit strange to me." Scott sealed the cabin door, started the engine and after a minute to warm up the motor and Julie's toes, piloted the chopper back to Suddenly.

David had walked home from school with only one text in his backpack: biology, but he had a small package of containers and swabs for DNA collection in with his book. He had finished his other homework during last period study hall. At the end of sixth period, Megan had gone to the hospital to work, so David concentrated on his studies during that last hour of classes. Danny's bike was leaning against one of the support columns of the front porch so David knew his brother was already home.

The door was locked so he used his key and entered. "Hey, Danny, where are you?"

He heard a muffled reply, "In my bedroom—reading about astronomy."

Megan had driven her father's jeep to Memorial Hospital and parked in the reserved section, not knowing if that was a privilege of being a candy stripper. She signed in at the reception desk and met with Nurse Berg, who had been waiting for her arrival. As they walked down the main corridor, Mrs. Berg commented, "I was told by Mrs. Hadley that you are her son's girlfriend."

"Uh-huh. Rick and I have been dating since the homecoming football game last year. Can you tell me how he is doing?" They walked a few more steps before the nurse replied, "I'm sorry, hon, but since you aren't family, I can't tell you any details, but I can tell you he's doing as well as could be expected. He had a terrible injury. He was very lucky that Mr. Loebner was able to fly him to specialists for the best care possible. We couldn't have done much for him here. That's all I can say—maybe that was too much."

Mrs. Berg put her arm around Megan's shoulder. "I'm going to start you off with an elderly patient that fell and hit his head. His name is Robert Ganz; he's in room fourteen—that's on the East wing; odd numbered rooms are on the West. You can talk to him if you like and pick up his lunch tray. Take the tray to the kitchen; they'll show you where it goes. Come see me after you do that—at the reception desk." Nurse Berg turned and made her way back toward the hospital entrance, occasionally stopping to look in on a patient.

Megan was all alone and she was acutely aware of her situation. She went forward a few steps, checked the room number and moved on to the next room, number 14. The door was halfway open and she hesitated, not knowing what to expect. Was the old man going to be presentable?

She pushed the door open so she could pass freely and stepped into the dimly lit room. The small amount of light from the draped window and the hallway was enough for her to make out the patient leaning against pillows and covered to his chest with a blanket and sheet. She saw the tray on the small adjustable table and advanced cautiously, watching the form in the bed for any movement.

"Who's there?"

"Oh! You scared me; I thought you were sleeping. I've come to pick up your tray from lunch."

"Well, for God's sake, turn up the lights so I can see you, or are you on a black ops mission?"

Megan laughed and found the light switch next to the door. She pressed the switch and the ceiling lights fully illuminated the sparsely furnished little room, hardly bigger than Megan's bedroom.

"Am I dead?" the old man said.

"What? No, you're not dead. Why would you say such a thing?"

"You look like an angel—you are beautiful—just like I have imagined an angel in heaven."

"What a nice compliment, Mr. Ganz. Thank you." Megan smiled and moved more directly to the tray than previously. As she scooped up the tray, she glanced at Mr. Ganz and smiled. Should she tell him to have a nice day? She felt very awkward; what could she say?

Fortunately, Mr. Ganz spoke, "Please sit for a minute, young lady, and tell me who you are."

Megan pulled the only chair from its position against the wall and sat down with the tray in her lap. She spoke for less than a minute before she ran out of things to tell the elderly gentleman. She sat smiling for a moment and stood up.

"Just wait for another minute, Megan Isaacs; don't run off. Do you have to be somewhere?"

"I'm supposed to take your tray to the kitchen."

CHAPTER 14

"I surely wouldn't want to get you fired, young lady. Perhaps we will talk some more at another time?"

"Yes, I'm sure we will. I want you to tell me how you hit your head, maybe later this afternoon, or day after tomorrow. I come to the hospital after my classes and only for a couple of hours Monday, Wednesday, and Friday. I'll see you again, okay?"

Mr. Ganz nodded and said, "Remember, you are my angel."

After delivering the tray, Megan found Nurse Berg talking to Nurse Larkin at the front desk. Megan waited for the conversation to end and said, "Mr. Ganz is really nice, Mrs. Berg; we had a little chat—he called me his angel. He wants me to come back to talk some more."

Nurse Berg smiled and said, "Did he say anything strange to you, Megan."

Megan thought for a moment and said, "Not really, except calling me his angel. But he explained why he said that."

"So he knows where he is?"

"I think so; that didn't come up. He asked me about what courses I was taking in school. I told him we'd talk about how he hit his head. He seemed all right with that."

"Okay, but if he says anything really strange, let me know right away—he could have a brain injury. If so, we'll have to conduct further tests. Let me show what you can do for the remainder of your time here today. Please come with me."

Midway down the hall, Mrs. Berg entered a code on the numerical lock and the door sprung open. Megan looked into the utility closet and saw a bucket on casters, a mop, a shelf containing cleaning supplies, and a pair of vinyl covers to fit over her street shoes. Megan glanced at Nurse Berg who was smiling, and said, "Where do you want me to start mopping?"

On the return flight to Suddenly, Julie gave Scott a quick tour of three other lookout towers before Scott landed at Cowpiddle Pond and shut off the chopper's engine. As the rotor wound down, they sat and conversed, expecting their talk to last only a minute, but they talked for nearly a half-hour.

"How did the boys take the death of their father?"

"Danny cried a lot at first, but David held it all in. He's been like a rock and I'm afraid he has been too serious about things. He sometimes says things to Danny—and even Megan, whom he adores, that are too critical, and seem to lack compassion. He wants companionship, but is afraid he might lose them."

"I can understand that; I lost a close cousin in Iraq. He was killed in a helicopter crash. He's one of the reasons I became a pilot."

"Oh! I thought you were a pilot in the war."

"No, I was in special forces. I went to flight school after coming back to the states. Flight training helped keep my mind busy and I think I've overcome my problems with forming relationships."

Julie looked at Scott and said, "I believe you have. My boys and I like you very much."

"That's good to know; it works both ways." He smiled and glanced at Julie's cast. "How's your ankle feeling?"

"My muscles are a bit stiff from sitting too long. I think you'll have to help me to the truck."

"Not a problem."

Scott dropped to the ground and motioned for Julie to sit on the edge of the canopy door. "Okay, lean forward and I'll catch you." When he had her in his arms, he lowered her slowly to the ground and when their faces were close, Julie kissed him. Scott held her tightly and gave her a lingering kiss in return. Julie's body shuddered slightly as she was slowly released from Scott's grip. Scott steadied her, locked the chopper door, picked Julie up, and carried her to the passenger door of the truck.

When they were in the truck, Julie smiled at Scott and said, "It's been a long time since I had that experience."

Scott started the truck and smiled back, "What experience are you talking about?"

"You want me to spell it out, huh?" She paused for a moment and continued, "Our kissing and being carried by a handsome man."

Scott chuckled and said, "Well, that was a new happening for me."

"What happening are you talking about?"

Scott glanced at Julie, who was smiling, "Being kissed by a beautiful woman."

"Hah! I find that hard to believe."

As the truck pulled into the Drums' driveway, Julie placed her hand over Scott's and said, "We'd better be careful about showing affection—I'm not sure how the boys will react."

Scott held Julie's hands in his and said, "*That* is going to be very difficult."

Scott stayed for dinner with the Drums and as they were having dessert, David mentioned the DNA project he and Megan had volunteered to carry out.

"We didn't do anything like that when I took biology; isn't it expensive?"

"I don't know how much it costs, Mom, but Ms. Sidwicke got the okay from the principal." David looked at Scott and said, "Do you mind taking the place of my father?"

"It's all right with me, but you realize the DNA will show that we aren't related."

"Yeah, my teacher expects that to be the case. That's part of the study. Everyone has to sign a permission slip, too. Mom, you'll have to sign for Danny and me."

Julie said, "Do you have the sample containers?"

"I'll get them. They're in my back pack." David skidded his chair back from the table and went toward his bedroom and the phone rang. Danny pushed away from the table and ran to the receiver on the kitchen wall.

"It's Mrs. Isaacs, Mom. She wants to talk to you."

"Hi, Sarah. Sure, come on over. Have you had dessert?—All right. We've finished dinner and are talking about DNA, too."

David went to the door and welcomed the Isaacs into the house. After everyone was seated in the living room, Sarah spoke up, "Julie, what do you think of this DNA thing? Do you think it's a good idea to have a teenage biology class looking at our identity?"

Julie hesitated, not wanting to embarrass her friend and next-door neighbor. She glanced at Scott, hoping for some support, not knowing how to answer. Scott accepted the nonverbal cue and said, "Maybe I can help you with that question, Mrs. Isaacs."

Scott had captured everyone's attention and explained, "I was in the Special Forces and the government had our DNA recorded—in case our remains needed identification. The reports cannot give any information unless the individual's name is present. No one can recognize their DNA data; it's not like a picture. Before I was shown my DNA profile, I had no idea what it looked like, but it is just a table of numbers."

Julie said, "Thank you, Scott. You certainly know more about DNA than I do."

"I have to thank you, too. I guess I have no reservations about the test. Megan, get out those swabs and take our samples. I'm ready. It doesn't hurt, does it?"

"Mom, it's just a Q-tip. I promise not to stick it up your nose."

When everyone quit laughing, Megan and David obtained a specimen from each person in the room, attached labels, and obtained signatures. Megan gave David her family's samples so he could turn everything in to Ms. Sidwicke at one time. She told David she didn't want to risk contaminating the DNA if she walked around with the sealed containers they might get damaged. Then she made a comment, "I was going to tell you about my job at the hospital, but Mrs. Wallen reminded me that my contact with patients could not be discussed with people outside the hospital unless they are family members."

"So, was your first day interesting? Was it what you expected?"

Megan smiled, "Part of it was; I had to mop the floors around all the entrances and exits."

"For the whole building? There are at least four doorways I can think of. Your arms and back are going to be sore tomorrow."

"There are eight of them, David. Some you don't recognize unless you're inside and there are two emergency doors that are hardly ever opened except by the safety inspector. It took me almost an hour to mop them all."

"Are you the only stripper?—I mean striper?"

She gave David a nasty look, "Very funny. Don't you ever quit? For your information, there are three of us, but I'm the only sophomore. The other girls are seniors and are going to attend nursing schools next year."

"You might want to be a doctor, Megan. You have the smarts to be just about anything you want to be, and doctors make a lot more than nurses, but they have a lot more responsibilities. Could you stand all the blood and guts?"

"I wouldn't have to be a surgeon, I could select an area that isn't so gruesome, don't you think?"

"I suppose—did you get pinched today?"

"David!"

David expected Megan to hit him and he moved away from her punch so it only grazed his shoulder. "You'd better not try MMA, Meg—you hit like a girl."

"I don't know what MMA is—what are you talking about?"

"MMA is mixed martial arts; it's similar to boxing, but they can wrestle, kick, and strike with very light gloves. Don't you watch it on TV sometimes with your father?"

"No. We watch educational shows like National Geographic and PBS, not dumb fighting stuff. Who wants to see two men beat each other up?"

"They have women fighters, too. They're pretty tough."

"Let's talk about something else. Has anyone at school asked about Rick?"

"Barbara and Christie asked me if you left study hall to see Rick; I told them he was still in Boise and you were a candy striper at the hospital. They just looked at each other, shrugged, and went into one of the quiet rooms to study, or talk."

"If Barb and Christie know that much, it will spread like wild fire. I'll have to be ready for questions tomorrow."

Megan didn't look like I had spilled the beans, so I guess I wasn't in over my head, but I said, "Did I tell them too much? I hope I haven't caused you any trouble."

"No, you're all right, David. Let's join our parents and see what they're talking about."

Danny had been excused to his bedroom to do some homework, and the adults had moved to the dining room table and were talking. Scott and Aaron were discussing real estate investments in Suddenly, and Julie was asking Sarah about the damage to their chimney from the lightning strike.

"There were a few bricks broken but it's only going to cost about a hundred dollars to fix the damage and our deductible is five hundred. Aaron thinks that's not bad. The loud noise scared the bejesus out of me; I felt like God was trying to strike us down. It was scary."

Megan bumped her shoulder against David's and rolled her eyes back. David put his hand over his mouth so he wouldn't laugh out loud.

The adults conversed for another ten minutes before the Isaacs' excused themselves and returned home. As they were leaving, Scott announced, "I have to leave for Spokane tomorrow and will be gone for at least a week, maybe longer. If you see someone in the apartment, you'd better call Sheriff Howell. When I return, I'll come by and introduce you to Spectrum. Oh, I forgot to ask if it's all right to have my dog in the apartment."

Julie was surprised that Scott hadn't mentioned leaving until now, but she said, "As long as your dog is potty-trained, it's all right with me."

Scott smiled and replied, "We're both trained, but if there's an accident, I'll clean it up."

"I should hope so," Julie said. "Have a good trip and hurry back. We'll all be missing you."

Chapter 15

Megan drove the Drum boys to school in the morning at 7:30. It was a little early for them, but better than walking seven blocks in the wind and light rain. Scott hadn't left for his chopper yet and when he stopped to say good bye to Julie, she offered to give him a ride to Cowpiddle Pond, she had to drive that way to visit the Walthams'.

They had lost a cow, apparently from a bear attack, and they wanted the bear hunted down and destroyed. Julie was going to have to tell them tracking the bear would have to wait until she got a walking cast on her leg in another week. In the intervening time Mr. Waltham would have to search for the beast by himself, but Julie had to warn him that hungry bears could be extremely dangerous, and it could turn and hunt the human, in spite of the rifle. She was going to insist that Gene Waltham wait until they could work together, but Gene might not listen to her.

Julie drove to the helicopter and stopped. Scott and Julie watched the droplets run down the windshield for a few seconds before Scott said, "Stay safe, be careful with your leg, and I'll see you as soon as I can complete my business." He leaned over, gave Julie a kiss, and exited the truck.

Julie watched Scott for a second as he walked towards the chopper, lowered her window, and yelled through the rain, "Fly low and slow—I don't want anything to happen to you. Hurry back!" Scott turned and smiled, waved, and climbed into his ship. When the main rotor began to turn, Julie backed out of the meadow and headed toward Walthams'.

Scott lifted off and gradually gained altitude as he headed northwest over the Bitterroot and Nez Perce national forests. Thirty minutes into the flight, he passed over the Selway River and a few minutes later, US Highway 12. The next major landmark was the Dworshak Reservoir which was a little over half way to his destination. The ninety minute flight had passed very quickly, Scott had been thinking about Julie and how he would tell her the truth about his name and mission. Spokane International directed him to land at the northeastern corner of the taxiway marked with an octagonal display of flashing blue and yellow lights. As he shut down the engine, he received a voice command from the tower, "Mr. Wilson, you are to report to a taxi at the western side of the terminal. I have ordered your ship to be refueled."

Scott said, "Thank you," popped the hatch, dropped to the tarmac, and straightened his clothes before walking to the waiting taxi.

"Destination?" The driver sat as if frozen in place, waiting for his fare's response.

"West end Kennels—you can take your time."

"Yes, sir. You just arrive in town?"

"Yes, but I've been here before—several times on business."

"Had a fare yesterday, same destination—woman, good looking—about your age. There some kind of animal thing going on?"

"Not that I'm aware of; I've come to pick up my dog."

"She didn't need a dog for protection—she was carrying."

"Maybe she came for a dog to fetch her casings."

The driver laughed, "Yeah, sure."

A couple of minutes later, having sat in silence for the remainder of the short ride, Scott was still thinking of who the woman was that had visited the kennel. Was the other visitor a civilian or another agent he hadn't met?

"Here you are, sir. Your fare has been paid. Thanks for talking with me; sometimes I get tired of driving people around without a peep."

Scott exited the vehicle, took a few paces, and heard the taxi leave before he entered the large, freshly painted light-green with white trim, steel building. The muffled sounds of a few barking dogs came from the rooms behind the reception counter. He was recognized immediately by the male attendant who said, "Good morning, Mr. Wilson. Spectrum will be available to you when you exit the facility. Please check in."

Scott moved behind the counter, looked into what appeared to be a camera lens about shoulder height centered in a metal door and said his name, "Scott Curtis Wilson." A metallic click was heard and the door swung open to an elevator. He pressed CONFERENCE and the small enclosure descended three floors and eased to a stop. The door slid open and he stepped out in front of a secretary's desk, unoccupied. The mouse looked lonely, waiting to be moved on the light-blue pad.

"Agent Wilson, please join us."

Scott looked up and straight ahead to his supervisor, Del Adams, waving for him to come ahead through the array of a half-dozen occupied cubicles, each surrounded by bullet-proof glass extending upward to six feet. Glancing at the occupants as he passed by their stations, Scott recognized only one, Tobe Lundene, wearing glasses and a mustache, evidently a partial disguise looking like a newspaper reporter. Scott wondered if Tobe was trying, but unsuccessfully, to resemble Clark Kent.

Del was talking to a woman, probably the one the cabbie had mentioned. She stood up as Scott entered the office and Del introduced Scott to Toni Thornton, just in from Omaha. She was good looking, not pretty, but well-proportioned for a six-footer. Her almost black hair was pulled back and braided from ear to ear making her look a bit like an American Indian. Scott guessed that she weighed about 165, but no appreciable amount of fat was evident. He thought Toni could take most men in hand-to-hand combat. He wondered if she was a good marksman, but he would lay odds that she was a crack shot.

"Sit down, I have something to go over with both of you."

It had been less than a month since Scott had seen Del, but in that time short time, his supervisor had aged five years. His hair was nearly white and straighter than the gray and wavy in the past. Del had always appeared much younger than his age of sixty-three. Scott was wondering if Del perhaps had cancer, but Scott was in no position to ask about his superior's medical status.

"The bureau has received information in the past week that two felons have been summoned to Dillon, Montana, not far from your present station, Scott. The Dillon police think a kidnapping is being planned, but the subject has not been identified."

"Someone from Dillon, or maybe Suddenly?" Scott queried.

"We don't know, but you two are going to find out and put a stop to it before things get out of hand. Secrets are hard to keep in those small communities. I want you to act as a couple and nose around—you'll be looking for real estate to buy so you can start a hunting and other outdoor activities lodge."

Scott saw the supervisor's plan as a significant danger to Julie's and his relationship, which he didn't want to jeopardize in any way. He had to make a suggestion, "Sir, I think it would be better if we would be a brother-sister team; we could work more independently that way, and we wouldn't have to act as husband and wife. I'm not a very good actor when it comes to roles where I have little experience."

Toni spoke up, "Sir, I agree with Scott."

Del thought for a brief moment and replied, "Well, you do as you like. You are both experienced operatives. You can stay near the airport at one of our locations, until you get orders from your shell company to proceed. Let me know as soon as you get instructions."

Toni stood and started out the door ahead of Scott, who shook hands with Del and said, "Are you all right, sir? You look a little tired."

"Ah, it's my daughter. She thinks her boyfriend is the living God and can do no wrong. He's a German industrialist and he's got her convinced she should go to Europe with him, but he hasn't asked her to marry him. I think he's just a rich asshole, looking for a toy to play with for a while, and then discard.   H   e needs to be taken down a notch or two, but I'm too out of shape to do anything."

Scott smiled and replied, "Toni and I can help you with that. Where can we find him? Does he frequent any health clubs or gyms?"

Del nodded, "He likes to box, but only after he thinks he can beat his opponent, and he is vicious. He's a regular at Eastside Ground and Pound—late afternoons. MMA fighters train there, but he doesn't take them on, just boxers."

"We'll pay him a visit; see if we can embarrass him."

"Be careful, Scott, he'll try to break your nose and knock you out."

"Don't worry about us. Oh, will your daughter be there?"

"Usually. He's a showoff and wants her to see him win. Seems to inflate his self-esteem. Like I said, he's a typical rich A-hole."

Scott and Toni had lunch near the airport and caught a cab to the Eastside athletic club. They walked around for an hour to settle their meal and returned to the club by 2:30. They were able to rent some shoes and gloves and watched athletes coming and going, lifting and sparring. It was approaching 3:30 when Scott recognized Del's daughter, Kathleen, entering the gym with a handsome young man dressed in a tailored business suit. He escorted her to a foldup chair adjacent to retracted wooden bleachers and disappeared into the men's locker room.

Toni poked Scott and said, "I think Del's daughter sees you, she's waving." Scott stood, waved back, and motioned for Kathleen to join him and Toni. A large older man began to follow her, but she told him to stay put, waving him back. He retraced his steps and sat down as Kathleen worked her way through mats and exercise bikes to Scott and Toni.

"Scott, it's so nice to see you—it's been ages. What are you doing here?"

"We came to see you, Kathy. Your dad said you might be here, so we thought we'd take a chance. It's good to see you. Who are you with?"

"Gerhardt Langer. He's my current boyfriend—a really nice guy—and rich, too." She smiled, looked at Toni, and said, "Who's your friend, Scott?"

"Oh, I'm sorry. This is Toni Thornton; we're working together on a project. Toni, I'd like you to meet Kathleen Adams, Del Adams's daughter."

Shortly after the two women shook hands and began a conversation about Kathy's degrees in psychology and fine arts, Gerhardt emerged from the locker room and called out, "Kathleen, come over here to watch me spar."

Kathleen looked at her boyfriend and yelled across the gym, "I'm coming." Then she glanced at Scott and said, "Nice to see you again, Scotty, and to meet your friend." She smiled at Toni, turned, ran back to Gerhardt, and gave him a hug.

Scott remarked to Toni, "He looks fit and must weigh about 210. Let's watch what he thinks is boxing."

"Yeah, I want to see how he moves; he probably has some bad habits."

The agents watched Gerhardt dance around the ring with a heavily padded sparring partner for two rounds, before the German took a break for wind and water. He spoke with the older man accompanying him and Kathleen, and a couple of minutes later, a young Afro-American boxer entered the ring wearing a face protector head gear. The young man was a bit undersize for Gerhardt, perhaps as much as twenty pounds, but Scott assumed the opponent had been paid to take a fall. A number of trainees had been assembled for the show.

The bell sounded and the two fighters traded jabs, but neither fighter landed solid punches until Gerhardt forced the smaller man against the ropes and kneed him in the left thigh as they clenched. The younger, smaller man yelled out, "I thought you wanted to box, I ain't doing MMA wid you." He turned away and started to get out of the ring, but Gerhardt hit him with a solid left uppercut and a right cross, knocking the young man to the apron. He almost rolled off the raised ring, but Toni had dashed over to the youngster and kept him from falling to the gym floor.

"Are you all right?" Toni said. "Your opponent needs to learn some manners."

"Uh, sure." He shook his head, glanced at her, and noticed she was wearing gloves. "You gonna try to fight him? You too little, lady, you'll get kilt."

One of the onlookers helped unlace the gloves, tossed them to another fighter, and checked Toni's gloves. He frowned at Toni and said, "You'd better not turn your back on him, he'll knock the piss outta you. Watch out, he mean SOB."

Scott had joined Toni and checked the gloves. "You serious about this? Why don't you let me take him on?"

"I've got this, Scotty. I'll soften him up for you. You can knock him out." She looked up into the ring and said, "Hey, Fritz, are you man enough to fight a girl?"

Gerhardt walked over to the ropes, leaned over and sneered, "You have your insurance paid up? You'll need it."

Toni swung one leg onto the apron, grabbed the lower rope, jerked hard, and let the rope pull her into the ring where she rolled to her feet and backed into a neutral corner. G e r h a r d t strode to the center of the ring and said, "I'll stand right here and you can have the first punch." He held his hands down to his sides and motioned for her to step forward and give him a free punch.

Toni moved slowly and feigned a punch with her right and kicked Gerhardt in the crotch as hard as she could. When he folded forward, she brought her left knee up and hit him flush in the face, causing him to fall to the canvas with blood gushing from his nose. He rolled to his side and got to his feet, staggering to the corner ropes for support.

"You crazy bitch! I'll kick the crap out of you for that." He tried to wipe his nose with his right glove, but winced with pain when his glove came in contact with his nostrils. "You broke my nose, you lousy bitch." He stumbled forward with his gloves raised, but Toni stepped quickly to the side when he was in range, and kicked his leg, which buckled and he fell down again. As he got up, she kicked him in the side of the head, but he grabbed her leg and she lost her balance. Gerhardt grabbed her other leg and began pulling her across the canvas and tried to stomp on her head but missed when she rolled sideways.

Scott had had enough; it was time for him to intercede. He entered the ring and stood in front of Toni, shielding her from any kicking from Gerhardt.

The German stepped back and said, "So, you want to fight like a man? I'll let you have the first punch, but no kicking, okay?"

Gerhardt assumed the same posture as before, but with blood dripping from his nostrils.

Scott moved forward, hit Gerhardt on the chin, twice in the belly, and on the temple before the playboy knew what had happened. The German collapsed on the canvas—out cold.

CHAPTER 16

A cheer went up for Toni and Scott as they left the ring and mingled with the athletes. A number of them, including Gerhardt's first opponent were patting Toni on the back and congratulating her on her initial well-placed kick.

Kathleen wasn't sure how to react, but had decided to try to help with Gerhardt when he was standing, supported by the big man that seemed to be a body guard. Kathleen asked one of the trainers if she could get some ice for Gerhardt's nose bleed. Scott and Toni were coming toward her and Gerhardt to view the damage to Kathy's boyfriend.

Kathleen said, "Did you have to do that to Gerhardt, Scotty?"

"No, we didn't have to do anything, but we did him and you a service. If he continued hurting people when their back was turned, eventually he would run into big trouble. We also thought you should know he's a sore loser. He can't take it when the shoe is on the other foot; he loses his temper and can't control himself. If you end up marrying him, you will undoubtedly suffer spousal abuse; he could even kill you and get away with it. It would be easy for him to dispose of a body—we know how to do that."

"Did Daddy send you here?"

"No, he just told us where you hung out occasionally, and I wanted to see you again. We had no idea Gerhardt was an ass, but we wanted to verify your dad's suspicions. I hope you learned what he's really like."

Kathleen looked at Gerhardt, who was holding an ice bag over his nose. She then got Scott's attention by touching his arm, and said, "Can you take me home? I want to get out of here."

"Sure. I'll call a cab. Toni and I have to go back to the kennel and pick up Spectrum."

"Spectrum?"

"He's my dog. I've had him about a year—he's my co-pilot." Scott laughed, "I haven't let him solo yet."

"How'd you come up with the name Spectrum?"

Toni was listening closely to Kathleen's question. She said, "I've got to hear this."

Scott sat down, removed his gloves and athletic shoes and looked up at the women, "I originally thought of Heinz, but that was too easy, you know, Heinz: 57 varieties of pickles; a mixture of different breeds, but I wanted something more scientific, so I chose Spectrum—a mixture of wavelengths of light."

Toni thought of the speed of light and grinned, "He's pretty fast?"

Scott shook his head and said, "Let's get our civvies on and take Kathleen back home; then we'll pick up Spectrum. You can race him if you like."

Toni, Kathleen, and Scott waited about five minutes before an Empire Cab showed up. Kathleen was home in about ten minutes, and in another ten, Scott and Toni entered the kennel. After a very short wait, Spectrum was led from behind the reception desk and ran to greet Scott, who had knelt to hug his dog. Spectrum whimpered and licked at Scott's face.

"I'm happy to see you too, big guy. Too many kisses, Spectrum. Save the kisses for Toni."

Toni joined Spectrum and Scott and held out her hand to the dog. Spectrum sat back and raised his right paw for Toni to shake, then he went quickly to the door to exit the kennel. He looked back at Toni and Scott as if to urge them forward and out of the building.

"I think he wants us to get out of here, Toni; he's been cooped up long enough—ten days without a ride in the chopper."

"No, ten days without his master—give yourself some credit."

The safe-house near the airport was a small ranch with no particular standout features; it fit the neighborhood as if it really belonged. There was a 2015 blue Honda SUV sitting in the driveway and the front door of the house was unlocked, but sheltered between the garage wall and that of a bedroom. There was a stump, the remainder of a once proud tree that once screened the front door from the sidewalk. As Scott opened the door, he entered cautiously, not knowing what to expect inside. Toni waited outside until Scott called out, "It's all right, no one's here."

Toni checked the layout of the house and reset the alarm system. It had been disarmed while they were making the transit from the kennel. She suspected someone at the kennel had deactivated the security system. Knowing the bureau's reputation, she theorized the house was replete with listening devices; she would have to be careful with what she said to Scott.

Scott was in the kitchen checking the contents of the refrigerator: frozen dinners, a dozen cans of beer, orange juice, chocolate and vanilla ice cream, a quart of each. There was a post-it note taped to the egg carton instructing that more food was to be found in the freezer in the garage.

"Toni—can you build a fire? It's a little chilly in here; the furnace is shut off. What do you want for dinner?"

"Okay. Have anything with chicken in it?"

"Be more specific—there's about five different kinds, all TV dinners."

"I don't care, but nuke two of them for me."

"You got it." Scott thought it was short of amazing that Toni wasn't particular about what she wanted to eat. He wondered about Julie; what would she have said? Julie probably would have said, "Anything is okay, just pick one." He followed the package directions and then placed the dinners in the oven on warm.

While they ate, conversation drifted to relationships. Toni was the first to breach the subject, "Have you got a special someone in your life?"

Scott was happy he didn't venture into the subject first. He hesitated a moment and then said, "I've just met someone, only about a week ago. We seem to be hitting it off. She's about my age and has two teenage boys. She's a forest ranger—lives in Suddenly, Montana. What about you?"

"I have a partner in Chicago, she works in the clothing industry—a designer. We've been together a little over three years now. No plans for marriage yet; our jobs are so different we haven't had much time together, but I really like her, and we enjoy each other's company." Toni glanced at Scott to see how he reacted and then said, "Does that bother you?"

Scott grinned, "No, we have something in common; we both like women."

Toni smiled and said, "I'll do the dishes. See if there's anything to watch on TV."

"What dishes? Everything goes in the wastebasket."

Toni laughed as she picked up the plastic waste and carried it into the kitchen. "Why do you think I volunteered? Remember, I don't do dishes."

Rather than watch TV, Scott attached a leash to Spectrum and started out the door. He heard Toni rushing around behind him and glanced back to see her putting on a jacket.

"Hey, wait for me!"

They toured the neighborhood for about thirty minutes with Spectrum, giving him a chance to run and fetch a rubber ball that Scott always carried in his luggage. When they returned to the house, there was a message from Del on the answering machine: Scott and Toni were to fly to Spirit Lake, Idaho, to meet with Scott's West-Com contact on Wednesday at 2:00 p.m.

Following two days of gray skies, rain, and boredom for the inhabitants, the clouds had lifted and the sun was beginning to dry the grass and evaporate the puddles along the curbs in Suddenly. Water vapor could be seen rising from rooftops, attempting to fool the inhabitants into thinking clouds were given birth from wet shingles.

David was sitting in Biology class waiting for Ms. Sidwicke to begin class, when he felt a finger poke in his left shoulder. He turned that way but got a giggle from Megan who was on his right side. He turned to his right so he could see his tormentor.

"Ha! Gotcha! I'll be working at the hospital today so you'll have to walk home after school. Don't get your pants wet; people will think you had an accident."

David grinned, "Have a good time at the hospital—don't kill anybody. I'll get home late today. I'm turning out for track—relay team."

"All right, may I have your attention?" Ms. Sidwicke was ready to get started. The class became quiet and faced the front of the room. "For some unknown reason, the DNA results will be available next Monday, much sooner than I expected. I will go over some data on Friday so you will be familiar with the way the results are presented."

David jotted a note to Megan: '*You'll find out if you're adopted,*' a smiley face, and passed it back to her when Ms. Sidwicke turned her back to the class. A moment later, he felt a sharp pain in middle of his back; Megan had poked him with a sharp pencil. He reached back to massage the wound, but couldn't touch it. He wondered if a piece of pencil lead had remained in his back. He squirmed a bit and then relaxed, thinking he had deserved getting poked.

Fifty minutes later, David and Megan were walking together down the hallway to their eleven o'clock: English.

"I think your pencil lead is lodged in my back, nurse. Check your pencil; see if the tip is missing."

"I didn't notice, David. I took notes with a ballpoint today. You deserved getting poked; you know that crack about being adopted bothered me."

"But you didn't have to poke so hard. When I get a chance, I'm going to pinch you on the butt—when you least expect it."

They stopped in the hall at the entrance to their class. "If there is some lead in your back, come over to the hospital and I'll remove it."

"No, it'd rather wear it, but if it causes cancer, you'll be sorry. I'll send your dad the medical bills."

"It won't cause cancer, pencil lead is made of graphite, not lead. I can take it out with a pair of tweezers."

"Yeah, I know. I just wanted to take your mind off of being adopted." David grinned, "We'll find out on Monday."

As soon as the two agents and Spectrum were in the air, Scott called ahead to the airport in Spirit Lake. When he entered the destination in his navigation computer it warned that he would need permission to land at Lakeshore Airport; it was a private field located on a farm two miles northeast of the small town. A short hop to Spirit Lake from Spokane, it would take only about fifteen minutes, hardly enough time for the engine to reach optimum temperature. As they came into view of Spirit Lake, a message was received that they had permission to land. They could borrow a private car if they wanted to go into town.

Upon landing at the south side, away from the flightpath of monoplanes, and at one end of the short airstrip, a large black SUV pulled up at a safe distance from the rotor. Toni and Scott climbed out of the cabin and Scott said, "Remember, you're Toni Loebner, my sister—just back from the UK. You were there to be in the wedding of an old college friend. Make up anything you like for the school you attended."

"Don't worry, I can handle the back story."

CHAPTER 17

The front passenger door slowly opened and a diminutive middle-aged man dressed in what looked to be an expensive pinstriped suit, white plastic rim glasses, short red hair and a bolo tie approached Scott and Toni. He carried a smartphone and handed it to Scott.

"Mr. Harnold wants to talk to you, Mr. Loebner."

Scott took the phone and listened to a voice he had never heard before.

"Who is the woman with you?"

"My sister, sir."

"You were told to come alone. Are we going to have trouble with you obeying orders?"

"I was told to ferry two operatives from the Canadian-US border to Dillon, Montana. I can't afford to be turned away from two men I do not know, therefore, I have asked my sister to ride along and watch my back. If I can't guarantee my own safety, the deal is off; find someone else to transfer your cargo."

"All right. No need to get testy. I see your point. My man will pay you half now and half when the cargo is on the ground in Dillon." Scott handed the phone back to Harnold's agent who listened to the cell a moment, dropped it into his breast pocket, and gave an envelope to Scott. The small man turned, walked back to the car, got in, and it sped away.

"Who is Harnold, Scott?"

"I presume he's part of the mob—rarely shows his face. He might have had his voice disguised."

"So you think you were talking to a woman?"

"Could have been. Let's get out of here and pick up the two characters we have to transport."

"Where are we going?"

"The border crossing at Eastport, Idaho. It's about a half hour from here, but we have to give them a one hour notice. I'll call ahead, then we'll walk into town, get some coffee and walk back. That will kill a little over an hour and then another half hour of flight time to the border."

"So we'll be at the border in about two hours?"

"That's about right; let's get Spectrum."

Megan skipped study hall again so she could get in two full hours at the hospital, but she hoped the mop would not be one of her medical instruments. She was looking forward to seeing Mr. Ganz to find out how he hit his head. She parked the jeep in the reserved area for hospital employees, giving little thought that as a volunteer, she was not getting paid for her services and didn't qualify for the special spot. She hurried into the hospital, signed in at the front desk, and rushed down the hallway's polished floor directly to Mr. Ganz's room to retrieve his lunch tray. She peeked into the room and saw the elderly man sitting up reading a newspaper. She checked her blouse, smoothed her skirt, and entered the room.

"Hello, Mr. Ganz. How are you doing today?"

He dropped the paper to his lap and said, "Ah, my angel has returned. I'm in good spirits today. You look beautiful—just like you did on Monday."

Megan giggled and replied, "Thank you, sir. What were you reading about?"

"I was checking up on my stocks in the market. One of them is having some problems—it's dropped ten percent in the last week."

"I'm afraid I don't know anything about the stock market, but my father would. He's a banker. Can you tell me how you bumped your head?"

He didn't answer immediately, but after a few second pause, he grinned and said, "I broke one of my mother's cardinal rules."

Megan frowned, glanced at the *Wall Street Journal* in Mr. Ganz's lap, and said, "What did she tell you?"

"To look both ways."

"You were crossing a street and were hit by a car?"

"No, I was walking along Stevens Road and I saw a dime in the street, not far from the curb, so I stepped into the street and reached down to pick up the coin and suddenly a car came around that sharp bend near eleventh. I jumped backwards, tripped on the curb, and hit my head on the sidewalk. Next thing I knew, I was here and a Doctor was looking into my eyes and asking me my name."

"And did you know your name?"

"Why, certainly: Robert Walker Ganz. I should have listened for a car, looked both ways before going for the dime. Those extra seconds would have prevented me from being in the street when that car showed up."

"The driver didn't stop to give aid?"

"Maybe, I forgot to ask how I got here." He turned his head and thought for a moment, "Can you ask for me?"

"But you didn't need that dime, did you?"

"Oh, heavens no. But you have to understand; I grew up during the depression when every penny made a difference. I've always been thrifty."

"Gosh, Mr. Ganz, you must be nearly ninety years old."

"I'll be ninety-three this year, young lady. I've outlived three wives. I remember my first wife the most, maybe because all the experiences were new to us."

"What was her name, Mr. Ganz?"

"Please call me Robert." He smiled, "Mr. Ganz is too formal for an angel talking to a mortal. Her name was Florence Singleton. She ran into me with her bicycle in London during the Second World War."

Megan thought for a minute and then said, "You were a teenager during the war?"

"I was twenty—in the signal corp. It was 1945. I met General Eisenhower, but I had a feeling he didn't like me. It was just a feeling though."

"What happened when Florence hit you with her bicycle?"

"I asked her if she had done it on purpose and she said yes. She thought I looked like a nice guy and she wanted to get to know me. Her parents were killed by German bombs and she was a nurse taking care of burn victims. We hit it off and stayed together for twenty years. She smoked cigarettes—died of lung cancer in 1966. Don't ever smoke, young lady."

"How did you know you were in love, Robert?"

"One day after we had been seeing each other for about two weeks, she confessed that she had been observing me for several weeks, but didn't know how to attract my attention. She didn't have any nice clothes or money to waste on makeup, so she decided to bump into me with her bicycle. When she got cleaned up, she took my breath away; I thought she was gorgeous and she was very smart—I like smart women. We didn't get married right away and when we did, we decided not to have any children. The war had been too hard on us to want children to live through another conflict."

"Did you stay in England for long?"

"About two years after the war we got married and moved back to the states—to New York City. She liked the hustle and bustle of the Big Apple, and I attended college on the GI Bill—got a degree in finance and began working at the stock market." He reached out to Megan and held her right hand which she had rested on the bed. "But tell me about you, angel; you must have some boyfriends."

Megan grinned and said, "Well—I have two, but one doesn't know it, and the other one is in the hospital in Boise. He had a terrible accident and might not walk again. Now I have a big problem." She became silent, expressionless, and sat looking away from Robert at the ceiling.

Robert tapped her hand and replied, "I think I understand your problem; the one in the hospital is more exciting, but perhaps a bit undependable and not as bright as the other boy."

"How did you know that?"

Robert smiled, "I've been around a long time, dear, and experienced many things. I can see the trouble in your mind by your expression—the furrows on your brow. Listen, you are very young and don't need to make decisions about getting married for several more years. You live in a small town where there aren't many choices. Are you planning to attend a university?"

"I think I want to go into the medical field, a doctor of some kind, but not a surgeon; I like children so maybe a pediatrician."

"What do your boyfriends want to study?"

"The one that got hurt, Rick, wanted to play football at a university. He thought the only way he could go to college was to get a scholarship. After football, his idea was to coach at a high school. But now, he won't be able to attend college, his parents can't afford to send him without an athletic scholarship; he might be confined to a wheel chair."

"What about the other boy, the one that doesn't know you like him?"

"Oh, you mean David. He's my next door neighbor and I've grown up with him. He showed me how to drive a stick shift the other day. We tease each other all the time. He's very smart and will probably get an academic scholarship to study engineering. He's my age; Rick is two years older."

"How deeply involved are you with Rick? Have you become intimate?"

"He tells me if I love him, I'll let him make love to me, but I don't want him to. There's no going back after having sex. He puts his hands all over me and I don't like it—I've told him so, but he keeps trying. I don't know what to do. Should I break up with him? What will people think of me when he's so injured?"

"I think I can help you, angel. You.ve got to get his mind on something besides sex. Tell him you won't have anything to do with him if he doesn't graduate from college. You have to think of your future, too. If Rick wants to go to college, I'll pay for all his expenses, but he has to pay me back after he get a degree, and it has to be a secret between you, me, and Rick. He can't tell his parents where he's getting the money. I don't know his parents, they might be good people, but I don't want any freeloaders. Can you keep the secret?"

Megan was shocked at what Robert had said. Did he have that kind of money? "Yes, I can keep it a secret. Should I be the one to tell him?"

"I believe that would be the best idea. I'll set up an account in Rick's name with your father's bank in charge of all the funds."

"Mr. Ganz—Roger, that is a wonderful idea. I'll tell Rick about it as soon as I see him." She glanced at her watch and said, "I'd better take your tray to the kitchen; I'll see you again on Friday."

"I don't think so, angel. My stay here has ended; I have much to do at home. My little R and R is over."

"Oh, I'll miss you. How do I contact you?"

"That's easy, dear, the registration desk has my number and address. They call me all the time."

"Why do they call you?"

"Administrative matters, angel; I own the hospital."

Spectrum sat behind Scott beside Toni as the chopper made the short trip to Eastport. Scott was directed to land at a specific site and was met by two border agents who conducted a quick but thorough inspection of the helicopter. After checking Toni's and Scott's passports and poring over Spectrum's veterinary papers, the new arrivals were allowed to enter the concrete and brick border complex.

As they approached the entrance, the automatic doors slid open. Toni chuckled and told Scott, "Reminds me of Wal-Mart." But there was no uniformed greeter, just several rows of waiting room vinyl-covered chairs and along a side wall, four vending machines. A sign hung from the ceiling informing travelers the direction to the restrooms. Two employees in uniforms were standing behind a registration/information counter.

Scott had surveyed the room quickly, but the two passengers were nowhere in sight; he had expected them to be waiting for their ride to Dillon.

"Spectrum, sit." Scott pointed at the first row of chairs and said, "Have a seat, Toni. Our passengers don't seem to be here."

Rather than sitting, Toni walked over to the vending machines and purchased a candy bar, tore off the wrapper and bit into the peanuts and chocolate. "Want something, Scott?"

"Yeah, two men to transport to Dillon. Nothing to eat, thanks."

Scott could hear two male voices coming from the far end of the waiting room and when he looked in that direction, he observed two men in suits, one in gray, the other in light-brown, coming toward him. Apparently, his passengers had been in the restroom. As they came closer, he concluded the suits were cheap, the stitching at the shoulders had puckered the material and the lapels were slightly wrinkled, probably as a result of eating and sleeping in the clothing they were wearing.

Chapter 18

The brown suit stepped up to Scott and introduced himself, "Bryan Manietta, how ya doin'? You our ride?"

Scott shook hands with Manietta, and then the gray suit, Martin Kalber. Scott glanced at Toni but she knew enough to keep a low profile until Scott had completely analyzed the nonverbal communications from the two men.

"Yeah, I'm your ride. I'm Scott Loebner. Any luggage?"

Kalber replied, "Cases are over behind the counter. The checkers are watching our stuff until we leave. You ready to fly us to this Dillon place?"

"Get your things and meet me outside at my ship. I've got to check the fuel; it's a two hour ride—tanks have to be full. Got something to read?"

Kalber laughed, "Hell, Manietta can't read; he'll just count trees or go to sleep—if he doesn't puke. I'll watch for planes that might hit us."

"Don't worry about that, we've got radar."

Toni watched as Scott and Spectrum left the building with the two men following closely behind. She waited beside the exit door until the two men and Scott were in the cabin and Spectrum jumped into the passenger compartment. When Scott started the engine, she made her way to the chopper and climbed in beside Scott.

"What the hell? Where'd she come from?" bellowed Kalber.

"She's my sister. She was in the restroom. Have some objections?"

Kalber sat back and the scowl drained from his face. "Well, no, but she surprised me. I didn't know there was another person going with us."

"Gentlemen, meet Toni. She doesn't particularly like men in suits."

Toni turned and reached back to shake hands when the men introduced themselves.

The chopper lifted off, moved eastward about two hundred yards, climbed to three thousand feet, and accelerated to cruising speed in a south-southeast heading.

Toni put on her headset and talked to Scott. "You sure they can't hear us?"

"Don't worry, the rotor noise interferes with normal conversation; they can't hear a thing we say."

"What's their back story?"

"Fishermen from Europe. They've been in Eastern Canada so might speak French and English, but I don't believe either one graduated near the head of his class. Actually, I think they're from Chicago or maybe Minneapolis, hired for a quick five or ten Gs for a week's work."

"I'll keep an eye on them, but they couldn't have any hardware. What are their orders?"

"Don't know, but I've been thinking that it's something not too complicated. When we get to Dillon, they'll probably get a call of some sort telling them what to do. We'll probably have to arrange for their transportation to another location—but that's just a guess."

"I'm going to take a nap; wake me when we get there."

"I forgot to ask you, can you fly a chopper?"

"No, I can't. Don't fall asleep."

Scott laughed. "Don't worry, I have enough caffeine in me to stay awake until tomorrow."

The jail on the outskirts of northern Butte was home to Stan and Tom while they served the two-month sentence for attempted robbery at the drug store in Suddenly. Stan had phoned his cousin, Chuck Nugent, and asked him to come with a friend to visit. Chuck and Sammy Arnold were waiting in the visitor's room as Stan and Tom were being processed for their allowed ten-minute visitation with relatives. They sat quietly for about five minutes, nervously bouncing their legs under a metal table that was bolted to the floor.

"What does Stan want us for, Nugget?"

"I dunno, but he's got something on his mind. Just wait and see, Sammy."

Another couple of jogs of the minute hand on the large wall clock occurred as the waiting continued, with the two visitors looking around the light-green walls and polished steel fixtures. A buzzer sounded, a large metal door swung open, and Tom, in a wheelchair, was pushed in by a guard and positioned across the table from the visitors. The visitors smiled and Tom nodded to the young men but remained silent.

Another door opened with a click and Stan walked in on crutches, thumped his way to the table, and sat down hard on a stool provided by another guard. When the guards had withdrawn to chairs beside the doors leading to confinement areas, Stan said, "Good to see you boys. Thanks for showing up. I've got a little job for you, and it should be fun."

Chuck was scanning the walls and guards and said, "Anybody listening to us?"

"Nah, this is low level security; just don't talk loud." Stan leaned forward, "Here's what I want you to do." He looked at both young men and continued, "I want you to grab a chick in Suddenly, take the doll to one of those fire lookout towers, and wait for five hundred grand to be delivered before you let her go. And absolutely no playing with the merchandise."

Sammy let a low whistle escape from between his teeth and lips and stared at Stan. "You're kiddin', right?"

"I'm dead serious. Here's how you do it."

Stan leaned a few inches closer to the two visitors, and Chuck and Sammy bent into Stan's near whispers so they wouldn't miss any details of the plan. When the ten minute visitation time expired, one of the guards came forward, tapped on the table, and said, "Time's up, gents; say goodbye."

Chuck gave Stan and Tom a thumbs up as the prisoners backed away from the table. The visitors turned, and took the exit from the interview room. Sammy and Chuck didn't utter a word until they were back in their truck, and headed home to make a list of items needed for the kidnapping.

Sammy said, "Is he nuts, Chuck? You sure we want to do this? We're gonna have to shell out several hundred bucks for rentals."

"You gotta think bigger, Sammy; two or three Benjamins spent and we'll each get back ten Gs—minimum."

"Well, as soon as we get the cash, I'm takin' my share and headin' to the Bahamas. You think they have one of those treaties?"

"Treaties? Oh, you mean extradition?" said Chuck.

"Yeah, one of those."

"Hell, I don't know, but you'll need a passport."

"It'll have my picture in it, right? I don't like my picture bein' took."

As soon as the free conspirators were back in downtown Butte, Chuck called the forest service in the Bitterroot region and asked if he could rent the fire lookout tower in Shadow Valley. He was told he would have to accept it as is because the ranger had not been able to personally inspect the tower since the previous residents had vacated last September.

"That site is difficult to access, sir. Do you have an ATV, an all-terrain vehicle?"

"Not a problem. My buddy and I can get in and out of just about anywhere. We're expert hikers and climbers."

"All right, then. Please send your monthly payment by Western Union to Bitterroot Ranger Station, Suddenly, Montana. Enjoy your summer of relaxation."

"Thanks, I'm sure we will." Chuck got off the phone and smiled at Sammy. "Let's get a truck and that ATV—the one with four seats, over at Mountain Rentals, then we'll have to get some food—enough for three for a couple of weeks."

"Yeah. I need some of that red licorice and some bug spray."

"Get what you want, Sammy, but remember, we're spending our money, so don't go overboard with junk food."

"Yeah, yeah. When do we pick up the doll?"

"If we have everything ready, we'll nab her on Monday. We'll have to find out where she lives and watch her house—figure out her schedule. We'll do that tomorrow and Friday."

"You know where that tower is?" Sammy said.

"We'll find out on the Internet tonight. Maps will be on the Bitterroot ranger site. Let's get goin', it'll be dark before long."

Fatigue from the two-hour flight to Dillon had caught up to Scott, and he was anxious to get the passengers put away for the night. The quarter mile walk from the landing spot to the Motel 6 gave everyone a chance to stretch their legs and fill their lungs with fresh air. Two adjacent rooms had been reserved for the four travelers, and in the morning when Scott went to the office to settle the bill for the overnight lodging, he was surprised to find that the bill had been paid. His employer's tentacles had been more far-reaching than expected.

Toni and Scott met with Kalber and Manietta for breakfast at a small, but clean, diner about two blocks east of the motel. The building was constructed and painted to resemble a railroad dining car, minus the wheels. They sat at the long counter and ordered. Kalber sat next to Scott.

Kalber took a drink of ice water, rubbed his eyes, blinked a couple of times, and said, "You know where lookout tower seventeen is?"

"I do. It's about eight miles from Suddenly—to the south southeast. Nice place."

"Me and Mannie want you to fly us over the place so we can see the surroundings, and then follow the road back to where you park the chopper."

Scott frowned and then said, "Are you going to meet someone where I land my ship?"

"Not someone, a truck. It's gonna be loaded with gear for us; you know, food, blankets, ropes—stuff like that."

"Ropes? You want to do some climbing? I know a better place than that."

"Nah. The rope's for tying somebody up—so she don't get away."

"Oh! You're gonna grab some woman for ransom?" Scott had finally discovered why the two men had been flown to Dillon: so they could make arrangements for a kidnapping.

Kalber's eyes surveyed the diner before he said, "You might as well know, since you're working for the same people as us. We're nabbing the daughter of the banker—he's loaded. We want three hundred grand for her safe return, and for each day he hesitates, we add fifty grand."

"Aren't you guys worried about the FBI hunting you down?"

"We're just little fish and anyway, we won't get caught. We figure it will be over in a day or two and we'll hightail it out of here—back to the big city. Anyhow, we aren't taking her across states lines, so no FBI will be involved."

Scott decided to stop talking for fear of raising suspicions, so he finished his breakfast in silence. He paid for the meals and they headed back to the chopper where a fuel truck was waiting to fill the tanks with high octane gasoline; AvGas wasn't available in Dillon. When the tanks were filled to the brim, the local service man had Scott sign for the fuel, climbed into his truck, and drove away.

The fifteen minute flight to Suddenly became extended to twenty-five minutes because of the passengers' request to see tower seventeen from the air and the eight miles of road leading from the site to their waiting pickup. Scott swung to the south of the town to avoid the unwanted attention of the inhabitants. As the chopper circled to the west over the timberland, Scott pointed out the dirt road the men would follow and landed at Cowpiddle pond. Just as Kalber had said, there was a black pickup parked under the nearby trees, almost completely concealed from the landing site and the access road.

Scott cut the engine when he felt touchdown and the two men gathered their luggage. Toni was first on the ground and she walked over to the black vehicle to get an idea of what was piled in the bed and covered with a blue tarpaulin. She lifted an edge of the cover and peered under to see cartons of soup, chunky style peanut butter, and loaves of bread.

"Hey, what are you doing? Don't mess with any of our provisions!"

She stepped away from the truck and said, "Don't sweat it, Mannie, curiosity is not pilfering. Besides, I don't like crunchy peanut butter." She joined Scott, who was checking over the chopper before locking it.

The two men tossed their belongings into the back seat of the crew cab, climbed in, and drove away without another word. Toni thought she saw Mannie, on the passenger side, give her the finger, but she decided he could have been waving.

"A couple of real nice fellows," Scott said, and they both started laughing. "We've got a fifteen minute walk to our accommodations, let's get started. We'll get something to eat when we get to my place. I'll introduce you to my landlord and her two boys. The younger boy is a really funny kid."

CHAPTER 19

uring the walk to the Drums', Scott briefed Toni on each member of the Drum family and their next door neighbors, the Isaacs.

"So, Megan is the target for the kidnappers, and you want me to keep an eye on her and disrupt the process?"

"That's correct, but absolutely no gunplay. If Megan gets hurt, it would be traumatic to all three families."

"Three families?"

"I forgot to tell you about Rick Hadley's family. He's Megan's boyfriend and was severely injured in a logging accident. He's hospitalized in Boise for leg reconstruction. His parents were devastated." They walked another two blocks before Scott said, "Drums' house is a block ahead on the left." He pointed and said, "It's the gray ranch with white trim. My apartment is in back—above the garage; you'll like it unless you don't favor wood paneling. I'll ring the bell to let them know I've returned." He pressed the doorbell but no one answered. Scott glanced at his watch and said, "I don't think anyone's home. The boys should be at school until three o'clock."

There was no sign of life in the house so Scott and Toni went around to the garage and entered the cold apartment filled with stale air. Spectrum searched all the nooks and crannies, sniffing as he inspected the apartment.

"Make yourself at home, I'll turn up the heat and we can have some lunch. Julie usually gets home between five and six o'clock. We can go for a walk or take a nap, or watch TV—whatever you want to do."

"You haven't mentioned much about the boys' mother. You like her?"

"She's great; I like her a lot, but I've had to lie to her about my job and my real name, so that's not going to be favorable. I think she's going to be irritated with me."

"You've been discussing marriage?"

"No. I've only known her for about ten days, and—watch your language around the boys."

"Okay, I'll try not to embarrass you. I guess I behave like a man sometimes—I work with them all the time and they talk like I'm one of the guys. I have to remind myself that I'm supposed to be your sister; I'll clean up my act."

While they waited for the Drums to return home, the agents played cards and watched an old movie. Scott occasionally checked the house to see if any lights came on, and he was rewarded a few minutes after three o'clock. He and Toni were going down the steps to announce their presence when a squad car abruptly appeared in the driveway and skidded to a stop. The driver struggled to shed the squad car and said, "Let me see your ID!"

Danny burst from the back door and yelled, "That man is okay, Sheriff Howell, he's renting the apartment from us, but I've never seen the woman before."

The sheriff put his hand up to stop Danny from getting any closer. "You stay back, son. I'll deal with these people."

The sheriff had one hand on his pistol as he moved a little closer to Scott and Toni. He spoke softly, "Please show me some ID."

Scott pulled his wallet from his left rear pocket and flipped it open so the officer could see his photo and affiliation; Toni extracted her laminated credential card from her right breast pocket and offered it to the sheriff.

As the sheriff examined the IDs, Scott volunteered, "We were going to visit with you tomorrow, sheriff. We're here to investigate a kidnapping."

"You're both FBI?"

"That's correct. We want to ask you to request our assistance with the kidnapping."

"I haven't been notified of a kidnapping; who's been made off with?"

Scott looked at Danny and then back at the sheriff. "Can we talk to you in private? The boy doesn't know we're FBI and we'd like to keep it that way for a while."

Sheriff Howell returned the ID cards and said, "Sure. Why not come down to the station and we'll have a good talk."

Scott noted more than a hint of suspicion in the sheriff's demeanor, but he knew they had more to discuss than what had been mentioned in the driveway. Scott and Toni started toward the police car and Danny ran up to Scott and said excitedly, "I'm sorry Mr. Loebner, I didn't know you had come back so soon, so I called the sheriff when I saw the lights on above the garage."

"You did the right thing, Danny. If your mom gets home before we get back from talking with the sheriff, tell her we'll see her this evening. This is my sister and my partner."

Danny gave Toni a quick look and said, "I didn't know you had a sister. See you later."

Toni and Scott got into the back seat of the squad car and waited for the sheriff to squeeze in behind the steering wheel and latch the extra-long seat belt. Toni looked at Scott and covered her mouth to keep from laughing out loud.

Five minutes later, the agents were sitting with the sheriff in a small conference room, usually used for interrogation of prisoners, in back of the first floor of the Court House and above the sheriff's office. The sheriff had provided coffee for Scott and Toni.

"Now, tell me about this kidnapping. It hasn't occurred yet you say?"

"It's planned for next week, but we don't know the precise date or time."

The sheriff took a sip of coffee and said, "Well, do you know who is going to be snatched?"

Toni reacted quickly, "The banker's daughter."

"Megan Isaacs? How do you know this?"

"We're part of the team that's going to do the kidnapping and hold her for ransom—three hundred thousand dollars."

Sheriff Howell slapped his knee, almost spilling his coffee, and laughed, "Is that all? I doubt if the bank has that much cash in the vault, and anyway, it wouldn't be Mr. Isaacs's money. He's not a rich man."

Scott and Toni traded glances and Scott said, "We'd better backup and tell the whole story, then you can ask us to help you with the problem. We can't officially work on the case until you ask us for help."

"I think this is going to take some time; how about some more coffee? And I've got a dozen doughnuts in my desk. I'll get 'em and we can relax and enjoy our talk." The sheriff struggled to his feet and left the agents for about a minute.

Toni chuckled and said, "Five bucks on Sheriff Howell eating six doughnuts."

"You're on!"

When the sheriff returned with a tray of chocolate-covered doughnuts, a stack of Styrofoam cups, and a large coffee dispenser, Scott gave a big grin to Toni, thinking he was going to win the bet. There were only six doughnuts on the tray and he was planning to eat at least one of them. Toni winked at him as if she knew something he didn't.

Scott began with an explanation of the shell company, West-Com, and how he became aware of the potential kidnapping. By the time he and Toni had explained their journey to Dillon with Kalber and Manietta, the sheriff was on his third doughnut. The agents were doing most of the talking, so they each had only eaten one, leaving a single ring-shaped cake on the plate. Scott watched as Sheriff Howell reach for it, but the big man decided to take a break.

"I'll be right back, hold your place." He exited the room with the empty tray, having left the sixth doughnut on a napkin next to the coffee dispenser. Five minutes later the sheriff reappeared with another six chocolate-covered pastries and a jar of strawberry jam.

While Sheriff Howell was gone, Toni showed Scott her notebook with three tally marks for the sheriff and one each for Scott and Toni. Scott shook his head at Toni's keeping track of such trivialities, but smiled and gave her a thumbs up for the correct count.

"Give me the names of those two men and I'll see what I can find out about them. I'll have my secretary draw up a request for aid from the FBI; we don't have enough man power to handle this type of thing alone. Where do I send the petition for assistance?"

Toni answered quickly, "The FBI Field Office in Spokane."

Scott nodded and said, "Oh, Sheriff, those men will be staying at tower seventeen. They're driving a black crew cab Chevy pickup with Idaho plates. They weren't armed when we picked them up, but they might be now. We didn't get a good look at the contents of the pickup before they drove away."

"I'll have Deputy Doureline watch for that vehicle. How do I contact you people? We don't have cell coverage here—too many trees for microwave or satellite coverage."

"Here's a number you can call to leave a message. It's a receiver in my chopper and is a secure line." Scott jotted down a number on a notepad and handed it to the sheriff, who glanced at the number, frowned at the strange series of numbers, and stuck the paper into his shirt pocket.

"Well, I think I have all the info I need; I'll take you back to the Drums', unless you want to be somewhere else. I noticed you don't have a vehicle to move around town."

"That would be fine, Sheriff, but there is one other item I think we'd better discuss."

"What have we overlooked?" said the sheriff.

"Don't you think we should tell the Isaacs what we have wind of?"

The sheriff took a big bite from doughnut number six and exhaled, blowing a morsel of cake from his mouth. He brushed off his shirt covering his extended belly, sipped from his coffee, and said, "I suppose we should let them in on what we are aware of. Bruce will want to know how much cash he'll have to come up with if Megan is taken."

Scott said, "I don't think it will come to that. Toni is going to be shadowing Megan until this thing blows over. She's armed and has great self-defense skills."

"You agents talk with the Isaacs and make sure they know numbers they can call in emergencies. This evening would be a good time. I'll see Bruce at the bank when it opens in the morning. If he receives any ransom notes, he should call me right away so we can stay on top of this." Sheriff Howell looked at Scott and Toni and said, "If that's it, I'll give you a ride home."

When Scott and Toni were walking up the driveway toward the garage, Scott took a five spot from his wallet and gave it to Toni who had extended her hand toward her partner as soon as Sheriff Howell drove away.

"Thank you, sir."

"How did you know he would eat six of those? That's over two-thousand calories."

"Don't you ever play a hunch? The sheriff must tip the scales at over three hundred pounds and he is certainly not in fighting shape. He didn't get that way by drinking diet sodas. If we ever get shot at, I'm getting behind Sheriff Howell."

Scott laughed but knew Toni had a sound idea. After climbing the steps, they were still smiling as he and Toni entered his apartment. Scott popped the door on the fridge and asked, "Want a beer?"

"Please." She cleared her throat and said, "When do I meet your fiancée?"

Scott had taken a drink of beer and choked. "Julie is not my fiancée." He looked outside and down at the driveway, "There she is now." Julie's truck had pulled into the driveway.

"So, she *is* your fiancée! I knew it. When you talk about her, you speak softly and your face lights up. Don't try to be coy with me, Scott. I can tell you're in love."

Scott knew he couldn't win when Toni was intent with her teasing, so he decided to ignore her bantering, but he had to introduce the two women and prevent Julie from misunderstanding what Toni was doing in his apartment. He thought he'd try to talk with Julie before Danny had a chance to mention the presence of Toni to his mother. He didn't think it was going to an easy explanation, and he wasn't sure how Julie would react. Scott had told Julie he didn't have any siblings.

Scott practically flew down the stairs and ran to greet Julie before she got in the house. He caught up with her at the front door.

"Oh! Scott, you scared me! When did you get back?" She took a step toward him and they hugged.

"A couple of hours ago. I have another agent with me, a woman. Her name is Toni Thornton, but she is masquerading as my sister. By the way, my real name is Scott Wilson."

Julie stepped back frowning, and said, "Wait a minute. You told me your name was Loebner, now it's Wilson?"

"I'm sorry, but when I first contact people at a new location, I have to give them my assumed name so no slip-ups happen."

Julie reached into her pocket and found her house key, which she inserted into the lock and opened the front door. She turned toward Scott and said, "I've got to clean up. I'll see you in the apartment in a few minutes."

CHAPTER 20

"**M**om! Scott's back and he has his sister with him, but I don't think she's his sister. I think she's his girlfriend." Danny had met his mother at the front door when he heard her key in the lock.

"I have to change clothes and then I'm going to meet his sister. Scott and I need to have a talk. Please get the groceries out of the truck. How was school today?"

"Okay. School was the usual—nothing happened. What's for dinner?"

"Pork chops. Don't put them in the freezer." Julie started for the bedroom, unbuttoning her shirt as she moved down the hallway.

"Are Scott and that woman coming to dinner?"

"I don't know Danny. Please get the groceries from the truck. We'll talk after I've changed."

Julie had insisted the doctor place a walking cast on her leg for two reasons, one of which was to facilitate dressing and undressing. She had purchased pants that were two sizes larger than normal so she could get her pant leg over the cast. Also, she couldn't do her job when she was forced to use crutches. After an X-ray, the doctor complied.

As Julie changed out of her work clothes, she wondered what this Thornton woman looked like. Was she good looking? Was she really another agent? Was Scott really who she thought he was? Why does my life have to be so complicated?

After washing her face and combing her hair, she heard David's voice. Danny was talking to David, telling him about the woman with Scott.

"Who do you think she really is, if she's not his sister?"

"She might be an old girlfriend —or a secret agent." Danny started laughing and David joined in.

"I like that—she's a secret agent. Great imagination, Danny."

Julie walked into the kitchen and commented, "I'm going to talk with Scott and his sister; I shouldn't be gone very long. Set the table for at least three, but we might have five for dinner—it all depends."

"Can we go with you?"

"No, this meeting is for adults only. Decide what vegetable you want and whether you want bread or buns."

She opened the slider, walked to the stairs at the rear of the garage, climbed the twelve steps, and tapped on the apartment door window. For some reason, Julie had expected the woman, Toni, to open the door, but Scott had heard footsteps on the stairs and was at the door.

The furrows in her brow gradually melted when he opened the door and said, "Come in Julie. I want you to meet Toni Thornton. She's FBI from Chicago posing as my sister, and also working undercover as an agent for West-Com."

Julie inched into the apartment and focused on Toni, who had just risen from one of the chairs in the kitchenette. Julie watched as Toni grabbed the remote and turned off the sound on the TV.

Scott guided Julie into the living area and introduced the two women. Scott watched and listened as the women sat down and started talking. He moved closer to the conversation and sat beside Julie, "I'd offer you something to drink, but don't you have to feed the boys?"

"Oh! Gosh, I told them I'd only be a few minutes. Why don't you join us for dinner? I always buy enough for a half-dozen or more, never knowing how much the boys will eat.

Scott gave a quizzical look at Toni and she nodded, "Okay, Julie, but you'll have to let us treat you and the boys another time."

"It's a deal. We'd better get down there before the boys have ice cream for dinner."

Scott was pleased, and a little surprised, that Toni and Julie had gotten off to a good start without any sparks flying. As dinner progressed, the women were talking like old friends. The boys showed interest in Toni and at one point, when there was a lull in the conversation, Danny asked, "Miss Loebner, are you a secret agent?"

Toni winked at Scott and said, "How did you know? Is it my slight accent?"

David and Danny were both shocked at Toni's reply. Danny was quick to ask, "Are you an agent from Russia?"

Toni pretended to be caught unaware of her discovery by Danny. "If you want to know the truth, I'm an agent of the KCB."

David said, "Don't you mean the KGB?"

"No. The KCB is another segment of the KGB, but we work out of Moscow—just like the KGB."

"So what does KCB stand for?" said Danny.

Toni picked up her serrated steak knife and pointed it towards Danny. "It stands for killers of curious boys." She grinned— Scott and Julie began laughing.

Danny said, "I guess you're not a secret agent."

"If I were, I couldn't tell you, Danny; that would have to remain a secret."

Julie broke the slight tension the boys had established. "Do you guys want dessert before you have to study, or do you want to wait 'til later?"

David answered, "I'll wait until later, Mom."

"Me, too. David and I will clear the table while you old folks talk."

"Thank you, honey."

"Mom!" Danny said plaintively.

Julie shook her head, smiled, and said, "Calling us old folks!"

Nothing but chit-chat was carried on by the adults until after the boys disappeared to their bedrooms to study for Friday's classes. When Scott, Toni, and Julie were alone, Scott brought up the subject of kidnapping.

He looked directly at Julie and said, "We have to let you in on our present investigation. Megan is the subject of an attempted kidnapping."

Julie appeared stunned, "What? Someone is after Megan Isaacs, my neighbor's girl?"

Scott nodded. "That's right. It's going to occur in the next week, but we don't know the precise time. Toni is going to be watching her, following so to stop the act before the perps can take her. We know the guys assigned to grab her."

"Can't you arrest them?" Julie said.

"I wish, but that would be equivalent to arresting democrats for disliking the president; half the country would be in jail or prison. Until the two guys do something against the law, we're impotent."

Toni smiled and teased, "I like your choice of words, Scott."

Julie sat quietly, pondering over the idea of Megan being snatched.

Scott asked, "What are you thinking?"

"David said on Monday, Wednesday, and Friday Megan leaves school early and goes to the hospital. I'm wondering if the kidnappers will grab her on the way or wait and take her from the hospital."

"They drive a black crew cab pickup so they could put her in the back and no one would see her. The men have explicit instructions to not harm her, or else." Scott looked at Toni, expecting a wisecrack, but she just grinned.

"I can cut my workday short after three o'clock and swing by the hospital to check on her. That would be tomorrow and Monday."

Toni spoke up, "That won't be necessary, but if you want to, it's fine with me. You have a good reason to be at the hospital."

Julie glanced at Scott and asked, "Have you talked with the Isaacs?"

"No, I thought we should do that together. You know them much better than I do and the idea of a kidnapping won't be such a shock if you're along. Toni can stay here with the boys and we'll talk with the Isaacs—right now."

"One last thing, Scott, should Megan know about this?" Julie's concern was evident.

"I think it would be a good idea, then she won't be surprised if and when it happens. She'll also know that she won't be hurt, so she can just relax and wait for us to get her out of trouble."

Toni said, "I'll watch TV until you get back. Don't tell Megan about me watching her, otherwise she might give me away—I'll be disguised as a nurse or a custodian. She might figure out that I'm not a regular at the facility anyway."

Julie grabbed a heavy sweater from the hall closet, and started out the entrance way, holding it open for Scott who joined her and pulled the door shut behind him. He felt the cool evening air, almost causing goose bumps on his bare arms. He wanted to put his arm around Julie's waist, but she was moving too quickly, covering the short distance between houses in a few seconds.

"You can break the news, Scott. I'll back you up. Sarah won't believe a word of it, but Bruce will be very worried."

"You think Mrs. Isaacs will think I'm nuts?"

"Uh-huh, sometimes she's one or more dimensions from reality."

Scott laughed as he put his right index finger on the doorbell and pressed. The muted two-tone sound announced their arrival and the door swung open before the ringing stopped. Megan must have been very near the door to have reacted so quickly.

"Mrs. Drum and Mr. Loebner, please come in. Mom and Dad are in the living room."

"Bring them in here, dear." Sarah Isaacs' voice could be heard over the sounds from the television.

Sarah and Bruce were sitting at opposite ends of the large sofa, each holding a cup and saucer, which they placed on the coffee table as they stood to welcome the neighbors. Sarah stepped forward and ushered Julie and Scott to the L-shaped sofa. "What a surprise! Can we help you with something?"

Scott turned to Megan and said, "You need to sit with your parents, Megan. I have something important to tell you."

"Oh, no! Has Rick died?" Megan was obviously upset and pulled her mother down to the sofa and grasped her hands.

"No, that isn't it. As far as we know, Rick is recovering in Boise. What we came to tell you is about you, Megan." Scott was scanning the Isaacs' faces, all presenting a look of concern.

He continued, "My name is not Loebner, I'm Scott Wilson, and I'm withthe FBI."

The Isaacs were all staring at Scott now; he had their full attention. "We have information that two men are going to attempt to kidnap you and hold you for ransom. They know your father runs the bank and they're going to ask three-hundred thousand dollars for your safe return."

Sarah said, "That's the most ridiculous thing I've ever heard. Do you believe what Scott just said, Julie?" Sarah moved to the edge of the sofa and stared at Julie.

"Yes, Sarah, one hundred percent. He knows who the two kidnappers are and he has a partner over at my place with the boys."

Bruce spoke up, "We don't have that kind of money. I don't now anyone in Suddenly that could dig up three-hundred thousand dollars. All our savings plus this house would only be about half that amount. I'd have to borrow all the money in the bank to reach that sum, and that would be illegal."

"I know someone that would have that kind of money," Megan said.

Bruce frowned and looked at his daughter, "You think the Hadleys' have that much cash?"

"No, Daddy, Rick's parents don't have much. Mr. Ganz owns the hospital. He's a nice old man."

Bruce said, "I've never heard of a Mr. Ganz. Are you sure of that name?"

"Yes. I talked with him twice—for more than an hour. He told me I can call him anytime; the hospital has his contact number."

Scott gave the Isaacs more information about the kidnappers: their description, names, and described the vehicle they were driving. Then he remembered where they were staying, but hadn't thought the kidnapping would ever proceed to an extent that knowledge of where they were living would be valuable. "The two men are staying at fire tower seventeen."

Megan said, "You said the men are about forty years old? Where are they from?"

"They're independent contractors from the East Coast, but maybe Chicago, or perhaps some other large city, but I didn't recognize any accent. They look to be about thirty-five to forty years old. One thing though, you're probably smarter than both of them combined."

Megan grinned, "Thanks." Her grin faded into seriousness, and she began to chew on the nail of her right little finger, "But Agent Wilson, what am I supposed to do?"

"Just be normal, and don't get too worried. We'll be after the guys—remember, we know where they're staying, and they think nobody knows that—except my partner and me. They have no idea we all know about their plan."

CHAPTER 21

ousin Chuck Nugent and his buddy, Sam Arnold, had driven to Suddenly Thursday morning, Chuck drove the small, freight-delivery-truck with the ATV and groceries, and Sam in a rented dark-blue crew cab pickup. Contrary to orders from Cousin Stan, Nugget and Sammy both had picked up small caliber handguns. Neither young man had spent any time in Suddenly.

Avoiding the town's streets and possible sightings by the keen-eyed, but flabby sheriff, they had travelled dirt and brush-littered back roads to within a half-mile of fire tower twenty. When they saw a road sign pointing toward Shadow Valley, 1 mile, they knew they were close to the tower they had rented.

According to the map he had drawn from the Ranger Station's web site, Chuck slowed the delivery truck near the first of three streams, pulled it off the dirt road behind a clump of trees, and cut the engine. Sam pulled up ten feet behind him.

Chuck stuck his head out the window and yelled back at Sammy, "Pull back about ten yards so we can unload the ATV!" He thought to himself, "What an idiot." After the ramps were pulled out, Sam drove the ATV out of the truck and over to the bank of the stream where he stopped and waited for Chuck to climb in.

"Get in the water and drive upstream until I tell you to pull out on the left bank."

Sammy shrugged and followed directions for about a hundred yards. "Hey, man, it's getting deeper!"

Chuck had his eyes on a wide spot in the water and pointed ahead, "Keep going! Pull off up there where the bank gently slopes into the water—near those big trees."

Sammy was happy he wasn't being criticized when he drove out of the water and stopped under some big trees. "Where to, boss?"

Chuck was following his plan to keep the trail of the ATV as hard to follow as possible. He glanced at his map and said, "Try to stay under the trees as much as possible and don't spin the wheels—go slow, especially when going uphill—straight ahead until we come to another creek."

Ten minutes later the two men arrived at a somewhat larger stream, twice as wide as the first, but much shallower. The banks were much rockier than before, and Sammy drove downstream this time, but only for a short distance before leaving the water and turning right—still staying under the trees as much as possible.

"Hey, Nugget, why are we staying under the trees? The driving would be easier out in the open."

"Look, Sammy, the ATV makes easier to follow tracks in the open. The needles and undergrowth beneath the trees help conceal our tracks. Okay?"

"Yeah, that makes sense—good thinkin'."

The third stream was completely dry, and few large rocks were exposed, which made the route along the bed fairly easy traveling.

"Stop!" Chuck shouted. The ATV skidded across a couple of feet of rock before coming to a halt. "Look over there." He was pointing up through an opening between clumps of trees. "That way, Sammy, that's our tower."

Sam turned into the incline of the hillside and up into the shelter of the trees, climbing the rise toward the structure which he had only seen the topmost part. It had looked small from the glimpse he had gotten from fifty or so yards away, but as the ATV brought the men through the stands of trees, Sammy's neck bent back as he observed the zigzag stairway to the little cabin perched on top of the sixty-foot high wooden beam structure. The first thing that entered his mind was the difficulty he imagined carrying all the food packed in the back seats up those many steps. He pulled up next to one of the corner posts and shut off the engine.

Sammy smiled and said, "Where's the elevator, Chuck?"

For a split second, chuck thought Sammy was serious, but when he glanced at his partner and saw the smile, he laughed and said, "I think it's on order, Sammy. Let's get up there and see where we're living for a week." Chuck stuck his right arm through a large coil of rope and started up the steps.

"Watch it on steps two and three, they're rotted out. We'll have to put some boards on those to keep from breakin' through and fallin'. We don't need any broke bones on this gig."

Sammy had grabbed a box of canned soup and followed Chuck. When he reached the landing at the top, he took a deep breath, exhaled and said, "Sixty-five steps. Man, I'm out of wind, and after only one trip. It's gonna take an hour bringing that food up here, and our legs will be shot."

"Don't sweat it, Sammy; why do you think I brought the rope up here? We're making an OTIS to lift the groceries."

"What the hell's an OTIS?"

Chuck giggled, "OTIS makes elevators, Sammy. Go back down there and I'll drop the rope to you. Tie some of the food to the rope and I'll haul it up. Should take about five lifts to get it all up here. Then we'll take a break, eat a sandwich, and get the place organized."

"Why don't you go down there, Chuck?"

"Who has stronger arms, Sammy, you or me?"

"Okay, I'll go down."

"Awesome idea, Sammy."

After filling the cupboards with food, Chuck and Sammy rode the ATV back to the freight truck and pickup. They left the ATV in the truck and Chuck drove the pickup into town to begin locating places of interest: the Isaacs' home, the high school, and the hospital, places they imagined Megan might be found. They had heard her boyfriend had been in the emergency ward after an accident.

Chuck called the high school from a convenience store and asked the secretary, "What time is the last class in the afternoon over? I need to pick my boy up and I forget what time."

"3:30, sir."

"Thanks."

Chuck bought himself a candy bar and some licorice for Sammy, got back in the pickup, and drove to the cross street where they could easily observe the Isaac's house. He parked along the curb, shut off the engine, and they waited. The time was 3:27.

Five minutes passed, then ten. Chuck glanced at Sammy who had lowered his window and tossed the licorice wrapper out.

"Hey! Don't do that! Get that wrapper and keep it in the truck. If someone saw you do that, attention would be fixed on us—plus you'd be leaving finger prints. You want to get us nabbed?"

Chuck watched Sammy retrieve the plastic wrap and nearly missed the arrival of a jeep with a girl driver and a boy sitting in the passenger seat.

"Sammy! Get in here! That's the chick!"

Both men watched the girl walk toward her house, but they missed seeing her go in the front door. A black pickup had moved slowly along the street and blocked their view for a few moments.

"I wonder who the boy is," said Sammy.

"Just a neighbor kid. I think she just gave him a ride. He went in the house next door."

"Chuck, do ya think the girl has a sister?"

"Nah, Stan said the girl is an only child—that's why he wants half a million, the banker don't want to lose his only kid."

They sat there for another ten minutes before Chuck said, "Nothin's goin' on here, we'll watch the school tomorrow and see if she goes somewhere else before comin' home. We have to be lookin' for that jeep, she'll probably be driven' it." Chuck started the engine and they drove away.

After Kalber and Manietta drove from the chopper landing site, they followed the road they had flown over a few minutes before landing at Cowpiddle Pond. Manny sat in the passenger seat watched the foliage, and kept an eye pealed for directional signs to fire lookout tower seventeen. He was a little nervous in the living forests, never having been outside the concrete forest of the big city. He noted squirrels, birds on the ground and in the trees, and one deer go bounding away from the rough dirt road as they moved away from Suddenly to the south.

A half-hour after leaving the chopper, the men, almost simultaneously, saw a sign indicating their tower was one mile away. Manny exclaimed, "Marty, did you see that sign? We're almost there."

"Yeah, Manny, another couple of minutes. We can't go very fast on this damn dirt road."

"Fast enough, I guess. It's damn bumpy."

The last two-hundred yards to the tower were taken very slowly, the road lacked guard rails, and if they deviated very far from the tracks already worn, the risk was great they would lose control of the truck and tumble down the hillside. Manny only looked out the downhill side of the truck once, swallowed hard, and quickly checked his seatbelt. He lowered his window to get some fresh air, and was happy to have Marty doing the driving.

At the bottom of the tower, there was room enough for the truck to turn around without fear of sliding down the side of the mountain. Manny got out of the truck, walked to the tower stilts, and gave hand signals as Marty backed the pickup bed close to the stairs. Manny grabbed the loaves of bread and started up the steps, counting as he climbed. The zigzag stairs went up three flights to the cabin at the top where he was surprised by the nice interior of the one-room efficiency apartment.

He put down the bread on the counter and heard Marty, "Hey, get your butt down here and get some more of this stuff. Some of it is heavy!" Manny started down the third flight and met his partner at the top second flight landing. He squeezed by Marty and descended to the pickup, grabbed their suitcases, and started back up the steps. Working together, it took about fifteen minutes to empty the back of the vehicle. While Marty organized the cabin's contents, Manny made some sandwiches for lunch.

After lunch, still in rumpled suits, the men drove into Suddenly to survey the town, specifically to locate the Isaacs' residence and the hospital, the two most logical places to grab the girl. The school was considered out of bounds—too many chances for them to be seen forcing the girl into the pickup.

Marty drove the periphery of the town taking note of the roads that might be used for a getaway if necessary. The main access routes were from the east and the north with dirt roads, almost like horse trails, that led to the nearby fire lookout towers. They saw some school buses dropping off students, apparently after school was over for the day.

"Hey, Marty, let's go by the girl's house. Maybe we'll see her coming home from school and find out what she's driving—if she has a car."

"Oh, she'll have a car all right; her dad has money so the pretty thing will be driving. Remember our file on her family? Didn't it say they have a jeep? Just the thing for a high school kid out here in the boondocks."

Marty turned onto Pinecone Drive and Manny read off the house numbers as they cruised the paved road.

"There it is: 6-3-4. A girl's getting out of the jeep and a boy, too, but he's goin' next door. She's looking good, Marty. She must have every boy in the school lickin' their lips."

Marty said, "There's a pickup parked on the left corner over here. Looks like two boys—probably spyin' on her. I bet I know what they're thinkin'."

"I don't think they have low T," Manny retorted with a snicker. "Hey, Marty, why don't we grab the girl right now? Only her and her mother will be home."

"But Manny, what about the two guys in the blue pickup, and do you have the masks?"

"You've got a point there. Nah, the masks are back at the tower."

Marty said, "Not too bad an idea though—not many peo-ple around on the street. Let's go back to the tower and get all our stuff ready so if conditions change, we'll be ready."

CHAPTER 22

Scott and Toni were up at seven o'clock Friday and had a quick breakfast in the apartment. The ground was wet and it seemed to have started raining early in the morning. The TV news and weather suggested it would rain on and off all day and perhaps not let up until Saturday noon.

Scott swallowed the last of his coffee and said, "Let's find Mr. Ganz and tell him what's going on."

"With no wheels? And in the rain?" Toni had frowned at the thought of traipsing around   without the use of an umbrella. She had not gotten used to the outdoors in the western states, having spent most of her life in Chicago, a few days in the Spokane area, and a day in Suddenly.

"I thought of that. We'll have Julie drop us off at the sheriff's office and have him find where Ganz lives. The sheriff or his deputy should provide a taxi ride to Ganz's home."

Toni shook her head wondering what was coming next that her brain and body would have to adapt to.

Julie had just gotten the boys out the front door headed to Megan's jeep when Scott and Toni met her at the front porch. She had stuck her hand out beyond the porch roof to judge how much rain was still falling when the agents appeared.

"Good morning. It's pretty wet out there, can I give you a lift?"

As Scott and Toni ducked under the roof, Scott said, "Morning, Julie. Yeah, we need to see Sheriff Howell."

Julie stepped back into the house and quickly returned, tossing the pickup keys to Scott.

"I'm not going anywhere 'til this afternoon. You can use the truck, but try to stay out of the mud." She laughed and said, "Say 'Hi' to the sheriff for me."

Ten minutes later, the agents were entering the Court House and checking the directory for the Sheriff's Office. Toni said, "Oh, yeah, it's below the little conference room in back."

There was an elevator, but the agents used the stairs. They entered the office and encountered a giant desk behind which a large woman in a flower print dress was typing on a computer keyboard. The secretaries' placard said, Mrs. Ginny Gumble.

Toni smiled and started to speak, but Mrs. Gumble spoke first, "Don't say it," and giggled. "How can I help you?"

Scott had ignored Toni's intention to say, "Gumball," and motioned toward Sheriff Howell who was leaning back in a large executive chair eating a doughnut.

"Who shall I say is here?"

"We're FBI agents and need to see the sheriff."

Rather than get up, Mrs. Gumble swiveled her chair and pushed her roller chair across the linoleum to the sheriff's door. "The FBI agents are here to see you, Henry."

"Thanks, Ginny. Send them in."

When Scott and Toni entered the sheriff's office, he stood, brushed doughnut crumbs off his shirt, and shook hands with the agents.

"What can I do for you today?" Sheriff Howell ran his tongue over his teeth and said, "Have a seat."

Scott glanced at Toni and grinned, focused on the sheriff, and said, "We'd like you to help us get in touch with a gentleman named Robert Ganz."

"Old man Ganz, eh? You think he can help with the ransom?"

Scott nodded, "Yes, sir. But we have no idea where he resides. Megan Isaacs told us he owns the hospital. Is that correct?"

"Yep. He's got more money than he knows what to do with, but he's a stingy old cuss. He's got a place in the Beaverhead National Forest—hard to get to by car, but you've got that chopper—should be a cinch, but you'll have to phone ahead. I'll get his number for you." The sheriff picked up his office phone and his secretary's phone rang.

"Yes, Sheriff."

"Ginny, please put in a call to Bill Nedfield, I need to talk to him."

Scott and Toni looked at each other and frowned. Sheriff Howell said, "Robert Ganz is an alias of William Nedfield. He probably has other aliases, too—for things I don't know about."

The sheriff and agents didn't have to wait long before Sheriff Howell's phone rang. Howell put the call on speaker phone and said, "Sorry to bother you, William, but I have two FBI agents in my office that need to talk to you. Can they fly out to your compound? They have a helicopter."

"What's this all about? I don't have any dealings that would interest the FBI."

Scott motioned to the sheriff that he wanted to talk to Mr. Nedfield, so the sheriff sat back and nodded to the agents.

"It concerns Megan Isaacs, sir, the candy striper you met at the hospital."

There was a moment of silence, then Nedfield exclaimed, "Oh! You mean my angel. Has something happened to that beautiful young lady?"

"No sir, not yet, but we would like to discuss the case in private—not over the phone."

"All right, you may come to see me. There's a pad on the roof. One of my staff will meet you. Can you give me an estimate of your time of arrival?"

"How far are you from Suddenly, sir?"

"Well, as the crow flies, about forty miles."

Scott replied, "We'll be there in about thirty minutes, sir."

"Fine. I'll be waiting. Goodbye." The phone clicked ending the call.

Scott looked at the sheriff, "He sounds pretty sharp. Megan said he is about ninety."

The sheriff smiled, "Yeah, he's too mean to die and he's got tentacles in just about everything you can think of. I wouldn't put it past him to have money invested in doughnuts."

Toni and Scott were taking off fifteen minutes after thanking the sheriff and leaving his office. A quarter of an hour later, they were in sight of the helipad at Nedfield's compound. Scott estimated the concrete wall surrounded four acres and dead center was a two story brick structure with a steel roof and solar panels on the four edges. The landing pad, painted like an archery target, was centered on the roof. From the chopper, he couldn't see any means of access to the building below. After landing and the main rotor had nearly stopped moving, the center helipad began to rotate. Toni was startled and reached over to grab Scott's arm. It was new to him also, but there was nothing to do but wait and see what happened next. The movement stopped after a ninety degree rotation had occurred. Scott noted a rectangular structure about the size of a hospital elevator had raised above the pad, a door slid open and a man approached the chopper. He motioned to follow him, which the agents did, and they descended into the structure beneath the landing area.

The elevator door slid open and a distinguished elderly gentleman said, "Hello, I'm William Nedfield; welcome to my home." He extended his right hand to Toni and then Scott.

They said their names and were led into a study where they were seated and asked if they would like something to drink.

"No thank you, sir. We had breakfast about an hour ago and are full of coffee. We have a story to tell you and would like to get your reaction." Scott leaned back and began telling Nedfield how the FBI became involved in Suddenly. When he had brought Nedfield up to date, he asked, "We want to know if you can put up the ransom money at a moment's notice."

Nedfield said, "Do I have any guarantee that the money will be reimbursed if lost?"

"The FBI will guarantee you will not lose a cent," Toni said. "Do you have enough cash to cover the ransom?"

Nedfield laughed heartily, "Don't worry about that, agent Thornton. I'm concerned about the young lady, Megan. She was very kind to me at the hospital and I would hate to see anything bad happen to her."

Scott added, "Toni will be shadowing her until this is over. Toni is a very capable agent; I trust her implicitly."

"I can see that she looks like she can take care of herself in a tussle, but what about firearms?" Nedfield's eyes were firmly fixed on Toni.

"Well, Mr. Nedfield, we don't expect any gunplay, but Agent Thornton is a crack shot, even if the target is moving."

Nedfield stood up and said, "All right, I'll have one of my aids alerted as to the cash needed. It will be marked—don't worry, the marks are undetectable with the human eye. I'll give you a number to reach me in case the funds are needed."

Scott and Toni had risen with Mr. Nedfield and Scott mentioned, "I didn't see any barbed or concertina wire around the walls. Don't you think the concrete barriers can be easily penetrated?"

Nedfield smiled, "The walls aren't to prevent people from coming in, Agent Wilson; they are to prevent fire from entering the property. We occasionally get animals trapped inside and we have to open the gates and shoo them out. I recognize the walls are not very high. I've had the trees cleared away from the walls out to fifty yards."

Scott smiled and said, "You are a very knowledgeable man, Mr. Nedfield. Thank you for your time. It has been a pleasure."

They shook hands and were led to the elevator. As they entered the lift, Nedfield said, "Say hello to Megan for me—I'll always remember her."

As the door began to slide shut, Scott said, "We'll do that, sir."

When back in the air returning to Suddenly, Toni couldn't keep quiet any longer, "Thanks for supporting me back there, Scott, but it wasn't necessary. Besides, what do you know about my skills with guns?"

Scott hadn't been thinking about Toni questioning what he had told Nedfield, but now he was being pressed for an explanation. "Did you notice that all the people we saw in the compound were men? And remember, Megan told us Nedfield had outlived three wives. I don't think I had consciously thought about it, but it seemed natural to reinforce your talents as a woman in his world of men. I guess I figured he thought of women as being weak or ineffective."

She laughed and said, "You have a very strong case of women's intuition. Is that why you've never married?"

Scott took his eyes away from the sky and grinned at Toni. "Boy, you sure know how to hurt a guy."

Toni responded, "I sure would have liked to have met your mother; I'll bet she was a riot."

"She was a realist and a very strong woman—not physically—mentally. I remember one day I was feeling bad because I couldn't do pullups like some of the other boys, and she told me, 'You're just as good as anyone else, Scotty; that's something you can improve. It just takes practice and will power.'" Scott glanced at Toni who looked deep in thought. "Then she said, 'Everyone has weaknesses and strengths, and both can be improved.'"

"Sounds like she was a great lady. Is she still living?"

"No. She passed when I was going into the army. Gosh, that was twenty years ago. She had an autoimmune disease. I don't remember what that was all about. I might have erased that from my memory."

"What about your father?"

"He died about ten years ago—of emphysema; he was a long time smoker and passed away when he was seventy-two."

"No brothers or sisters?"

"Nope, just me. What about your family? Any siblings?"

Toni didn't have a chance to answer, Delilah was descending to the landing spot at Cowpiddle Pond and Scott's full attention was on sitting the chopper down safely and without any jarring bumps, so she hadn't replied. As they buttoned up Delilah and were walking to Julie's truck, Toni commented, "I had a sister, but she was killed in a freak accident. I don't like to talk about it." She paused for a moment and then continued, "Could you please drop me off at the hospital? I need to talk with the people in charge, and I'll find something to eat there. You need to get this truck back to Julie. You can have lunch with your sweetie."

"I don't know about that. Ever since we came back from Dillon with those suits, she seems to have changed. You think she's found someone else?" Scott climbed in the cab and slammed the door a little harder than usual. They rode to the hospital in silence.

When Scott dropped Toni off, he said, "Call the house when you're ready to come home; someone will pick you up. Oh! Maybe you can hitch a ride with Megan—you'd better let her know who you are. I imagine she'll be wary of strangers." Scott watched Toni dash through the light rain and disappear into the main entrance of the hospital.

CHAPTER 23

A few blue spots had begun to appear in the sky and a beam of sunlight illuminated the driveway at the Drums' when Scott arrived, returning the state vehicle. A knock at the door wasn't answered, so he turned away and went to his apartment for lunch. He didn't feel like expending any effort to make a sandwich, wondering how Julie was. He decided to have a beer and tore open a bag of potato chips. The quiet in the bachelor pad and his thoughts of Julie were suddenly interrupted by a clap of thunder that startled him so thoroughly that he hit the floor. The abrupt noise was reminiscent of the sound of a rocket propelled grenade explosion and he had dropped both beer and chips when he dived for cover.

Rapping at his door was not machine gun fire and he began to laugh, then seeing the beer starting to puddle on the floor, he said, "Oh, crap!" and quickly up righted the bottle and reached for a towel.

Julie could be heard from outside, "Scott, are you all right?"

"One moment!" Scott answered, as the beer was being soaked up by the dish towel. He wiped the floor, tossed the wet towel into the sink, and opened the door. Julie was standing there with a towel wrapped around her head being pelted by rain. He pulled her into the apartment, wrapped his arms around her, and before she could utter a word, kissed her. She kissed him back, smiled, and as they separated, she said, "Thank you. What were you doing on the floor?"

He cleared his throat as he felt a flush moving across his face. "The thunder—it sounded like an RPG and I hit the floor—

spilled my beer—but I cleaned it up. Come in, I've been thinking about you most of the morning. He led her into the living area and they sat on the couch.

"That clap of thunder frightened me, too—it shook the house. I had no idea loud noises might affect you." Her wrinkled brow exhibited her concern.

"It's a little embarrassing sometimes, when in the presence of others, but it only seems to happen when my mind is distracted by something very important."

Julie grasped his hands in hers, grinned, and said, "And what might that be?" Julie was reminded of the time her husband proposed, but she felt more like a school girl having a crush on a boy, not a grown woman with children, searching for a husband—and father for her boys.

Scott leaned back against the sofa cushion, sighed, and said "I'm getting out of the FBI."

Julie frowned and stared into Scott's eyes, "Really? What will you do?"

"Well, I need some advice. What do you think of me joining the Forest Service—becoming a ranger? Would there be a chance I could work with you or at least nearby?"

She wasn't so excited about what Scott had said, but she asked, "Can you get transcripts from college and recommendations from the FBI? I can get the application forms, but you'll have to go through a training program—I believe it takes about 300 hours."

"The transcripts should be easy—the agency has an extensive file on me, all the way back to high school."

She put her hand on the wet towel covering her hair and stood up. "I heard your knock when I was in the shower. I need to finish cleaning up and go to work. Can we talk about this some more?"

"Sure, and I'll tell you about our trip to see Mr. Ganz. That was very interesting. Toni's at the hospital introducing herself and memorizing the structure of the building. She'll start watching over Megan this afternoon."

"Okay, sounds good. I'd ask you to have lunch with me, but I've got to get to work. See you this evening." She rushed down the stairs, every other step a clunk of her cast.

Scott watched her cross the patio, open the slider and disappear from view. He suddenly realized he still had her keys in his pocket, so he would give her another ten minutes to get ready, time enough to finish his beer and eat a few potato chips. He'd watch for her as she approached the pickup, and run to meet her. He wondered why Julie hadn't been more enthusiastic about his idea of becoming a ranger.

The ten minutes seemed to drag by, like waiting for a fish to strike, but using the wrong bait. The rain was now stuttering, coming in miniature volleys synchronized with erratic puffs of wind. Bright sunlight was beginning to glare off the cement driveway then quickly dimming from eclipsing by fast moving clouds. He heard a door slam, and Julie appeared moving toward the truck. He reached her as she opened the driver's door.

"I forgot to return your keys; thanks for the use of the truck." He handed her the keys and she said, "You're welcome." He started to turn away, but stopped and said, "Julie?"

"Yes?" She looked up from the little cluster of keys.

Scott kissed her and said, "Have a nice day."

She laughed, "I will now. See you and Toni later—for dinner—about six-thirty."

The state truck wound through the dirt roads toward tower twenty in Shadow Valley. Julie knew she wouldn't be able to reach the tower without a four-wheeler, but she might contact the renters and see if they needed anything after resisting the temptation to leave the tower and make the trip to town after all the rain. She knew all three streams would be swollen with runoff for another twenty-four hours, maybe longer, depending on how much more precipitation arrived.

The road came close to the first creek where a large turnout existed, so she drove there, but no one could be seen. She lowered her window to let the cool, clean, mountain air fill her lungs. With her chest protector in place and her sidearm easily accessible, she walked to the noisy stream, observed the depth and width, and then returned to her truck, but she could see where the grass and ground had been disturbed on the other side of the road, so she walked over to take a look. The large depressions in the ground could only have been made by a truck, one larger than a pickup. She measured from the center of the front wheel ruts to the middle of the back wheel indentations to get an idea of the wheel base, then she walked along the tracks to see where they led.

She didn't have to walk very far, maybe two hundred yards, before she came upon a blue pickup and a small freight truck, fairly well hidden, out of sight from the road. She assumed these were the two vehicles that were initially parked just off the road. She photographed the trucks and their license plates and returned to her vehicle. No other tracks could be seen. Driving off road was a violation; she would be issuing summons to the vehicle's owners. Next stop was the sheriff's office to have the VINs checked with the State Department of Motor Vehicles. Hopefully, Sheriff Howell would not have gone home early.

Toni looked out the hospital windows and watched an older-model jeep roll into the parking lot at 3:14. She focused on the driver, dressed as a candy striper and wearing a rain coat, approach the hospital front entrance. Toni swished the mop across the floor tiles and dipped it into the bucket of dirty water as the young lady rushed past her to the check-in desk. Toni was positive she had just seen Megan Isaacs for the first time.

The mop and bucket were quickly stored in the custodian's closet and Toni consulted with the admissions attendant to ascertain Megan's location. Toni headed toward room 139, located in the west wing, a little over halfway down the side hallway. As she passed room 129, Megan appeared in the hall carrying a bedpan covered with a white towel.

Toni called ahead, "Megan, we need to have a talk."

Megan continued walking backward toward the hospital bathroom, keeping her eyes on the woman who had just spoken.

"Who—who are you?" She backed to the wall, but kept moving away from Toni. She took a quick glance at the lavatory door.

"Don't be afraid, I'm Scott Loebman's partner—FBI. I'm staying in the apartment with Scott—above the Drums' garage."

"You said you wanted to talk; let me get rid of this." She held up the bedpan and laughed. "We can talk in the nurse's break room—but only for a few minutes. I have things to do."

Toni waited outside the bathroom, heard a toilet flush, and about twenty seconds later, Megan reappeared in the hallway. Megan shook her hands as if to remove body waste and chuckled. "I always wash my hands after going in there. Come on, I'll show you where the break room is."

The room for relaxation was a regular patient's room that had been refurnished and repainted; a vending machine and coffee maker were in one corner next to a sink. Toni and Megan sat at a small table.

"My name is Toni—I've been assigned to keep an eye on you until this kidnapping thing is over. We hope it will be behind us in a few days, but we expect that two men will try to kidnap you from the hospital early next week: Monday or Wednesday. I wanted to let you know who I am and why you see me around all the time. Just ignore me and carry on with your normal duties."

"So I shouldn't talk to you or anything?"

"That's right. Sometimes I'll be dressed as a custodian, like now, or maybe a nurse or a doctor carrying patient files or a clipboard. If anyone asks who I am, just say you don't know."

"That'll be easy—I don't know most things around here," Megan grinned. "Is that all?"

"Oh, one more thing. Can you give me a ride home when you're through with your shift?"

Megan stood, smoothed her skirt, chuckled, and said, "No problem. I drive that little jeep that's parked in the lot."

"Okay. Thanks, Megan."

As Megan pulled into the Isaacs' driveway a few minutes after five o'clock, she caught sight of a dog running out of the Drums' driveway toward the street, but it was a momentary distraction from parking the jeep. Megan and Toni got out of the vehicle and Megan said, "Did you see that dog? Where'd it come from?"

"That's Scott's dog, Spectrum. I'll introduce you." Toni whistled and in a few seconds, the dog came running around the corner of the Drums' house. A moment later, Scott came running after Spectrum, but he slowed to a walk when he saw Megan and the agent. Toni knelt and began stroking the dog's back and Spectrum licked her face as she turned her head to avoid a wet tongue.

Scott said, "Spectrum, sit!" He followed with, "Shake hands."

Megan leaned forward, shook the dog's raised paw, and said, "It's nice to meet you, Spectrum. You are a beautiful dog." Megan stood up but Spectrum leaned into her legs.

"I think he likes you, Megan. Now you have a four legged animal boyfriend. Here's his ball, give it a toss, and see who he returns it to."

Megan took the ball and turned to throw it across the other neighbor's yard, but she saw David coming down the street so she wound up and threw it as hard as she could toward David, but Spectrum beat David to the ball and came back to give it to Scott.

Almost home, Julie saw the gathering in the Isaacs' driveway and gave her horn a beep as she turned into the driveway at the side of her house. She joined the group at the Isaacs', pulled Scott aside, and whispered, "I have something to tell you that may be important; join me in the kitchen."

Scott recognized the urgency in Julie's demeanor and excused himself from Megan and Toni, who were still involved with Spectrum, and followed Julie into her home. Danny was coiled on the sofa, had his shoes off, the television on, but he was reading from a large book, not paying attention to the program. He glanced up and waved when Julie and Scott came in the house.

Julie pointed at the kitchen table and Scott sat down. She scooted her chair close to Scott and said, "I saw something a bit strange today—near Shadow Valley and tower twenty."

She looked at Danny briefly and then back at Scott, "I found a delivery truck and a dark-blue pickup parked behind a cluster of trees, out of sight from the road. It looks as if someone is trying to hide them. What do you think is going on?"

"Who are they registered to?"

"I don't know. I took the VINs and license numbers to Sheriff Howell, but the DMV in Helena was already closed for the weekend. I won't know who they belong to until Monday."

Chapter 24

"That's not much to go on, Julie. Did you take a look in the back of the truck?"

"No, it was locked, as was the cab of the pickup. So, do you think I'm nuts—maybe my sore foot has affected my brain?" She gave a nervous laugh, "Perhaps this kidnapping plan has set off my warning lights?"

"No, you might be on to something. I'd be suspicious of those vehicles being parked off road like that, too. Who's renting tower twenty?"

"The Ranger Office said the renters are two young men, Peter Young and John Palmer, from Butte. They're only renting for a week, which makes me wonder if they're just smoking some weed and don't want to get caught."

"Let's ask Toni and your boys—see if those names ring a bell. I guess we should check with Megan, too." Scott rested his left elbow on the table with his chin in his fingers looking at the marble table top, but not seeing it, just staring. He looked at Julie, "Isn't tower twenty in Shadow Valley? It takes an ATV or a good hike to get in there, doesn't it?"

"That's right! I'll bet the truck had an ATV in back. If they took the ATV out before it rained, I wouldn't have seen its tracks. They must have the ATV at the tower, so that isn't unusual at all. But why would they have tried to hide the trucks? I can't figure that out."

Scott grinned, "Let's wait until Monday and get the results from Helena. What's for dinner?"

"Oh! I haven't even thought about it—would you like to pick up some pizza? Get two large ones—any topping except anchovies—the Drums don't care for those little fish. Take the pickup and one of the boys. I'll get cleaned up and set the table while you're gone."

Scott looked serious, "You expect me to pay for it?" He started laughing before Julie could react.

She stomped her good foot and said, ""Don't do that; I can't tell when you're kidding!" She tossed him her keys and started down the hall to her bedroom muttering, "What am I going to do with him?"

Megan, Toni, David, and Spectrum were still gathered on the Isaacs' driveway when Scott reached the state truck. He waved at the group and yelled, "David, come with me to pick up some pizza. Bring Spectrum." Scott watched as David said something to Megan and Toni, turned away from the women, called Spectrum, and ran to the pickup.

Scott waited until David and Spectrum were in the cab beside him before asking, "Where do we get the best pizza?"

"PieRama, over on fourth and main, but Mom usually gets frozen ones and we cook 'em."

"Fourth and Main it is." Scott backed the pickup into the street and headed toward Main.

Five minutes later, Scott and David were at the counter ordering three large pizzas. Scott let David select the toppings so nothing would be left over for more than a day. He was sure no slices would remain uneaten longer than Saturday noon. They sat down in a nearby booth to wait for their number to be called.

Scott scanned the occupants of the restaurant but didn't recognize anyone. There were two families in adjacent booths and two men sitting near the side door in a third booth.

"When will you get the DNA results, David?"

David was watching one of the girls behind the counter. "We're supposed to find out about the family DNA on Monday." David took a drink of water and continued, "I've been teasing Megan about being adopted, but here's little chance of that."

Scott was curious, "Why tease her about that?"

David laughed—kind of an uneasy snort, "She doesn't look much like her parents—for sure nothing like her dad."

"Well, you don't look much like your mother; why would she resemble her father?"

"I don't know—I meant it to be funny; just a tease, but she kind of took it the wrong way. I told her I wasn't really serious, but she seemed a little worried—until I assured her that her parents were her real parents."

Scott had turned serious, "What will she do if it turns out her parents aren't related to her genetically?"

David sat there and shuffled his feet for a moment before answering, "She'll really be pissed at me for including her in the student activity, and then she won't talk to me until after all hell breaks loose at home. I'll probably hear some yelling coming from her house, her dad will retreat to the bank, and her mom will start crying. Then she'll come see me."

Scott smiled at David's response, thinking the kid knew Megan very well. "You really like her, don't you?"

David nodded and said, "What's not to like? She's beautiful, smart, and fun to be around. We've grown up together—neighbors our entire lives. I wish she liked me as much as I like her."

"I can't give you much advice about women, David, I've never had any time to have much involvement. All I can think of is wait and see, don't rush into things; let them develop normally—be patient, don't force anything."

"Number 76!"

David looked at his ticket, "That's us. Let's get our pizzas."

The three pizzas stacked on David's lap were giving off an amazing aroma that penetrated the entire pickup cab. Scott felt sure that when Julie drove the truck the next day she would still smell the odor from the delivery. He grinned when he imagined Spectrum being able to follow the scent along the streets back to the pizza parlor for two or three days.

As David and Scott walked toward the front door, they could feel a few drops of rain—Mother Nature was not through with the environmental car wash. Scott held the door for David, entered the foyer, closed and locked the door behind him; when he saw Danny homed in on David, he said, "Stand back, Danny, don't touch those boxes, they're radioactive."

Danny ignored the strange warning, saw the labels on the boxes, and said, "Mom! They got the good stuff!"

David let his brother take the top box to the table, lift the lid, and gaze at the tomato sauce, strewn with lumps of hamburger and quarter-sized discs of peperoni.

Julie came to the table with a tray of drinks and told Danny, "Get your nose out of the pizza, take a seat, and act like a human being—no foolishness, buster."

David put the other pizzas on the kitchen counter and worked his way around the table until he was beside Scott. He whispered, "I think Mom had a rough day—she's irritated about something."

Scott took a chair between David and Toni and waited for everyone to be seated. After two of the pies had vanished, Scott, using the edge of a fork, tapped on his water glass and said, "I have something to talk about and I would like everyone's opinion." The room became so quiet that he could hear David's and Toni's breathing. "I'm thinking about quitting my work with the FBI and start training to be a forest ranger. What do you think?"

David and Danny spoke in near unison, "FBI? You're with the FBI?" David cocked his head and stared at Scott, "You said you worked for West-Com."

"Sorry about that, but I couldn't tell you the truth until we had another problem under control—or at least understood the threat." Scott watched Julie raise her eyebrows and glance at her boys to monitor their reactions. "Toni is with the FBI, too; she's working with me on the case." Everyone looked away from Scott and shifted their eyes to Toni. She nodded while still chewing on pizza.

Danny said, "I'm kind of confused; is *anybody* working for West-Com?"

Julie had to laugh and she said, "Scott and Toni are both working for West-Com, Danny."

Danny scratched the back of his head, "Mom, I don't get it."

Julie looked at Scott, raising her eyebrows, asking for help.

Scott decided to explain the entire thing to the boys. "Okay, my name is Scott Wilson and Toni is Toni Thornton; we're not related, but both of us are agents with the FBI. When the agency discovered there was going to be a kidnapping by the West-Com organization, I answered their ad for a helicopter pilot. After the kidnapping, I'm supposed to fly two men and the victim to a safe place and wait for the ransom to be paid."

David stood up, frowned, and said, "Wait a minute. Who is supposed to be the victim? Is it one of us?"

"No—it's Megan, your next door neighbor."

David stared at Scott, "Megan? Does she know about this?"

"Yes, and we know who the kidnappers are, but we can't do anything until they do something illegal."

"Hmm." David appeared deep in thought and then suddenly said, "She didn't tell me about it. Hey! I can be with her over the whole weekend. Would anybody mess with her if I'm with her?"

Scott didn't have time to reply before Toni did, "I'm going to be watching her from the time she leaves school until she arrives home. I was with her at the hospital today; I'll be there on Monday, too, and on Wednesday, if that's necessary. If you were with her, David, the kidnappers would notice that something different was going on and they might not do anything—and—we don't want you to get hurt."

"Okay. Do you know what they want?"

Toni said, "Yes. They want three hundred thousand dollars for Megan's safe return."

David whistled as he exhaled, and then said, "Megan's worth more than that! But where will the Isaacs come up with that kind of money? Their house isn't worth more than two hundred thousand, and Megan told me once that they don't have much in savings."

"We're not concerned about the money; we'll pick up the kidnappers and Megan as planned, but they won't know Toni and I will be flying them to the FBI office in Spokane; they won't have any opportunities to get away." Scott sounded very confident with the FBI plan; the team of agents had thought of every conceivable problem that might arise and how to overcome all obstacles. The West-Com organization was near the end of its existence and the members of the group had no idea they were to be arrested in a few days.

The remainder of the evening was spent playing games and watching movies. At nine o'clock Julie announced it was bedtime for her, she had to work all day Saturday monitoring rain gages, inspecting bridges, and checking reports of sightings of cougars and bears. Scott was the last to leave after helping clean up the kitchen. Julie escorted him to the back door where Scott said, "Thanks for having us stay for dinner, and let me know if I can help with anything tomorrow." He bent down and gave her a kiss.

She responded, "You're a really good kisser—and thanks for buying us the best pizza in town. Good night."

The rain had let up and Scott had a relaxed stroll, breathing in the cool fresh air as he made his way to the apartment above the garage.

Chapter 25

Scott and Toni were up at 6:30 Saturday morning, but there was no evidence of any activity in the Drums' residence. Scott didn't want to wake Julie and ask for a ride to the helicopter even though he knew she had a workday. The agents ate a quick breakfast and set off walking to the chopper with Spectrum sometimes following, sometimes running ahead marking trees as if he knew where they were going. The streets were still damp, but the sky was blue, no sign of clouds, and sidewalks were nearly dry after the Friday night drizzle.

Toni kicked at a pinecone, sent it skittering across the street, and said, "Do you think Kalber and Manietta will nab Megan tomorrow?"

"I'm not sure what they're up to. We need to light a fire under their butts so they do something soon so we can get this concluded and go back to our normal locations. I need to talk to Del and hand in my resignation; I think I can do that in Spokane. I'll have to fill out a stack of forms; I hope it's all computerized."

Toni said with a big smile, "Are you going to take the chopper with you when you resign?"

"I wish. I'll have to give up Delilah—she's a high maintenance lady—too expensive for me. My salary as a forest ranger will be about half of what I make now."

"Delilah for Julie—sounds like a very good trade."

"I think so, but it depends on her."

"You don't need to worry about Julie; I've seen the way she looks at you."

They had been in the air only a couple of minutes when Toni cleared her throat and said, "Scott, you know where we're going? I don't recognize anything."

Scott smiled, "Sure, tower seventeen; we're almost there. See that tree over there—the one with the double branches at the top? The tower is a little to the east; there, I can see it now."

Toni glanced across Scott's lap and could see the tower roof with the number seventeen prominently displayed on the cedar shingles in white paint. "How did you do that? I have a good sense of direction, but nothing like what you can do from the air."

"I can't explain it, Toni; but I seem to have a very strong ability for dead-reckoning. I think it's something that develops when flying—it's done unconsciously, but once in a while I remember odd landmarks."

"Well. Whatever it's due to, it's remarkable."

Scott circled the tower as he dropped in altitude and set the chopper down about fifty feet from the tower. Before the main rotor stopped Kalber and Manietta were walking toward the helicopter, dressed in sweatshirts and jeans, quite a change from the poorly tailored suits they wore the last time the agents had seen the men. They could probably pass as mountain vacationers if they hadn't been wearing highly polished street shoes.

Toni and Scott met the kidnappers halfway between the chopper and the tower.

"What are you guys doing here?" Kalber said.

Scott replied, "We wondered when you're going to snatch the girl; I have to have the tanks full when we leave the area. I don't want to have to land in a populated area to get fuel— someone might see the girl."

"Hell, did someone change the plan?" Kalber folded his arms across his chest, stepped back a pace, and frowned. "We're always the last to find things out."

Manny said, "Yeah."

"We're going to fly out of here with the girl and drop her off when we know the ransom has been paid. Will you nab her Monday?" Toni stared at Martin Kalber, waiting his answer.

Kalber stood there for a moment thinking, "Depends on the damn rain. We don't like driving on these slippery dirt roads. What if we have a wreck and the girl gets hurt? We're suckin' sand if that goes down. We won't get paid and might even get caught!"

"I checked the weather this morning to determine flying conditions until next Wednesday. We're to get a little more rain tonight and then it will dry up until Tuesday night."

Kalber looked at Scott, "And is that accurate? You know how weather reports are—good for about ten minutes." He chuckled and Manietta joined in with a loud laugh.

"It's flying weather, so it might not correspond with ground level conditions, especially in the mountains. We should be all right though." Scott was talking with his hands grasped behind his back, looking Kalber in the eyes, standing in a rock solid position.

"All right, then. We'll pick her up Monday as she leaves the hospital—about five o'clock, and bring her here. We'll even provide dinner for her; everyone likes peanut butter and jelly sandwiches. We'll leave the ransom note at the hospital's front desk; Manny's working on it."

Scott glanced at Toni, who nodded, and then he said, "Everything is set. We'll be out here to pick you up around a quarter after five; be ready to go—have the tower scrubbed, no prints, and burn all your waste materials."

"Don't worry about that, boss. The place will be spic and span; nobody will know we were ever here, not even that broad that hired us."

"We'll see you with the girl on Monday, ready to fly out of here." Scott waved at the men and he and Toni returned to the chopper, took off, and headed back to Suddenly.

"Did you catch what Kalber said?" Toni yelled over the sound of the engine before she put on her headphones.

Scott was already pondering: what woman could have instigated the plan to kidnap Megan? He hadn't heard Toni's question, his senses were concentrated on flying Delilah, thinking about getting her refueled, and trying to anticipate what supplies would be necessary if they had to ditch in the mountains with five people on board, two of whom would be antagonistic. When he had mentioned good weather for the next four or five days to Kalber and Manietta ten minutes ago, he had lied, he had no idea what actual conditions would prevail.

"Well, what do you think?" said Toni. They were wearing headphones now.

Scott glanced at Toni, "About what?"

"You didn't hear me? I asked you if you heard what Kalber said about a broad hiring them for the kidnapping. Wouldn't the woman have to be someone from Suddenly?"

Scott nodded, "That would have a high probability. I can't think of anyone that might benefit other than the Hadleys, but I haven't had enough time to get to know the entire community. There might be someone out there that is jealous of Megan: a classmate or maybe a mother of another school girl."

As the agents started back to the Drums' with Spectrum on their heels, Toni said, "Can't we rent a car? There's got to be a rental here in town; we can't borrow your sweetie's truck to get around all the time."

"Yeah, there's a dealer on Main Street: Harley's Car and Truck Fleet. He caters to hunters and fishermen, but rents to people while their vehicles are being repaired after accidents."

Toni looked at Scott and grabbed his arm, "Is it far from here?"

He kept on walking, but when he reached the corner, he made a quick left and Toni fell behind a few steps. Scott laughed but Toni caught up in a couple of steps and punched him on the shoulder. The agents had shifted direction toward Main. "All right, let's rent a car—a cheap one; we'll save the agency some cash."

Toni blurted, "We'll get two sets of keys."

Scott could hear the excitement in Toni's voice and saw a smile grow out of a slight grin. He sensed that she knew just what she wanted to drive, but what was in the fleet at Harley's was anyone's guess. They would know what they had to choose from in a few minutes.

When they turned onto Main, Toni squinted and pointed down the street. "There's Harley's on the corner, but I don't see any fleet," she said sarcastically. The large blue and yellow vertical sign stuck out over the sidewalk. Only a blind person could miss it. As they got closer, Toni announced, "The lot's in back of the storefront—next to the alley. Sorry, Harley." There was a painted sign on the side of the building, shaped like an arrow, pointing down the side street. The sign could only be seen when close to the intersection.

The agents had been on the small lot for about ten seconds when they heard, "What can I do for you fine people today?"

Toni said, "We'd like to rent a car for a week; what have you to offer?" She was looking at a white Jeep Cherokee; marked on the windshield: '05, loaded, low mileage, V8, 4x4, extras.

"How about this little beauty?" Harley opened the door of a tiny light-blue Honda that had some small dents on the driver's side.

"What year is that? It looks pretty old," said Toni.

"1999, but it's got good tires and has good gas mileage. For a week it would be just $125."

"No disrespect Harley, but we're both about six-feet tall. If we were your size, we might fit, but we'd need a shoehorn and Vaseline to get into that little bug." The top of Harley's head almost made it to Toni's shoulder. Toni looked at Scott and he was holding back a laugh with his hand over his mouth. "Show us that Jeep Cherokee; it's about our size."

"Well, that's gonna cost about $250 a week—that's a fine car."

Toni said, "We'll take it."

Harley stared Toni in the eyes, "You people got some ID?"

Toni and Scott both showed Harley their official papers and he nearly choked, "Y—you're FBI agents?"

"That's right. We're in town to investigate price gouging. What was that price again?"

"Oh! I think I gave you the two-week price; one-week would be $125 and I'll fill the tank for you."

"All right. Let's go inside, sign the papers, and we'll be on our way." Toni winked at Scott and smiled.

Toni drove the rental to the Drums' and parked on the street so Julie would have full access to the driveway for her pickup, and the Cherokee wouldn't be hemmed in by the state vehicle.

After midnight Sunday morning a light rain fell and the temperature dropped to near freezing; a Canadian cold front had dropped south, below the border, fifty miles farther than the weather predictions had estimated. When Scott woke up around seven o'clock and looked outside as he made coffee, he couldn't see past Drums' house ten yards away. The trees in the neighbors' corner lot appeared ghostly in the thick fog. No vehicle movement could be heard, which was not unusual for a Sunday morning when most residents slept in.

"Turn up the heat, Scott! Aren't you cold?"

Scott was standing in his jeans and T-shirt waiting for the carafe to accumulate enough coffee to make one cup. He began to count down slowly from thirty. He would pour coffee into a mug whether the liquid level had reached one cup or not. Toni would have to wait for the second cup if she wanted her morning caffeine fix. Scott knew she wouldn't be getting up from her cot until the furnace warmed the apartment to at least seventy degrees. Toni grew up in Florida and had a great dislike for cold weather. Scott wondered how she ever maintained life in Chicago.

Scott was wondering how Julie's day went on Saturday, but hadn't spoken to her since the Cherokee had been rented. He grinned when he imagined Julie wondering whether there were now more agents staying in the apartment. He had begun to think about making breakfast when a rapid knocking occurred on the apartment door.

Toni pulled the blankets over her head and said, "You get the door, please; more cold air will be coming in, and I don't need any more goosebumps."

There was frost on the interior surface of the glass windows in the door, obscuring the person outside, but Scott thought it was Danny, due to the size of the image transmitted through the haze of frozen water.

Scott opened the door and Danny stepped inside. "Mr. Wilson! You need to turn up the heat, Ms. Thornton will freeze her... ah, will freeze—both of you will. Mom wants you and the others to come down for breakfast." Danny was glancing around the apartment. "Don't you have some other agents with you?"

"Just Toni and I are here, Danny. We rented a car yesterday—from Harley's."

Danny laughed, "Mom thought some other people came in the Jeep. Well, come on down, the apartment will warm up while you have something to eat."

Toni stuck her head out and said, "Do you like the fog?"

Danny grinned, "Yeah—it's kind of spooky."

Chapter 26

Fog engulfed the neighborhoods of Suddenly until late Sunday afternoon when a slight breeze brought in warmer air from the southwest. The town had been deathly quiet for most of the day, except for a minute or two from the wailing of a police siren. The agents, the Isaacs, and the Drums chose teams and spent the afternoon playing board games and answering trivia questions. When Julie ran out of snack food, the time for dinner was approaching, but no one was hungry. The Isaacs returned home and Toni commented that she had to go for groceries; the agents had run out of bread, eggs, and potato chips.

Julie said, "If you don't mind, I'll go with you. Our little party wiped out my cupboard of snacks and we're almost out of milk, and I've got to get meat for dinner for this coming week."

"Let's go now; I'll drive the Cherokee and save the state some gas money."

While shopping, the women separated, pushing carts up and down the aisles, and met again at the checkout. Julie turned to Toni and said, "See those guys over by the meat section? Are those the two men that are doing the kidnapping?"

Toni glanced around, briefly looked closely at the two young men, and replied, "Never seen them before; our guys are older, probably by fifteen years."

"I just wondered, I saw them watching me."

"They're just on the prowl, Julie. You're a pretty hot chick."

Julie chuckled and said, "I don't want a one night stand—I want to check their license plate when we get outside."

As they loaded the Jeep with groceries, Julie scanned the parking lot and saw one pickup, but it had an Idaho plate. She was disappointed that she hadn't discovered the drivers of the pickup and the truck unsuccessfully concealed in the trees not far from tower twenty.

"That's not the vehicle I'm looking for, wrong plate and wrong color."

"Don't sweat it, Julie. We'll figure it out tomorrow after we discover the owner of those trucks when we contact the DMV in Helena. That's the first thing I'll do in the a.m."

Julie grinned, "Toni, the state offices don't open 'til nine o'clock."

"Okay, I'll see the Sheriff, have doughnuts and coffee, then I'll call the DMV; that should be around ten o'clock."

Danny had gone to his room to do some reading. Scott and David were sitting in the living room talking.

"So what have you got planned for school tomorrow?"

David grinned, "We're supposed to get the result of the DNA tests in Biology, so I'm calling it D-day. I'm sure I already know the results, though. I think Megan is a little worried, probably my fault. I think I told you about that."

"I don't think you need to worry about that." Scott stood up and hurried to the front door. "I think the ladies have returned. Come on, let's help them with the groceries." Seven sacksful were on the kitchen counter before Julie had a chance to put anything away. She opened a cabinet door and started emptying the nearest bag as Scott watched where things were going.

Toni called from the front door, "Scott, that's all Julie's. I've got four more bags for us out in the car. You owe me twenty bucks."

Megan was anxious as she combed her hair Monday morning. Third period Biology was on her mind, specifically the results of the DNA tests. Her bedrock thoughts told her that her mother's and father's samples would confirm that they were her biological parents. She almost wanted to get mad at David for suggesting she might be adopted, but David was always teasing her, and she respected him in many ways—especially for his sense of humor, most of the time. He was trying to be funny and had no intention of hurting her. She knew he loved her.

She ate a piece of toast, buttered, and spread with strawberry jam, drank a glass of milk, grabbed her jacket, and went out to the jeep after saying good bye to her parents. Danny and David were waiting in the jeep.

"How long have you guys been out here?"

"About an hour," Danny said.

David laughed and said, "Only a couple of minutes; you're right on time. You look nice."

"Thanks. All buckled in?"

"Yep, let's hit the road. Are you excited about the DNA results?"

"Oh, yeah. I forgot about it." She lied to David so he wouldn't start with the adoption routine. "Ms. Sidwicke will be telling us all about the relationships. I'm sorry you had to have Mr. Wilson substitute for your dad. I think he likes your mom."

"Yeah. Mom seems to be happier when Scott is around. I'd like to see them get married; Danny would have a man to show him things—instead of me; I'm still learning myself."

Megan turned into the parking lot and shut off the engine. "What about it, Danny? Would you like Scott to be your new father?"

"That'd be okay with me—I like Mr. Wilson, he's cool. David always wins when we argue." Danny jumped out of the jeep and said, "Hope you live through biology class!" He ran to the entrance and joined some of his friends who were going into the building.

Megan got out of the jeep, stuck her keys in her pants' pocket, and said, "What did he mean by that?"

"I'm not sure, but he's always thinking of some smart comment. I don't think he knows anything about DNA."

They walked in the building together and Megan said, "I'll see you in biology."

Classes seemed to drag for Megan and she was almost late for biology, but just made it before the bell rang. David heard her sit down behind him, but didn't turn around; he was watching Ms. Sidwicke sorting through some papers at her desk in front of the chalkboard.

When she stood up, the class was quiet, all gossiping came to a halt.

"I have the results of David's and Megan's DNA samples, but I think there is some mistake. First, I'll show you that Megan and her mother are related, which we know. Then I'll show you the relationships for David, his brother, and their mother."

Ms. Sidwicke had made transparencies and displayed the results on the screen that hung from the ceiling in front of the class above the blackboard. After pointing out the parental relationships for the children and their mothers, she hesitated for a moment and then continued after changing the transparencies.

"Okay. David apparently mislabeled Mr. Isaac's and his substitute father's samples, because the stand-in's DNA indicates he is Megan's father."

Megan whispered to David, "David, what did you do? Why would you have changed samples like that—just trying to mess with me?"

David turned to look at Megan, "Megan, I—," he wanted to tell her it wasn't a mistake but held back. Megan's lips were pressed together, her frown made her normal pretty face turn homely. He'd have to talk with her after class. He refocused his attention on Ms. Sidwicke.

"David, you mixed up Mr. Isaac's and your stand-in's samples. That was just a careless mistake, but understandable," said Ms. Sidwicke. "I'll show you why there is only an almost insignificant chance that the substitute is not Megan's father."

David sat there mystified, not paying any more attention to Ms. Sidwicke's words. He couldn't think of anything else, Scott was Megan's father! How could that be? But more importantly, how was he going to convince Megan that Mr. Wilson was her biological father?

When class was over, Megan darted out the door before David could say a word; she obviously didn't want to talk to him.

He thought she would be cooled off by lunch time. He would talk to her then. Maybe, if they could work together, they could figure out the puzzle.

At twelve o'clock, Megan usually met with David and they had lunch together, but when David saw Megan going through the serving line, she was with two girls, and didn't seem to be watching for David. He sat alone and decided to not invest any more energy trying to talk to her at school. Hopefully, they would see each other this evening when he would have his mother to assist with the communication effort. He had to get Megan to listen to him.

It was three o'clock and Megan carried her books out to the jeep and started toward the hospital on Washington Avenue. She still had her thoughts on David's messing with the DNA samples. If he loved her, like she thought, why would he do such a thing? She had only driven about three blocks when a dark-blue pickup pulled alongside of her and an older man stuck his head out of the window and yelled, "Pull over!"

She ignored him, thinking he was just some crazy fool, and stepped on the gas, but the pickup stayed in position and got closer, someone was forcing her off the roadway! She was startled when she glanced sideways and recognized the man; it was John Kennedy, and he was pointing a gun at her head. She had to pull over.

Seconds after she had the jeep stopped, two men jumped out of the pickup, one wearing a mask of John Kennedy, and the other's face was concealed with a mask of Richard Nixon. Both men had handguns and Megan suddenly realized she was being kidnapped; she had been warned that it might happen. She had no alternative; she had to cooperate.

"Outta the jeep!" Nixon demanded.

The next thing Megan heard was car stopping behind her. She glanced back as she got out of the driver's seat. It was Toni! She was slowly approaching, her eyes dancing back and forth form one man to the other, but she didn't have a gun. What was Toni going to do?

"What's going on here? You're blocking the road."

Kennedy pointed his gun at Toni and said, "Get over here if you don't want to get shot." He motioned for Toni to stand next to Megan.

"Stand back to back—and don't move."

Kennedy pulled handcuffs from his pockets and cuffed Toni's right wrist to Megan's right and their left wrists together. Nixon pushed the two women into the back seat of the crew cab and said, "Sit still and keep your mouths shut; we're takin' a little ride."

The women had to sit sidesaddle to avoid painful tension on their arms, but they could see they were headed south out of town. When the road turned from asphalt to dirt, the truck stopped and Nixon put burlap bags over Toni's and Megan's heads. The pickup began to move again, and the trail became noticeably bumpy, the road noise loud enough to give Toni a chance to whisper, "These aren't the guys I told you about."

"Who are they, Toni?"

"I don't know."

"Shut up!" Kennedy yelled. "Keep your damn mouths shut!"

Megan had put the DNA results completely out of mind; now she was scared. This was not what Scott and Toni had planned on—these guys had masks, guns, handcuffs, and bags over the women's heads so they couldn't tell where they were going. Megan began to concentrate on the turns the truck was making, trying hard to recall if she had been on this road before. The truck came to a stop very suddenly and then slowly began to go slightly uphill over very bumpy terrain. Megan realized they were off the road now.

A minute or so later, Toni and Megan were taken from the crew cab and buckled into the back seat of a small vehicle, but the women weren't sure what they were in until the engine started; they both guessed an ATV. When the vehicle entered the first stream, Megan began to think of where a stream was so close to the road they had been travelling. When crossing a second creek, she was fairly sure they were approaching Shadow Valley. She began to concentrate with every brain cell she could muster.

The third stream crossing confirmed where they were, Megan was almost positive they were near tower twenty and Shadow Valley. She prayed that before long she would be telling Toni what she knew.

The two men guided Toni and Megan up three flights of wooden stairs to the cabin perched on the top of the tower. Having their wrists handcuffed together made the climb awkward and time consuming, but Megan counted the steps as they ascended the structure. She remembered David telling her once that there were forty steps to the top of tower twenty. She grinned when they reached to top step, exactly forty above the ground. They were at the Shadow Valley fire lookout tower, just as she thought.

Their captors had said few words as they climbed, but when they entered the cabin, one of the men said, "Give me the keys, Nix."

The other man answered, "Take off the cuffs, shut the door, and lock them in there."

Kennedy poked a gun into Toni's ribs and said, "Don't try anything or you're dead."

When Megan and Toni heard the lock close on the outside of their compartment, they pulled off the bags that covered their heads. Toni blinked her eyes and looked around, "Do you have any idea where we are?"

Megan smiled, "I know exactly where we are. We're at the top of tower twenty overlooking Shadow Valley, about seventeen miles by dirt roads from Suddenly."

"That's good—you need to tell me everything you know about this place."

Megan wasn't so afraid now, being with Toni, and knowing where she was had allowed her confidence to be regenerated. She chuckled, "That won't be difficult. It's got some interesting history."

CHAPTER 27

Toni assigned Scott the job of contacting the DMV in Helena and she took the Cherokee and followed Megan and the boys to school Monday morning. She checked in with the school office so the administrators and secretaries wouldn't be curious about her hanging around the school. She walked the halls and memorized the layout of the building, then went outside and committed the school grounds and nearby buildings to memory. She had parked the Cherokee next to the Isaacs' jeep and took a nap in the rental, awaking at noon when some students began retrieving their cars to leave campus for lunch.

Julie dropped Scott off at the sheriff's office and drove ten miles north to investigate a report of a moose with an arrow through the back of its neck. Some kid or a hunter that was a lousy shot wounded the animal, but apparently the moose could have cared less. Someone called it in so Julie had to investigate. Hunting moose out of season was a crime.

Scott went in the court house and found Sheriff Howell typing with his forefingers at his computer keyboard. He had just entered the license plate numbers of the vehicles Julie had found about a mile from tower twenty.

"Morning, Agent Wilson—have a doughnut and take a seat. I'll have some info on those vehicles in a few seconds—if the DMV computer isn't down."

Scott helped himself to a chocolate doughnut and sat across the desk from the sheriff waiting for an answerback from Helena. He didn't have to wait long before the sheriff said, "Those two vehicles belong to Mountain Rentals in Butte. Let's get in touch with them."

Sheriff Howell picked up his phone and dialed, listened for a few seconds, punched the number three on his phone, waited a few seconds and said, "This is Sheriff Howell over in Suddenly, can you fax me a photo of the renter of your delivery truck, Montana plate number MX 13367?" Sheriff Howell pressed the speaker phone button so Scott could hear the conversation.

"No."

"What do you mean, no?"

"Well, we have an old VHS tape system and can't copy from it. If you want to see what the customer looks like, you'll have to come see us."

Scott motioned to the sheriff that he would fly over to view the tape.

"All right, I'm sending a man over to see you. He's FBI."

"FBI? Sorry we can't give you better service, Sheriff. We'll be waiting for your man, but we'll be out for lunch at noon—back at one o'clock."

The sheriff shook his head. "Who am I talking to?"

"This is Lee Heimbigner; I'm the general manager."

"Thank you, Mr. Heimbigner. Bye."

The sheriff hung up and focused on Scott. "You want to fly over to Butte? I'll take you to your chopper."

"Thanks, Sheriff. I'll take photos of the screen with my cell and come right back after refueling. I should be back by three o'clock. Please tell Julie where I went if she gets in touch with you."

"I'll do that. You ready?"

Scott stood and zipped up his jacket, "Let's go."

Sheriff Howell grabbed a doughnut off a plate on his secretary's desk as they left his office. It was gone before he turned the key on the ignition.

Scott said, "I need to pick up my dog at the Drums'; it'll only take a minute."

Spectrum was always excited when Scott fetched him during the day; he knew they were going for a ride in the chopper. Scott put Spectrum in the cruiser's back seat.

"What's the dog's name?"

"Spectrum—he's a mix—loves to fly."

The sheriff chuckled, "I hope someone sees the dog in back; they'll think I have a K-9 unit. He looks like a German Shepard."

Scott smiled, "I should check his DNA and find out who his mother and father were."

"Where'd you get him?"

"He was in a kennel in Spokane. I was with my boss when he was getting a dog for his daughter. I saw Spectrum staring at me and squirming as he sat in the middle of his enclosure. When I stopped and looked at him, he got up and his tail started wagging. He was analyzing me, just as I was studying him. I decided to adopt him right then."

"Ah, instant love—just like you and Julie?" Sheriff Howell smiled.

"I don't think that's reciprocal, Sheriff. I told her I wanted to quit the FBI and become a ranger and she didn't sound very enthusiastic about the idea."

"You don't have to listen to me, Scott —I'm not any expert at love and emotions, but I imagine Julie is thinking about how her husband died. He was a ranger. She might be worrying that it could happen a second time and she might have to give up finding a man to share the rest of her life and help raise her two boys. If she lost again, it would be devastating."

"Let me out here, Sheriff. I'll go the rest of the way on foot and think about what you said." Scott got out of the police car and walked around to the sheriff's window. "You're a good man, Sheriff, but try to cut down on the doughnuts. Come on, Spectrum, we've got to see a man about a suspicious customer. Bye, Sheriff."

Sheriff Howell watched as Scott and Spectrum climbed into the cabin and the main rotor started moving slowly, then began turning so fast the blades became a blur. After the chopper lifted into the air, Sheriff Howell turned his cruiser around and headed back to his office, feeling good about what he had related to Scott concerning Julie.

The half-hour flight to Butte was uneventful, giving Scott time to think about the sheriff's words. The sky was clear and with Spectrum watching, there was little chance the helicopter would develop problems while Scott's mind wandered. A few minutes before approaching the Butte airport, three miles east of the city, Scott had made up his mind to proceed with his resignation from the bureau and pursue ranger training. He hoped Julie's reservations would change, but if not, he would have to move on to another location, perhaps at Glacier National Park. He was ready for a land job.

He set the helicopter down near the refueling area, went in the terminal and made arrangements for gas and a car rental. Twenty minutes later, he was parking his Ford Taurus in front of Mountain Rentals. It was almost eleven thirty.

He approached the sales counter where an attractive blonde smiled at him. "May I help you?"

"I'd like to see Mr. Heimbigner." Scott smiled back and reached for his ID.

The young woman glanced at Scott's wallet. "What is this about, sir?"

"I'm here to view a tape of a customer that rented a delivery truck about a week ago."

"Oh! You're the man from Suddenly. Daddy told me an FBI agent was coming in to view a tape. I can help you with that. I'm Gretchen, follow me."

Scott held up his ID and said, "I'm Scott Wilson. I need a photo of the person that rented the truck with license number MX 13367." Scott was led to a back room about the size of an efficiency toilet where a tape player and television set were located. Gretchen ran her fingers over the VHS tapes and pulled three from the previous week. She ran the oldest one first at fast forward, shelved the tape and loaded another into the player.

About half the tape had been scanned when she stopped the rapid playback and pressed PLAY.

"There they are! Those two guys rented the truck. They were smart asses."

"Can you hold that frame?" Scott withdrew his cellphone and got ready to take a close-up picture of the TV screen.

"No, but I can slow it down so you can get a clear shot."

"Great! That's all I need." Scott snapped two pictures and said, "Thank you very much. How old do you think those guys are?"

Gretchen took a close look and answered, "Hmm, mid-twenties—maybe a bit older."

A gong sounded and Gretchen explained, "That's so we shut down and go to lunch."

"Have you plans for lunch?" said Scott.

Gretchen shook her head, "I usually get a sandwich over at Jeremy's Bar and Grill; it's only a block from here."

"I have some questions for you; can I buy you lunch?"

"Sure! I'll get my jacket."

Scott was half-way through his chiliburger before he said, "What can I get as a gift for a lady friend?"

Gretchen's cheerful expression suddenly changed to her business face. "How well do you know this person? How old is she?"

"I met her a couple of weeks ago; she's about my age—she's a forest ranger."

Gretchen was very quiet for almost a minute as she chewed and thought. She swallowed and said, "How about a nice pair of fur-lined leather gloves? You can get them in almost any color and size at Betty's Boutique."

"That sounds like a good idea, thanks. Where is Betty's?"

"Finish up and I'll show you. We can take your car.

Betty's was ideal for the Western woman, according to Gretchen. The boutique carried cowboy boots, leather pants, saddles, coats of all types and materials, and a large section of undergarments and accessories. Gretchen walked directly to the gloves and held her right hand up to Scott, "How big are her hands?"

Scott judged Julies' fingers were longer than Gretchen's, which seemed rather small, and he said, "Bigger than yours by about an inch or so."

Gretchen grabbed a pair of gloves and gave them to Scott, "These will fit her; what color?"

"Light-gray and black; one pair of each."

Gretchen said, "Okay, pay for them and let's go back to Dad's store. I have to get back to work. I wish I could see your helicopter." She chuckled, "I've never done it in a helicopter."

Scott had to laugh at the thought; maybe ten years ago, but Gretchen was too easy. The difficulty of the hunt makes the conquest much more enjoyable. On the way back to Mountain Rentals, Gretchen volunteered some useful information.

"I've been thinking about that guy that rented the truck. I think he was a drop out in high school—tenth grade. I believe his name is Charley Nugent."

"Thanks for your help, Gretchen, with the gloves and the ID of the renter. I enjoyed having lunch with you." Scott pulled up to the curb at Mountain Rentals.

"Thanks for lunch, Mr. Wilson, and I wish I could have gotten in your helicopter. I've never seen one up close and personal. Bye." She grinned, quickly exited the Taurus, waved, and darted into the two-story concrete building.

Scott drove out to the airport, turned in the Ford, and signed for the fuel. Spectrum was waiting, focused on him, and barking, as he walked toward the chopper. They played ball for about five minutes before Scott said, "Let's get out of here, Spectrum. Suddenly needs us back. Shall we go see Julie and the boys?"

Spectrum barked twice, jumped into the chopper, and sat in the copilot's seat. Scott radioed for permission to take off and about thirty seconds later, he was cleared for the return flight to Suddenly. Instead of taking a direct route home, Scott decided to follow Interstate 15 to Dillon, then swung almost directly west on route 278 to Suddenly. He was watching for the delivery truck on the offhand thought that he might see it being returned to Butte, but nothing developed. Scott landed at Cowpiddle Pond at 2:20 p.m. and called Sheriff Howell for a ride to the police station.

"I've got a name, Sheriff—Charles Nugent."

"Good work; we're making some progress. Let's see if the computer can tell us something about Mr. Nugent. Want some coffee?"

"Sounds good, but no doughnut; I had a big lunch."

The sheriff drove through McDonald's and then to his office. Scott sat across the sheriff's desk petting Spectrum as Howell entered the name Charles Nugent into the state crime register. A few seconds after Howell's fingers stopped their movements, the sheriff sat back wearing a big smile. "You're gonna like this Agent Wilson. Nugent is a cousin of Stan Cardiff. He's one of the boys that tried to rob the pharmacy a few weeks back. Megan sprayed them with pepper spray. Those boys were more than a little pissed."

"Where are the hoodlums now?"

"They're spending two months at the correctional facility outside of Butte. Nugent still lives in Butte, so they could have concocted a kidnapping."

CHAPTER 28

"Sheriff Howell—you there?" Deputy Doureline's monotone base cut into the conversation between the sheriff and Agent Wilson.

"What have you got, deputy?"

"I've got two abandoned cars parked alongside the road at Washington and Ninth Street. One of them is that girl's jeep; you know, Megan Isaac's. Her books are in the front seat but she's not here. The other car is a white jeep Cherokee. I found a thirty-eight under the front seat; no driver."

"Deputy, that driver is FBI; she's supposed to watch over the Isaacs' kid."

"Should I ticket the cars?"

The sheriff gritted his teeth and shook his head. "No. An FBI man will pick up the Cherokee and I'll find someone to get the jeep. 10-4." Howell sat back with his hands behind his neck, "Well, I'd guess those women have been kidnapped."

Scott frowned, "That was supposed to have taken place later this afternoon. I'm wondering what changed their minds."

The phone rang in the secretary's office. Sheriff Howell looked at her through the glass wall and saw her signal for him to pick up.

"Sheriff Howell here." He listened for a few seconds and replied, "Don't handle that letter and have it delivered to my office—right now. Why don't you bring it over Mr. Isaacs? We need to talk."

The lawmen had to wait a few minutes before Mr. Isaacs walked up to the secretary's desk and was directed into the sheriff's office. The bank president handed a business size envelope to Sheriff Howell without speaking a word and sat down as if he were exhausted from the two-block trek. He looked as if he were in pain; he was clearly upset.

The dirty envelope was opened, read, and handed to Scott, who raised an eyebrow when he saw the figure $500,000. "I don't think this came from our guys, they were going to ask for $300,000." Scott focused on Mr. Isaacs and said, "When did you get this?"

"One of the managers handed it to me a few minutes ago. Someone left it on the counter at Miss Sanchez's window. She thinks it might have been there for thirty-minutes or longer and could have been put there when she was very busy. She was running both the drive-up and her counter position."

Scott looked at Bruce Isaacs, "You have a lobby camera, correct?"

"Yes, sir."

"We'll go over the recording and see if the person that dropped off the envelope can be seen. Don't worry about your daughter, my partner is probably with her at this time. We believe they were taken together."

Mr. Isaacs seemed to show some relief when he heard Scott's words, but then he said, "What am I going to do about the half-million?"

Sheriff Howell responded, "We've got until Thursday noon to get the money together, if we have to go that route. Agent Wilson says Mr. Ganz can cover it immediately, and the FBI will pay him back if it is lost. But let's not worry about that now. We're going to locate your daughter and Ms. Thornton, and see if we can capture the kidnappers."

Scott saw Julie appear at the secretary's disk and motioned for her to come into the sheriff's office. The sheriff's phone rang as Julie stepped into the sheriff's office. He smiled and hung up. "What can I do for you, Julie?"

"Nothing, Clint; agent Wilson motioned me in."

Sheriff Howell scratched the back of his head and said, "Oh," and glanced at Scott.

Scott stood up, gave Julie his chair, and said, "I think you should know about this note that Mr. Isaacs just received at the bank." He handed her the envelope and the three men waited for her to finish reading the note which was made up from words cut from the local newspaper. "I doubt if they graduated from high school; they can't spell."

"I flew to Butte this morning and found out one of the renters of tower twenty is Charles Nugent; he's a cousin of the Cardiff brothers—currently in jail north of Butte."

Julie's frown turned to a questioning look as she cocked her head to the side, "Cardiff? Oh! Those guys tried to rob the pharmacy!"

"Exactly, I think the cousin must have visited the brothers and they hatched the kidnapping plan. Sheriff, can you contact the jail and see if Nugent visited his cousins recently?"

"I'll do that right now. Why don't you gentlemen pick up those abandoned cars? If that visitation occurred, I think we know where the women are—tower twenty."

Scott looked at his watch, noted the time was 4:07 p.m., and commented, "I'll be back after I pick up the Cherokee. Bruce, will you be at the bank?"

"No," he sighed, "I've got to tell Sarah what has happened. She'll need me with her. She worries all the time about Megan, except when she's with David."

Julie dropped Bruce and Scott at their cars and headed home with the agent following in the Cherokee. As he drove, Scott was thinking about Toni trying to escape from her captors, but decided she wouldn't want to leave Megan alone and to get away with Megan would be too dangerous for both women. He assumed the kidnappers were armed and stupid; anything might set them off. With the cars parked, Scott talked with Julie at the curb.

"I've got to fly out to tower seventeen and see what my guys are up to—make sure they don't have Megan and Toni. Do you want to come with me?"

"Let me visit with the boys for a minute and I'll be right with you. It's too early for dinner."

Scott put Spectrum in the apartment and returned to the car. He got back into the Cherokee, started the engine, and waited about thirty seconds before Julie reappeared, got in the passenger seat, and fastened her seat belt. "Did you find the moose with the arrow in its neck?" Scott pulled away from the curb and drove west toward Delilah.

Julie watched Scott as he made his way through some scattered traffic, smiling. She wondered if the smile involved her. "I spent three hours looking for a moose with an arrow in it and came up with nothing. I think it was a goose chase, not a moose chase," she chuckled.

"You sound in good spirits."

"That's because I'm with you."

"Thank you, I'm glad I'm good for something other than chasing kidnappers. He reached over and gave her arm a little squeeze."

When in the air and skimming no more than fifty-feet above the trees, Scoll said, "Look under your seat, I got something for you when I was in Butte."

Julie felt around beneath her chair and found a gift wrapped box about the size of a brick, but very light in weight. The only things she could imagine might be in the container were socks and handkerchiefs; Scott wouldn't be buying her underwear—unless Toni had clued him in, and she didn't go with him to Butte. Julie gave him a questioning look, but he didn't look back; he was concentrating on flying.

All of a sudden they were descending—before she had the box opened. She set it beside her on the floor and watched the ground come up to meet them. Scott cut the engine, released his restraint, and opened the cabin door. "Stay here, Julie; this won't take long." Julie observed two men coming down the tower's stairs, the leading one waving to Scott. They shook hands and Scott seemed to be talking uninterruptedly until one of the men threw up his hands and threw something on the ground. Both men appeared displeased. Again, Scott seemed to take over and pointed at the helicopter. The men backed away, turned, retraced their steps, and started climbing the tower's stairway.

Scott yelled something at the tower and returned to the chopper. As he took his position, he said, "They don't have the women; they were just about ready to pick up Megan. They're really pissed, but they're going to help us get the women back."

"What's the new plan?"

"It's too late to do anything today. I noticed there's a front coming in from the North. Did you notice those dark rain clouds? I'm going to fly out here in the morning, get these boys, and see what develops at tower twenty."

"They want to help get Megan and Toni?"

"When I told them what had happened, they made the offer; so they can get their ransom. They could care less what happens to the other guys—they want me to get guns."

"You're not, though, right?"

"No way. I've got my own gun and Toni's, but I don't expect I'll need them."

Scott started the engine and lifted off, wondering if Julie had opened her package. When he glanced her way, he saw the decorative box sitting on the floor. She hadn't opened it yet, but by the time he was landing Delilah back at Suddenly, the wrapping had been torn from the box.

As the rotors were winding down, Julie grabbed Scott's right arm and said, "Thank you for the beautiful gloves. Now I'll have to figure out a place to go to wear them; they're too nice for everyday use."

Scott smiled and patted her hand, "I wanted to get you something for your birthday and for Valentine's Day; I missed both of them."

"Scott, you didn't even know I existed then."

"I still missed them and I wish I had known you. When *is* your birthday?"

Julie smiled and wondered if she should tell him and give away another of her secrets. She decided to let him wonder for a while. She didn't know when his birthday was so that would give them something to trade. "I'll let you figure it out—you can do some detective work."

Back in the Drums' house, Julie asked Scott to stay for dinner.

Scott said, "What's on the menu?"

"Does that make a difference?" She snapped back and then grinned.

"I might be allergic."

"You have allergies?"

"No, but I might have one if I haven't eaten something before."

"Waffles, bacon, peas, and corn."

Scott laughed, "Okay, I'll stay for dinner. Thanks for inviting. Can I help?" Scott was leaning against the door jamb, grinning, and watching Julie looking into the refrigerator.

"Mom, I have something to talk to you about—it's important—Mr. Wilson's involved."

"Can we talk about it while we eat?" Julie was holding a package of bacon and a dozen eggs.

"I—I guess so," said David.

Halfway through eating dinner, Julie said, "What did you want to talk about, David?"

"You remember the DNA project that Megan and I took part in?"

"Sure. Did you get the results?" Julie looked at her son as she held a piece of bacon in her fingers.

David glanced around the table to make sure everyone was sitting down. "Uh-huh. Mr. Wilson is Megan's father."

Julie and Scott started laughing; Julie dropped the bacon in her plate and said, "You must be kidding—did you switch the samples?"

"No, Mom. There's no mistake. Megan accused me of mislabeling the samples, but I didn't. Ours were labeled in capital letters and Megan's were labeled with her handwriting. There was no mistake, but she won't listen to me. I want you to go over to the Isaacs' with me and talk to Megan."

"She's not home, David. Megan and Toni were kidnapped this afternoon."

David jumped to his feet dropping his fork on the floor, "What? When were you going to tell me?"

"I was going to tell you about it after dinner—after we all ate quietly. We believe Megan and Toni were taken right after three o'clock classes were over—when Megan was on her way to the hospital. Toni was following her and got involved."

"What's being done? How do we get them back?"

Scott spoke up, "We think they were taken to tower twenty. We're going over there in the morning."

"I want to go, too."

Scott saw Julie shake her head, so he said, "I don't think you could do anything, David, and you have classes to attend."

"Tuesdays are a breeze: study hall and PE. If I miss them, it won't make any difference, and I might be able to help—we could use the drone to look into the tower to see who is there."

"He's got a point, Julie, and he'd be far enough away to not be in any danger. Good thinking, David."

"What about this DNA thing? Could you have made a mistake, son?"

"No way. But I can't figure out how it happened. Mr. Wilson has never even met Mrs. Isaacs before, have you?"

Scott didn't answer immediately, his thoughts were on rescuing Megan and Toni.

Chapter 29

"There is one possibility, but it's very slim," said Scott. "How old is Megan?"

David answered immediately, "She's sixteen, same as me. Why?"

"Well, about seventeen years ago I was in the Atlanta area taking basic training for the army. Four or five of us went into the city but we didn't have much cash, so we were paid for donating semen to a sperm bank. We had to answer a bunch of medical questions such as eye color, hair color, what childhood diseases we had—things like that. We got paid for giving samples. We went to a bar and played pool, had a few drinks, even though some of us were underage, and tried to find some girls. Jim Thatcher was the only one that had a date, and they got married later on."

Julie thought she knew what Scott was going to say, so she added, "You think Sarah Isaacs had artificial insemination and your sample was used?"

"That's what I'm thinking. I wonder if Mrs. Isaacs was treated there, or somehow got my sample from another medical center. Do you know if she was ever artificially inseminated?" Scott waited for Julie to reply, but he thought of something else, "If she did, does Bruce know about it? Maybe she wants to keep it a secret. What do you think, Julie?"

"I believe we should keep the results quiet for now. I'll do a little investigating and see what I can shake out of the laundry." She looked at the boys and said, "None of this should escape this room, all right?"

David said, "All right, but what if Megan won't talk to me ever again?"

"You need to tell her you made a mistake, but it wasn't intentional. I'll back you up."

"I'd be lying, but thanks, Mom."

"Can we count on you, Danny?" Julie said.

"Sure. I don't know anything about sperm. I haven't had biology. Are those swimmers?"

Julie said, "Maybe Scott can tell you about that." She grinned, glanced at Scott, and winked.

It was 7:00 p.m. and a discussion between Chuck Nugent, Nixon, and Sam Arnold, JFK, was going on at tower twenty. It was chilly, the sun had dropped below the topmost tree branches an hour earlier.

"I've been thinkin' JFK, we can't keep the broads here. We told the banker to deliver the money here and we'd release the women. We can't do it that way."

"What do we do, Nix?"

"You're gunna take them to one of those old ghost towns and leave 'em with enough food a water for a couple of days and then come back when I send you the word that I've got the ransom."

"Ghost town? That don't sound too good for me. You know ghosts give me the willies."

"The one I'm thinkin' about ain't really a ghost town, four or five people live there. I was there once a couple of years ago with some other guys and chicks. That girl I was with was *fine*."

"This place got a name?"

"Yeah, Southern Cross. It's about seventy miles from here near Georgetown Lake. But there ain't no roads; you'll have to take the ATV and drive in—leave the truck at the lake; it's just off route one. Don't sweat it, I'll draw you a map. You'll leave in the morning and get there around seven o'clock."

"Takes two hours?"

"I expect—no direct roads to the place—I'll show ya on my map."

"Want to tell the women?"

"No, let's give 'em a surprise," Nix cackled. "We'll give 'em some food and a couple of blankets and a coffee can to pee in—and a roll of toilet paper. We'll lock 'em in the back of the truck."

"They can't see in that truck."

"Well, shit—give 'em a flash light, too, and a couple of bottles of water. Want to make 'em comfy," Nix smiled.

"You'll help me get 'em in the truck?"

"Sure JFK. We'll cuff 'em together until they're in back, then we'll toss in the key and lock the door."

Toni and Megan had been laying on cots, walled off from Nix and JFK, but they could hear some of the murmurs beyond the wooden structure. Toni had her ear against the partition but couldn't make out many of the garbled words.

"What are they saying?" said Megan.

"Something about a truck and toilet paper, but that's about a ll I could understand."

"Do you think Agent Wilson knows we're here?"

"If Mrs. Drum and Scott put their heads together, they'll figure it out before tomorrow noon. I'd bet on that."

"Did you hear that?"

"What?"

"That scratching noise—listen."

Toni held her breath, moved away from the wall, and exhaled slowly.

"There! Did you hear that?"

Toni nodded, "What is that?"

Megan smiled, "I think a critter is trying to get in the tower cabin. We might have some fun."

"Hey in there! Whatcha doin'?"

Megan yelled back, "What are *you* doing; we're not doing anything. We heard you scratching something with a knife." Megan looked at Toni and smiled, then whispered, "I've got this."

The scratching became louder and then they heard a whine, almost a crying—like from a baby.

"What the hell is that?" One of the men called out.

Megan grinned and nearly started laughing. She yelled back, "I think it's a baby bigfoot—you know a whole family of them has been reported in Shadow Valley and tower twenty— that's where we are, isn't it? Open the door and I'll tell you a story about this place."

"I don't think so." They heard another scratching. "What kind of story?"

Megan winked at Toni, who smiled.

"It's about bigfoot. Something that a gigantic being might have done—a couple of years ago."

There was a pause and some mumbling was heard by the women. "Step away from the door. I've got a gun."

Megan and Toni sat side-by-side on one of the cots and watched as the small door opened slowly. They saw a man's chest and trousers and a pistol gripped in his right hand.

"What's this story you're talkin' about?" said JFK.

Megan moved a little closer to the door. "Well, about two or maybe three years ago, loggers in Shadow Valley got rained out. They parked their equipment and drove into Suddenly to wait until most of the rain had evaporated. Two days later they returned to find one of their trucks turned on its side and large footprints all over the place." Megan paused, glanced at Toni and gave a thumbs up. "When the loggers investigated the truck, they found clumps of hair and blood on the engine and on the doors to the cab."

"That's bull shit—that never happened," said Nix.

"Well, a zoologist came out from the university in Missoula and said the hair and blood were not human. Didn't you read about it in the papers?"

JFK said, "You might have missed it, Nix. You hardly ever read the paper."

There was a pause and then the scratching and whining returned. The noises seemed to be getting louder.

"I think that's a baby Bigfoot; it might be hungry—probably smells the food up here, but don't open that door, a full size Bigfoot might be with the little one. If it gets its arm through that door we've had it." Megan turned and whispered to Toni, "I think it's a dog."

Toni and Megan both jumped when the bang of bullet fired from less than ten feet away.

Nix said, "That'll keep whatever it is away. If that didn't chase it away, I've got eight more ready for it. I'm not screwing around with that bull shit. Have you got any more to tell us, little lady?"

"No!" Megan was shocked and scared by Nix's reaction to the scratching noises. JFK slammed the door on the partition and snapped the lock shut, isolating the women. Megan and Toni lay on their cots pondering what had just taken place. They knew the kidnappers meant business.

It was 4:30 a.m. Tuesday morning when the women were abruptly awakened by a loud banging on their partition wall.

"Get up, ladies, you're gonna go for a ride. Put on your heavy clothes, the cold out there this early in the mornin' is gonna wake you up good." The two men were laughing; Megan couldn't tell who had made the announcement.

Toni said, "Wrap your blanket around your shoulders and tie it in front. We'll sit together and try to keep warm." She stepped through the small door into the larger portion of the cabin where the two masked men were waiting with handcuffs and guns. Toni almost laughed when she saw how stupid the two kidnappers looked in their oversize masks of dead presidents. Nixon handcuffed Megan's left wrist to Toni's right and JFK put sacks over the women's heads.

"Got that backpack, JFK? We don't want two frozen chickens in the back of the truck."

"I got it, Nix. Let's get outta here."

The women were led down the flights of stairs and shoved into the back of the ATV. When their seatbelts were fastened, one of the men placed a fairly heavy bag between them on the floor.

"Don't lose that bag, ladies, your life depends on what's in there."

Megan couldn't tell who had spoken; the masks distorted the men's voices. She whispered to Toni, "Where do you think we're going?"

"I don't know, but hang on tightly; these idiots don't have night vision. If one of us falls out in a stream, we both get wet."

The engine roared to life and the ATV surged ahead into the predawn darkness. Megan could hear the water rushing around the wheels of the vehicle as they crossed the first stream, and a few minutes later, another bumpy ride through water, this time deeper.

She leaned toward Toni and said, "One more stream and we'll be close to the road." Just as she had predicted, after fording some rushing water, the ATV tilted up and the engine roared; they were climbing the bank to the road. More bumpy travel followed, but for only a short distance. The ATV stopped abruptly.

"Pull those ramps out and unlock the door, JFK."

The screeching sounds of metal on metal could be heard along with two thumps, then the noises of the rear truck door swinging open. The ATV was driven into the truck and the engine shut off, creating a deathly silence. The driver dismounted and shuffled down a ramp, the noises informing the women what was taking place. With the ramps stored, the rear door slammed shut. Megan was beginning to shiver from the cold and worry about what was next.

Toni pulled the bag from her head and helped Megan do the same. Still in the back seat of the ATV, both women reached down for the bag between them at their legs. Their hands bumped and Megan said, "Go ahead, Toni, I think you can feel for what's in the bag better than I can."

"Ah—a flashlight. Here, you take it. Turn it on so we can see what's in here."

The truck began to move and Megan almost dropped the flashlight as the truck moved over the rough ground and reached solid ground.

"I think we're on the dirt road now, Megan; it's not so bumpy."

The light came on and Megan directed the beam into the large bag. Toni pulled out two blankets and a roll of toilet paper, followed with an empty coffee can. Toni held up the can and remarked, "I guess I know what that's for; I'm going to need it in a while. What nice guys, they gave us some bread, peanut butter and a spoon—no knife. That's about it."

"No key for the handcuffs?" said Megan.

"Not in the bag—shine the light around and see if there's anything else we can use."

Megan pointed the light at the floor of the ATV and was disappointed at the lack of anything but dirt and a couple of small pebbles. Then she aimed the beam at the backdoor of the truck. When the light moved across the truck bed, Toni said, "There, Megan!" She pointed in the corner. "There's something shiny on the floor. Let's find out what it is. If it's a nail, maybe we can use it to undo the handcuffs."

Megan handed the light to Toni and slowly climbed from the ATV trying not to pull on the cuffs linking them together. Toni sat side-saddle and stepped away from the vehicle so they could move together to the shiny object. Megan bent down and picked it up. "It's a key, Tony! They wanted us to remove the cuffs!"

The truck jolted, almost causing the women to fall, but they steadied themselves against the side of the truck. Toni said, "Listen—we're on a highway; the road is smooth. If we meet some people, we can get away and call Sheriff Howell; he'll contact Scott and Julie."

Megan held out her arm and Toni unlocked the handcuffs and tossed them on the floor of the ATV. Megan climbed back into the machine, wrapped one of the blankets around her legs, and sat down. "I'm cold! How long have we been in here, Toni?"

"I think about thirty minutes. You think you know what road we're on?"

"Uh-huh, highway 278. It never has much traffic, but it's still early in the morning."

"Are there any towns along the road?"

"If we're going north, we should go through Wisdom before long. The truck will have to slow down—maybe stop for a light."

CHAPTER 30

Within ten minutes traffic could be heard passing the truck and in few more minutes, the truck stopped for about thirty seconds and then resumed travel.

"That must have been Wisdom; we're going north on 278," said Megan. "I'm really tired, Toni. Could you sit beside me while I sleep?"

"That's a good idea; I'm a little sleepy, too. I hope we aren't getting gassed from carbon monoxide. If we get headaches, we're getting poisoned, but there's nothing we can do about it." Toni glanced at her watch; it was 5:45 a.m.

Toni shook Megan when the truck came to a halt and the engine stopped. "Megan! It's a quarter after seven and the truck just stopped." Toni turned on the flashlight.

"Can you hear anything?"

"Nothing. There doesn't seem to be any traffic. I woke up when the truck stopped."

The women were startled by the sounds of the ramps being pulled from under the truck bed. They tossed back the blankets and waited for the door to swing open. When daylight hit their eyes they both blinked and squinted as the door swung wide open. They watched as JFK walked up one of the ramps into the truck with his gun drawn.

"Stay right where you are, ladies. I'm putting cuffs back on you—different key. Don't try anything. Megan, come here." He motioned with the gun and Megan followed orders. Once the cuffs were on the women, he marched them down the ramps, and with a piece of rope, tied them to a small tree a few feet from the truck.

Toni watched as JFK vaulted into the truck and drove the ATV down the ramps and over to the women. She had scanned the area to the horizon and didn't detect any people, buildings, or vehicles, yet they were next to a paved highway. The truck was parked about twenty feet off the road. JFK pushed the ramps up, locked the truck's rear door, dusted off his pants, and smiled, "We're going for another ride—to visit some ghosts."

With Toni and Megan secured in the back seat, JFK began driving cross country, generating his own road. The ATV snorted a few times as it chugged up and down some small hills and across a meadow and skirted two small lakes somewhat larger than Cowpiddle Pond. About ten minutes went by as the passengers were jolted around with JFK apparently having little concern for the women's comfort. A dirt road, overgrown with weeds and wild flowers ended up at some ramshackle buildings, and half-a-dozen modern looking tents. One of the old single story buildings had a sign hanging from a chain at a sharp angle. The black and white sign said, "JAIL."

No one greeted the newcomers but Megan could smell bacon. Smoke was coming from a chimney that poked through the top of the biggest and most worn tent. JFK escorted the women into the old jail, put them in the one remaining intact cell, and used the handcuffs to lock the iron cage.

JFK laughed and said, "Make yourselves to home, ladies," and left the premises. Arny pulled off the mask, stuffed it in his pocket, and followed the scent of bacon.

Scott fed Spectrum and had breakfast with the Drums. Danny was excited about flying the drone over the trees to look in tower twenty, hoping to see the kidnappers, Megan, and Toni.

"Mom, are you coming with us?" Danny's excitement was apparent in the sound of his voice.

"You're going to school, bub. I can't let you go with Scott and David; it might be dangerous. I'm going to watch for activity around that delivery truck."

"But Mom, I can fly the drone better than David can."

Julie looked at David and he nodded, acknowledging what Danny had stated.

"Come on, Mom, let me go with them. I won't even get close to the tower; will I, Mr. Wilson?"

"That's true; we'll be a quarter of a mile away on the ground with the chopper. I can receive the drone's TV signals on Delilah's computer screen. He'll be all right, Julie."

"Jeez! Three against one. Well, you can skip school, but only today."

Danny put his arm around Julie's waist and said, "Thanks, Mom."

"Okay, but you follow what Mr. Wilson tells you."

Spectrum, the boys, and Scott took the Cherokee to the helicopter and transferred the drone and controller to the passenger compartment. After a warmup, Scott took off and flew slightly above the trees to minimize the noise from the rotors. He remembered seeing a small clearing not far from tower twenty, dropped the chopper to the ground, and cut the engine.

"Okay, Danny, fly your drone above the trees and look for the tower. We'll watch the drone's position on my cockpit screen. Fly the drone straight up and swing the camera around—see if you can get a shot of the tower."

Scott pointed in the direction of the tower and Danny flew the drone vertically to several hundred feet, tilted the camera, and sighted the tower. Keeping the drone at high altitude as Scott suggested, Danny positioned the craft directly above the tower and then dropped it to about ten feet over the roof and held that location. He looked at Scott and said, "What do I do next?"

"We need to look in the windows, so start on the shadow sides and tip the drone so the camera is pointed at the windows, then move around the tower as quickly as possible. We don't know what will happen if the drone is spotted."

David said, "Can we record the scan?"

"That's being done, David."

David glanced at the console and noticed the RECORD light blinking. He thought, "This chopper has awesome technology." He smiled as he watched the images on the screen as Danny piloted the drone around the tower. All of a sudden, a man wearing a president Nixon mask appeared with a gun and took a shot at the drone and missed.

Scott said, "Evasive maneuvers, Danny!"

The drone shot straight up and moved to the side of the tower opposite the gunman.

"Better get out of there; I think we've seen enough," Scott said.

The drone climbed in altitude to make striking it with a bullet from a handgun almost impossible, and returned the craft to the helicopter. Danny brought the drone in for a perfect landing and turned off the four motors.

Danny and David were watching the slow motion playback of the recording from the drone's TV camera while Scott asked questions. The entire sequence of pictures showed only one person, the man hat shot at the drone. Scott enhanced the recording and replayed it, but with the same results.

"So other than that partition, did you see anything abnormal in the tower?" Scott said.

Both boys answered, "No," as they shook their heads.

A buzzer sounded and a red light on the console began blinking. Scott said, "Hello, Julie."

"Scott, the delivery truck is gone! What have you found at the tower?"

"There's one man at the tower—he took a shot at the drone but missed. Danny brought the drone back unscathed. We're about to take off. I'm going to swing around toward Butte and see if I can find the truck. Do you mind if the boys go with me?"

"No. If you take them home, you'll waste too much time. Go after that truck; that's where Megan and Toni are."

"Okay. Have Sheriff Howell put out an all-points and maybe we'll find it if I can't see it from the air. I'm playing a hunch and going towards Butte."

"All right, good luck!"

Scott started the rotors and said to David, "Where's the nearest highway going towards Butte?"

David thought for a couple of seconds, "State highway 278—directly east, and farther east is Interstate 15."

"You guys belted in?"

Scott heard the boys say, "Yes, sir," in unison and took off. When he was at 500 feet, he tilted Delilah and headed northeast at cruising speed. Four minutes later, Delilah was over highway 278.

"Boys, keep a lookout for a delivery truck going north." Scott was flying west of the road at about 500 feet in altitude and following the highway; Danny and David were watching out the right side windows and could see both lanes of the road.

"How fast are we going, Mr. Wilson?"

"About 150 miles per hour, Danny."

"It doesn't seem like we're going that fast."

David said, "Look at one car down there and watch how it seems to be going backwards. We're going pretty fast, Danny."

Danny watched for a moment, smiled, and said, "Yeah, I guess so."

They flew for another ten minutes in quiet before Scott said, "I'm calling Mountain Rentals in Butte and telling them to call me when that truck is returned. I want them to make sure they get a good picture of the guy."

Scott punched ten numbers into his keypad and waited about five seconds for a ring tone. A woman answered, "Mountain Rentals, Gretchen speaking."

"Hello, Gretchen. This is Scott Wilson. How are you doing?"

"I'm fine—I didn't expect to hear from you again. Are you going to give me a ride in your helicopter?"

"Not today. I want you to call me if that delivery truck is returned today. Do you have my number on your phone?"

"Yes, but it's kind of a strange number."

"Yeah, it's my phone on the chopper. I've got two young men with me to help look for the truck in the highways. When that truck is returned, please send me the mileage that was put on since you rented it out—it's very important. Also, please get a good picture of the guy that returns the vehicle."

"All right, Scott. I'll do my best. Bye."

"Bye, Gretchen."

David looked at Scott and raised his eyebrows, "She sounds awesome."

"She is, but she's too young for me and too old for you."

David smiled and looked back at the road below. "There's a truck! Could that be the one?"

"Let's check the license. Binoculars are under your seat."

Scott dropped the chopper to 100 feet over the highway and began to overtake the small truck from behind. David was focusing the lenses and said, "It's got Idaho plates, Mr. Wilson."

Scott took Delilah back up to 500 feet and continued following the road. Now they were on route 569 and Scott was losing hope of sighting the truck; they were moving north of Butte and travelling along route 1, passing over the little town of Anaconda when Danny yelled, "There's another truck, but it's coming toward us!"

"Check the license, David!" Scott dropped in altitude and flew a mile west and then turned and came back to the road, catching up with the truck from behind."

David read off the numbers of the Montana license and Scott said, "That's it! Good work, boys! Now, where has it been?"

Danny was bouncing his left knee and had started to bit a fingernail, "Aren't we going to stop it?"

Scott couldn't look away from flying, but he said, "What if the girls are in the back and the driver has a gun? I'm not sure we could stop him from hurting Megan and Toni."

David nodded his head, "We can't risk hurting them, but we can follow him and he won't even know it; don't you think?"

"Exactly. I've got our coordinates, so we can come back here and search for the girls if they aren't in the truck. We'll stay behind him at two-thousand feet—he'll never know we're tailing him. If he goes directly to the rental dealer, we'll know the girls aren't in the truck."

Danny added, "Don't lose him, David."

Fifteen minutes later, after easily following on Interstate 80, the truck entered Butte and Delilah dropped in altitude so buildings would not hide the progress of the truck through city streets. When the truck pulled into Mountain Rentals, Scott hovered Delilah for a few seconds, then went to 3,000 feet, and retraced the path they had followed from Anaconda.

David was watching state highway one almost devoid of traffic after passing over Anaconda and about ten minutes later, Philipsburg.

Scott decided to land at Philipsburg and ask some questions. He chose a spot that would draw attraction from the local police, the parking lot in front of the grade school. Less than five minutes after set down, a police cruiser appeared and a local lawman, with his hand on his holster, approached Delilah.

Scott popped the door on the canopy and stepped out. "Stay in Delilah, boys."

"Say, what's the idea of landing on school property and scaring the children?"

"I'm with the FBI. I'm looking for two kidnapped women and they might be nearby."

"Got any ID?"

Scott pulled his wallet from his left back pocket and gave it to Sheriff Kindahl. The sheriff focused on Scott's ID and handed it back.

"Okay, Agent Wilson, what can I do for you?"

Scott saw the sheriff looking at Delilah and commented, "Those are the Drum boys—they're helping me as spotters. They're neighbors of one of the kidnapped women."

"Those are Julie's boys? I haven't seen them since the funeral. They sure have grown!"

"You know Julie Drum?"

Chapter 31

"Oh, yeah. She's the prettiest ranger in the whole state of Montana. Has she remarried yet?"

Scott smiled, "No, but I'm working on that. Sheriff, we're looking for a delivery truck that might have come through Philipsburg this morning. Have you got eyes on traffic through town?"

Sheriff Kindahl's face exploded into a broad grin, "You're in luck, son. We just installed cameras on the main drag last month to catch speeders—helps pay my salary. Nobody gets through town without us getting a picture of him—or her."

"Can I look at this morning's traffic?"

"You bet. Bring the boys and I'll give 'em something to chew on. They're still growin'."

Scott walked over to Delilah and motioned for the boys to come with him. The sheriff took the trio to the station and Scott reviewed the morning's traffic. The procedure only took a few minutes, barely enough time for the boys to drink a can of pop and eat a candy bar, but they managed. No trucks other than a farmer's flatbed were on the digital recording.

"Well, Agent Wilson, your truck hasn't been through my town. I'll take you back to your helicopter."

As they returned to the grade school, Scott asked, "Where could two women be kept incommunicado between here and Anaconda?"

Sheriff Kindahl rubbed his chin with his right thumb and forefinger and replied, "Two places, and they're close together: Georgetown Lake, and Southern Cross—it's a ghost town."

"Ghost town?" There was sudden excitement in Danny's voice.

"Oh, there's about half-a-dozen souls out there looking for gold and silver. They earn a hundred bucks a week or so, and once in a while find a nugget that keeps them excited. I believe that old jailhouse is still standing, after more than a hundred years. Last time I was out there, those old iron bars were getting pretty rusty."

The sheriff pulled up next to Delilah and said goodbye and good luck to Scott and the boys. The Drums' yelled, "Thanks, sheriff," as they climbed into the chopper. Scott waved but it was more of a salute—an acknowledgement of cooperation.

Once in the air, it took less than five minutes to find the old ghost town and land, stirring up a swirling cloud of fine dust particles. No one appeared from the tents, Scott assumed the occupants were at their claims, so he began walking up a gradual incline toward the old jail house.

A shot rang out and he dropped to the ground. He was in the open without any cover, so he rolled to his feet and ran inside the jail. He heard another shot and a thud when the bullet struck an outer wall of the old brick lockup.

Toni called out, "Scott! How did you find us?"

Crouched just inside the door frame, Scott was breathing hard, "Tell you later. Who the hell is shooting at me?"

"We don't know, Mr. Wilson. No one has said a word since the kidnapper left." Megan sounded sincere and Scott had no reason to doubt her.

Scott stood up and peered out from the door opening. "Hey! You with the gun! You're shooting at an FBI agent. Hold your fire! I want to talk." Scott couldn't see anyone with a gun, but there were many collections of debris to hide behind outside the old building.

David called out from the chopper, "Behind that pile of wood, about fifty feet from where you are, Mr. Wilson! I think it's an old man with a rifle."

"Can you start the engine, David?"

There was a ten second delay before an answer was heard. "Yes, sir. We've figured it out."

"Keep the rotor speed under 500—you won't lift off. Go ahead."

David sat in the pilot's chair and very nervously started Delilah's engine and the main rotor began to turn, very slowly at first, but picked up speed as David watched the controls. When the rotor was whirling about 300 revolutions per minute, a dust cloud began to form obscuring the jail from the wood pile and tents.

A few seconds later, Scott appeared at the chopper and climbed in behind David, popped open a tool box, grabbed a large screwdriver, and two handguns. "You did great, David. Give me about fifteen seconds and cut the engine." Then he vanished into the dust cloud.

"Are you counting?"

Danny was grinning, "Yes, sir, Captain Drum." Ten seconds later, Danny said, "Now!"

Delilah's engine lost power and the rotor blades began to slowly lose speed after David pressed the kill button.

Scott covered his nose and mouth with his shirt collar and scrambled into the old jail. He gave Toni one of the hand guns and said, "Watch the door while I get you out of the cell." He put the screwdriver through one of the handcuff links and rotated until the chain snapped, then he broke the second handcuff chain and pulled the door open. The women gave Scott a hug as they walked from the cell.

"Are you all right?" Both Megan and Toni nodded and said, "Yes."

"What do we do about the shooter, Scott?"

"I'd like to talk some sense into him, but he's probably brain washed into thinking we're not who we claim to be."

Megan said, "Do you think David and Danny could talk to whoever has the gun? Danny's with David, Isn't he?"

Scott mulled over the idea for a few seconds and said, "We can't risk one or both of the boys being shot. Toni and I are going to have to do this job." He looked at Toni, "Do you think one of us could get out of here through the back window? Are those bars really solid?"

Toni took the screwdriver from Scott, reentered the cell, and began to dig out cement that was holding the iron bars in place. "This is going to take about ten minutes, Scott. The cement is loose around the metal. I can get out if I get two of the bars out."

"Great, you can flank the shooter when I draw his fire."

Toni worked feverishly for about five minutes before the first metal bar was dislodged. The scraping and prying had been done quietly to keep from raising any suspicion from those on the outside, but the second window bar was set much more firmly in the cement than the first metal bar had been. She was going to have to pound on the screwdriver to chip away at the concrete.

"Scott, give me one of your shoes; I need a hammer."

Megan laughed when Scott didn't ask why his partner wanted one of his shoes; he leaned against the wall, pulled off his right shoe, and tossed it to Toni. Toni wrapped the bar with one of the blankets, and set to work driving the screwdriver deeply into the cement.

Scott feared the noise Toni was creating, when she was hammering on the concrete, was still too loud so he said, "Megan, sing something—it doesn't have to be good, just good and loud."

"Silent Night" was chosen by Megan and Scott was going to complement her following the standoff. Although she was nearly yelling, she was doing an admirable job, and he joined in when he could remember the words. He had sung in church when a boy, but had never had the nerve to sing without a choir to cover his somewhatt monotonic voice.

Fortunately, the singing was not necessary for long. Toni had made some judicious choices hammering the screwdriver and a large chunk of concrete was dislodged, taking with it the bar that had restricted her passage.

When she had wiggled her way through the opening and dropped to the ground, Scott called out, "We are armed FBI agents, do you still want to continue this?"

"I don't believe you!"

"How much are you getting paid to keep these women from going home to their families?"

"Almost a year's work at the claim, if you want to know."

"That's ransom money—you'd have to give it back—and then face charges for interfering with government agents seeking victims of a kidnapping. Do you want to risk spending five to ten years in a prison?"

A few seconds passed before a reply, "I'll take my chances."

"Okay, I'm coming out!" Scott left the building, running to his left, shooting rapidly at the wood pile and Toni ran to the right to flank the shooter. Scott hit the ground behind a rock just large enough to offer protection, took a few deep breaths, and reloaded with a new clip.

A moment later, Toni's voice was heard. "I've got him, Scott!"

Scott joined Toni, who towered over the shooter, the rifle leaning against the wood pile behind Toni. The old man, unshaven for weeks, wearing sweat-stained clothes, had his hands in the air and was squinting at the agents.

"What's your name?" said Scott.

"Ed Fender, what's yours?"

"Agents Thornton and Wilson: FBI." Scott flashed his ID and said, "Can you read?"

"Hell, yes, I can read. What kind of a question is that?"

Scott grinned and said, "You apparently fell for some garbage that was fed to you by a kidnapper. I just wondered. What did he offer you for watching the women?"

"I should have known it was too much to be legal—five thousand dollars and let them go Thursday night."

"You'll never see that guy again, Mr. Fender, unless you visit him in prison."

As the conversation with the miner continued, Megan appeared from the jail and met David just outside the doorway.

Megan hugged David and said, "It's good to see you, but I'm still mad."

"I understand, Meg. I'm just glad you're all right. We were all worried about you and Toni. Did you know that you're worth half a million dollars?"

Megan laughed, "Is that all?"

David put his arm around her shoulders and began walking toward Delilah where Danny and Spectrum were waiting. "I'd have paid a million to get you back."

The teenagers and Danny watched Toni and Scott talking with the bearded man for another minute and then observed the agents shake hands with the man and approach the helicopter. Toni hopped into the chopper and Scott climbed into the pilot's seat, started the engine, made sure everyone was secured, and took off.

As soon as Delilah reached cruising speed, Scott called Sheriff Howell and gave him the good news. Half an hour later, Delilah was landing at Suddenly. Julie's truck was parked next to the Cherokee and she was watching as the chopper touched down. When the dust and debris had settled, Julie rushed toward Delilah to welcome everyone home.

She could see that everyone was all right, but she said, "Are you all okay?"

Danny was first to hit the ground and he wrapped both arms around Julie. "Mom! Scott and Danny were awesome!" Then it struck him that Megan and Toni had assisted, too. "Everybody was awesome! I want to learn to fly! Flying is so cool!"

Scott was the last to exit Delilah, and after sealing the doors, he gave Julie a kiss and said, "Your boys were great, Julie. I'll tell you the whole story if you haven't heard everything from the others by this evening. Right now, I think we're all hungry. Let's go home."

Toni drove the Cherokee with the young people and Scott rode with Julie to the Drums' driveway. As soon as the Cherokee stopped, Megan was out the door, running to her house and not looking back. Scott and Toni followed her to make Mr. and Mrs. Isaac aware of the situation.

The front door was locked; Megan pounded with her fist and then used the brass knocker. After the second knock, the door opened and Mrs. Isaac's stepped out and hugged her daughter.

"Oh, thank God! You're all right! Bruce! Megan's back!"

Megan began to cry, but only for a moment. She wiped her eyes and said, "Mr. Wilson and the Drum boys found us. Toni and Mr. Wilson got us released from the rusty old jail in that ghost town."

Mrs. Isaacs stepped back from Megan, but still held her daughter's hands and said, "I don't understand. Why don't we all sit down and you can tell me the whole story?"

After everyone was seated in the Isaacs' living room, Megan told her parents the entire story from start to finish. Afterwards, Toni said, "I don't think I could have related our experience any better than you did, Megan. Good job!"

Megan smiled and replied, "Thank you."

Bruce Isaacs stood and said, "I want to thank you for bringing my daughter home without injury, agents. I commend you for doing such a good job. What is being done about the kidnappers?"

Scott and Toni stood and Scott said, "We're getting a photo of one of them and the other one will be taken into custody soon. We'll let you know what the next step is as soon as we have the perpetrators. At trial, we might need Megan to testify."

CHAPTER 32

M r. Isaacs said, "I'm sure that won't be a problem, will it dear?" He put his arm around Megan's waist and gave her a gentle hug.

"No, I'll testify, but I never saw their faces, Daddy. They wore those stupid masks."

"Well, we'd better be going. Have a good evening with your parents, Megan." Scott ushered Toni to the front door and they started to the Drums' to see what Julie had for dinner.

The agents had only taken a few steps when Toni said, "What about our boys out at tower seventeen?"

"Oh, crap! I forgot all about them." Scott glanced at his watch and said, "We've got another hour of daylight; let's fill them in on what's going on. I'll tell Julie we'll be back in an hour."

Toni got in the Cherokee and started the engine while Scott went in the Drums' house. Two minutes later, they were on their way to see Delilah. The engine hadn't had a chance to cool to ambient temperature, so they were in the air quickly and landed at tower seventeen five minutes later. They climbed the tower to talk with Kalber and Manietta, who were surly about the plans being changed again.

"Sit down boys, I've got something important to tell you." Scott and Toni flashed their IDs and Scott said, "We're federal agents with the FBI, but since you haven't done anything illegal yet, we can't arrest you, but we would like you to assist us in capturing the kidnappers that took Toni and the Isaacs' girl."

"What? You mean someone else took the girl?" Manny said. The two men looked at each other in disbelief, end then shifted their gazes to Scott.

"I thought there was somethin' funny with this gig. Didn't I say that, Manny?"

"Yeah, I remember—you said that."

"So what's in it for us if we help you?" said Kalber.

Scott replied, "Reduced sentences from the federal judge."

"You just said we weren't being arrested."

"That's right, not for kidnapping, but for being part of the West-Com organization. We've got enough evidence to put you away for about ten years."

Kalber looked at Manietta and, Manny nodded. "Okay, what do you want?"

Scott said, "Two things: the first is to help get the guy in tower twenty to surrender, the second is to identify the woman that you talked to on the phone about the kidnapping."

Scott and Toni sat down to explain the details of the two schemes the agents had in mind. The agents had about five minutes to discuss their plans and then took off in Delilah. They would pick up Kalber and Manietta, who were anxious to get started, at 8:00 a.m. the next morning, and fly to tower twenty at Shadow Valley.

Scott and Toni were ready to leave the apartment at 7:00 a.m. They had finished dressing, checking their guns, and eating while discussing their plan of attack on the tower. Since there was only one man to worry about, they felt it was going to be a relatively easy arrest, especially with the assistance of the men from West-Com. Then they would initiate their plan to expose the woman that had hired Kalber and Manietta.

Toni dropped Scott off with Delilah and then began to drive to the location where the delivery truck had been parked. Scott flew to tower seventeen to pick up the two West-Com operatives who were itching to get started with something they loved to do—intimidate and make life hell for someone. Just as Delilah was landing about a quarter mile from tower twenty, Scott received a message.

"Scott! I just found a Yamaha cycle parked in the back of that blue pickup the kidnappers used when they took Megan and me captive."

"Thanks, Toni. That means we have two men to deal with and at least two guns. Can you find your way to the tower? Delilah is parked a quarter mile south and we're ready to move now. We might need your gun."

"Wait a minute! Julie just pulled up. Let me talk to her; hold on." There was about a minute of silence and Toni came back on line. "Julie has a handgun, a rifle, and a slingshot."

"Okay, but I don't want her out here. Tell her to stand watch at the pickup—she can disable the bike and the truck; we don't want these guys getting away. You can bring the rifle and the slingshot; we can use them."

Toni said, "One last thing, Scott. Sheriff Howell says those guys' names are Chuck Nugent and Sam Arnold—they paid the Cardiff brothers a visit in jail a couple of weeks ago, and then rented the vehicles from Mountain Rentals. Some girl remembered them and looked them up in some high school annuals; they said some disgusting things to her."

"Tell Julie thanks, and when you get close to the tower, call for Spectrum, he'll lead you to us."

"All right, I'll see you when I see you."

It was nearly fifteen minutes later when the three men and Spectrum were close enough to the tower to see movement through the observation windows. Scott gave Kalber and Manietta some instructions, and when they moved out, he sat down with Spectrum behind a large tree to wait for Toni to call out for the dog. He didn't have to wait long, maybe five minutes, before Spectrum's ears picked up Toni's voice. Scott couldn't hear a thing except for the normal slightly audible sounds of the forest and breaking twigs from Kalber's and Manietta's movements.

"Spectrum! Fetch Toni."

Spectrum leapt to all fours and disappeared into the trees in seconds. Nearly a minute lapsed until Scott heard Toni's movements signaling her approach. Spectrum came through the trees and underbrush with Toni following a few meters behind. Toni was crouching, moving from tree to tree until she saw Scott and then held her position behind a mature tree. Scott motioned for her to stay down just as the clatter of rocks striking the base of the tower were heard.

Scott mimed the action of shooting a slingshot and Toni tossed the Y-shaped apparatus to him. Several more rocks struck the support beams and stairs before one of the tower's occupants came out to investigate. When the young man looked over the railing at the ground below, Scott shot a pebble and struck the fellow on the shoulder.

"Jesus! What the hell was that?" As he began to rub his collarbone, another pebble struck home, hitting near his right elbow. He yelled out "Shit!" and disappeared into the cabin.

Scott motioned for Toni to join him. He reached down and gave Spectrum a pat, "Good boy."

Toni was chuckling when she joined Scott. "I think you got their attention. What's next?"

"I think you should call out their names and let them know you and Megan are free. We'll see how they react."

"Hey Chuck and Sam, we know who you are. Megan Isaacs and I are back home so you aren't getting any ransom for us. You might as well surrender. Toss out your guns; you are outmanned."

"Bull shit! We don't even know who you are. You're just pulling our chain. You can go to hell."

"You put me in that old jail with Megan over at the Southern Cross ghost town. My partner came in his helicopter and rescued us. The old miner with the rifle backed down when he was surrounded. He didn't want to tangle with the FBI." Toni waited a few seconds for a reply and when she got none she said, "The old miner's name is Ed Fender."

There was no response from the tower for about a minute and then one of the men appeared at the railing and yelled down. "If we give up, what happens then?"

Scott took over from Toni and said, "If you want leniency, you'll tell us who else is involved and what the plan was."

"What do you mean by leniency?"

"As long as no one is hurt, the minimum sentence is five years, but a judge could reduce the sentence for cooperation, but that's not guaranteed." Scott was citing the state charges, not the federal ones. "Unload your weapons and toss them down to us. We'll take you into town to Sheriff Howell."

The agents waited for another minute before two handguns were dropped to the ground. Toni quickly gathered them and returned to her safety position as Scott watched the top of the tower for any aggressive behavior.

"Okay, we're coming down—don't shoot!"

Toni yelled back, "Keep your hands up—away from your body!"

When the kidnappers reached the ground, they were handcuffed. Kalber and Manietta made their way from the edge of the forest and joined the foursome at the bottom of the tower.

Scott whistled and after a short wait, Spectrum had not returned from the forest. Scott called out, and after another pause, the group of six began the trek back to Delilah; Scott whistled occasionally for Spectrum to follow. When they reached the chopper and everyone was ready to return to Suddenly, Scott walked away from Delilah and made one last call for Spectrum, but the dog did not return.

"Scott, Spectrum will be all right. Let's get these guys back to the sheriff, then we can return and look for your buddy," said Toni.

Concerned, but realizing he had a job to carry out, Scott followed Toni's suggestion, started the engine, and again waited, longer than normally, for the engine to warm up before taking off. With no sign of his dog, Scott began to worry that Spectrum had somehow been injured and could not return in spite of the whistles and calls.

Ten minutes later, Delilah was again on the ground and the captured kidnappers were transferred to the Cherokee. Kalber and Manietta climbed into their pickup and were waiting instructions from the agents. Scott locked the chopper and walked to the pickup as Kalber put down the window. Kalber said, "What do you want us to do?"

"We need to ID the woman you talked to on the phone when you set up the kidnapping. Drive out to the Hadley place— it's a mile or so north of the city limits, and talk to Mrs. Hadley."

Manietta said, "What're we gonna talk about?"

"Well, ask her if she would like to buy a set of encyclopedias or a monthly subscription to a new set of cookbooks. I don't know— just make up something. If you want to get thrown out, ask her if she would like to buy a burial plot for her son at the cemetery."

"What if the woman's not home?" said Kalber.

"Say you'll come back at a later time, which is true."

"Okay. Then what?"

"You know where the Isaacs' kid lives?"

"Sure, she's the one we were gonna grab."

"Go there and do the same thing that you did at the Hadley place, but be nice if she reacts badly. I just want you to hear her voice."

"After that, come down to the jail. My partner and I will be there talking with the sheriff."

Kalber nodded, put up his window, and drove off with Manietta, who appeared to be taking a nap.

Scott slid into the front passenger seat of the Cherokee and said, "Let's take these two to the sheriff. He's got several vacancies. Maybe he'll give them doughnuts for lunch."

Toni laughed, heard the click of Scott's seatbelt and drove away from Delilah toward the business district. When they arrived at Sheriff Howell's office, Ginny Lloyd, the sheriff's secretary, handed Scott a message scribbled on a Post-It and said, "The sheriff will be right back, he's down the hall."

Scott glanced at the note, but couldn't read the scrawled message. He handed it back to the secretary and said, "Could you please translate it for me?"

Ginny smiled and said, "Julie Drum has your dog and his female friend. She's taking them to the vet to patch them up."

"Thanks, Ginny."

Sheriff Howell approached Ginny's desk carrying a cup of coffee and commenting, "It looks like you have some desperadoes for me to hold for you, agents. Did you get my message, Scott?"

Scott grinned, "Yes. Thanks, Sheriff. We had to leave the tower area to bring in the kidnappers before I could find my dog. He went off into the woods and didn't come when I called."

"I don't think you need to worry. Julie said the dogs were a little scratched up, that's all. They're over at Wayne's Animal Shelter. Wayne Patton's the local vet; a good man. He'll be retiring soon."

"Where's the shelter?"

Sheriff Howell pointed with his big right index finger as he said, "Two blocks west and two blocks north—on the corner. Julie's waiting with the animals."

"We'll come back to press charges. Thanks again, Sheriff"

Scott turned to Toni and said, "Let's find out what Julie brought back."

Chapter 33

Scott was in the driver's seat as the Cherokee moved slowly through the downtown streets. He now understood why Spectrum hadn't come when called, but he wondered what the dogs' injuries were. As he and Toni pulled up at the curb in front of the shelter, Toni said, "Has your dog brought home strays before?"

Scott smiled, "Nope. He must have found someone he really liked."

Toni continued, "Why would a female dog be out in the forest alone?"

Scott shook his head, "Must have been abandoned or the owner was injured and couldn't take care of the dog. Maybe Julie or the vet will have some ideas."

As the agents entered the waiting area, Scott saw Julie sitting with Spectrum at her feet. She was looking through a magazine. She stood up, tossed the periodical on the adjacent chair, and approached Scott.

"Spectrums okay—just a few scratches on his paws. The other dog was shot, poor thing. Doctor Patton's operating right now. He's removing the bullet."

"Did you look for Spectrum?"

"No, he came up to me and whined—wanted me to follow him, so I did. He took me to the injured dog. It was near the second stream, not far from the tower. It was all wet from the cold water and shaking, just lying there like she was waiting to die."

Toni joined in, "I'll bet that was the dog that was scratching at the tower door when Megan and I were captive. One of the men shot through the door to scare off whatever was there."

"I think you're right. She was nothing much more than fur and bones; I carried her back to the truck and brought her here with Spectrum."

Doc Patton appeared and explained, "I removed a .38 slug from her back. It hadn't penetrated far into the muscle—only required a couple of stitches; I'll keep her overnight and give her some good food. She must have been on her own for about a month to lose that much weight. Whose dog is it?"

"We don't know, but I'll take her home until I can find a good home for her. My dog seems to like her."

"We can make a bed for her in the garage, Scott. My boys have always wanted a dog. I'll find out if they want to take care of this one. She looks pretty mangy right now."

"I gave her some antibiotics and powdered her to kill off the fur mites. Her fur should grow back before long."

Julie shook hands with the doctor and said, "Thanks, Doc. Send me a bill for everything."

Scott turned to Toni and gave a quick tilt with his head as Julie headed out the door. Toni called Spectrum and followed the ranger.

Scott handed a credit card to Doctor Patton and said, "I'll take care of it. Julie has enough to do with raising her boys. I'll pick up the dog in the morning."

When Toni and Scott got back to the sheriff's office, Kalber and Manietta were waiting on the cement bench by the entrance.

Scott said, "What'd you find out?"

"Never heard those voices before—neither one."

Manietta agreed, "I didn't hear them voices before either."

"Damn. I thought we had this just about all wrapped up." Scott scanned Toni, "Any other obvious suspects?"

She shook her head, "None that I can think of."

"Let's do some brain storming after dinner. Hopefully we'll come up with some fresh ideas," Scott said.

Kalber was beaming with a gigantic smile the others couldn't miss. "I'm going into that   bank tomorrow and see if I can't get a loan."

His partner's mouth fell open. "What? You want a loan? What for?"

Kalber cuffed Manietta on the shoulder and said, "I don't need a loan—there's a bunch of women workin' in that bank. What'll you bet that banker is damn tight with at least one of 'em."

Toni smiled, "I think we were just analyzing the surface, Scott. Our friends appear to have more experience with this sort of thing than we gave them credit for."

Manietta was obviously excited, "We might get out of jail time, Kalber. You've been puttin' your brain to work again. We don't even have to beat up nobody."

Toni whispered to Scott, "I think we're working with two of the three stooges."

Scott chuckled and said, "I think they might have hit on something. Let's relax tonight and clear our heads—see what they come up with tomorrow."

Before the stooges left for tower seventeen, Toni told them to wear their suits when   they went to the bank in the morning.

"When does that bank open?" said Kalber.

Scott replied, "Mr. Isaacs goes to work at ten o'clock. Make sure you talk with his secretary."

"Yeah, we'll listen to all of the women; we've got lots of dumb questions for 'em. Isaacs won't fund us," Kalber grinned. "Nobody around here needs a garbage pick-up service for a hundred bucks a month."

"Okay, we'll see you about noon tomorrow."

David was preoccupied during dinner and could hardly wait for the adult conversation to terminate. After he helped clear the table, he said, "Mom, can we go over to the Isaacs' and talk with Megan? It really bothers me that she doesn't believe me about the DNA samples. Could Mr. Wilson come, too?"

Julie looked at Scott, "You know what he's talking about, Scott?"

"Yes. She thinks he switched my DNA sample with Mr. Isaac's. Do you think Megan will be traumatized when she finds out I really am her biological father?"

"She won't believe it because her parents have never told her that her father isn't her biological father. She'll be more upset about them never telling her than thinking I switched the samples. Can we go talk to them?"

"Okay, let's get this over with. Toni, can you stay here with Danny while we're next door?"

"Sure, Julie. Good luck with Megan, David."

Sarah greeted Julie, Scott and David at the front door and ushered them into the living room. Bruce popped up from his recliner and shook hands with the guests. He motioned with a sweep of his hand for them to sit down.

"What is this visit all about, Julie?" said Bruce. "Have you found out more about the kidnapping?"

"No. It's something else."

Sarah sat down beside Bruce and put her hand on his arm. "I think I know what this is all about."

Bruce was befuddled. "You've got me buffaloed. What's going on?"

Sarah squeezed his arm and said, "Remember, Megan said she and David were doing a project for biology class? It was using DNA to determine relationships of family members."

"I guess I wasn't paying much attention—probably thinking about the damn bank business. So she found out?"

"Well, I—I guess she did."

David said, "Can I interrupt, Mr. and Mrs. Isaacs?"

Everyone shifted their attention to David, who continued, "The results of the test showed that you, Mr. Isaacs, were not Megan's biological father, but what was so surprising was that Mr. Wilson is her biological father."

The Isaacs' gasped, "What? How could that be?"

David frowned, "Didn't Megan say anything?"

Sarah said, "She said you mixed up the samples on purpose and she was mad at you for kidding around. I didn't think anything of it; I just thought it was a mistake of some sort and let it drop."

"Did I hear David's voice?" Megan appeared from the kitchen holding a glass of water and when she saw Julie and Scott with David, she said, "What's going on, Mom?"

"Sit down, honey. I have something to tell you."

Bruce spoke up, "We have some history to let you in on—something we might have told you before, but now that you're older, it's about time."

Megan held the glass in both hands and sat on the edge of the sofa cushion and frowned. "What is it?"

"I'm not your father, Megan, that is, not your biological father. Apparently, Mr. Wilson is your biological father."

"Daddy, what are you saying? You are my father."

Sarah took over, "David didn't switch the DNA samples, dear. Your father had a severe case of the mumps when he was in his twenties and his sperm count is almost zero. After five years of trying to get pregnant, we had some tests run and discovered the problem, so I went to a clinic and had artificial insemination performed."

Bruce commented, "They told us we would probably never know who the donor was, but your biology project defied the odds. Mr. Wilson is your biological father, we just discovered it." He smiled and said, "Think of it this way, Megan, you are the only girl in Suddenly that has two fathers."

Sarah exclaimed, "What a terrible time for you to make a joke, Bruce, can't you see that Megan is a little shocked about the news?"

"Oh, I'm not really shocked, Mom; I'm trying to figure out how to apologize to David. I haven't been very nice to him—thinking he had switched samples and when he tried to tell me he didn't, I wouldn't talk to him." Megan moved over beside David and put her hand on his shoulder, "I'm sorry I didn't believe you, David, but you *have* played some pranks on me in the past."

"Yeah, I guess I was partially at fault." He stood up and put his arm around Megan's waist, "I had to make sure that it didn't hurt our friendship. That's why I asked Mr. Wilson and Mom to come over with me."

Megan smiled and said, "Now I have a new worry. What do I do with two fathers? Do I give them equal time?"

Everyone laughed and then Megan said, "David, have you studied for the English quiz tomorrow?"

"Not yet, but thanks for reminding me. I'd better get back home and do that, but before I go, I want to thank your mother and father for meeting with us tonight. I feel much better now that we all understand the situation."

As everyone moved toward the front door, Scott drifted back, and mentioned to Bruce, "I'd like a word with you."

"About Megan?"

"Nothing like that. If she wants to know more about me, that's up to her. What I wanted to ask you about is with regard to your staff at the bank."

"Okay, what would you like to know?"

"Have you had any problems with any of your employees—anything at all?"

Bruce stiffened, scratched his scalp, and said, "You think someone in the bank is behind the kidnapping?"

Scott nodded, "That's right. If you can't recall anything right now, think about it—maybe something that happened three, four weeks ago. Let me know if you come up with something." He moved to the door, turned, and said, "Thanks for your time. We'll talk some more." The two men shook hands and Scott hurried out the door to catch up to Julie and David.

When he passed Megan and Sarah standing on the porch, he said, "Good night, ladies."

He heard Megan say, "Good night, Dad," and the women laughed.

Scott caught up with Julie as she was entering her front door and she held the door open for him. As they walked down the hallway, Julie commented, "I was surprised how well that went. I thought the Isaacs were going to have all kinds of problems finding out you were the sperm donor for Megan, but Bruce, especially, took it as matter-of-factly as I could have imagined. It didn't seem to bother him at all."

"That surprised me too. I did learn something very important; the Isaacs had nothing to do with the kidnapping, but I think someone in the bank is responsible."

"Any ideas?"

"Nope, but tomorrow noon I think I'll find out who it is. Kalber and Manietta should give us some clues."

Toni was watching TV alone. The boys had gone to their rooms to study. Julie headed toward the kitchen saying, "Anybody want a drink?"

Toni answered, "Sure, anything with booze in it will be fine." She turned off the television and joined Scott at the kitchen table. She could hear Julie extracting a tray of ice from the freezing compartment and the slam of the refrigerator door.

"What's on tap for tomorrow?"

"I've got to pick up Spectrum's friend at the shelter, bring her back here, and wait for those two knuckleheads to report what they've found out about the voices at the bank."

The half-full glasses of bourbon on the rocks were more than enough to loosen the agents' tongues, especially Scott's, and he entertained the ladies with some tales from his time in army flight school. After a second round of drinks, the members of the trio were nearly asleep. The agents said good night to Julie and climbed the stairs with some ungainly footwork to the apartment over the garage.

CHAPTER 34

Scott heard water running and scratched open one eye, blinked twice, and focused on Toni in the kitchenette. She had on her usual jeans and sweatshirt plus a light jacket. She hadn't turned up the furnace.

"One egg or two?" she said, as she turned around holding a spatula in her right hand.

"What time is it?" he asked. "Two. Thanks for asking."

"It's seven o'clock. Better get your ass out of bed and get dressed, I've got the morning all worked out."

"What? Did you even sleep?"

"Like a baby. And I had a great dream—at least I think it was a dream."

"Tell me as I get dressed and wash my teeth." Scott rolled out of bed, grabbed clean under ware, and went in the bathroom, leaving the door ajar.

"How many pancakes can you eat?"

"Four to six; depends on the size. So what are you thinking?"

"I'm thinking our two lamebrains are just going to stir the pot, so I'm going to the bank and observe the reactions of the employees when our retards start asking questions. Someone at the bank is going to get spooked, and I'm going to follow whomever it is."

"Okay. That leaves me without wheels and with a new dog to walk home."

"Buy a leash, Scott. Geez!"

"I'll take Spectrum with me and we'll walk back here. If it's too much for the new dog, I'll carry her."

"It's not that far—only eight or ten blocks. Butter or margarine?"

"Butter. You have a hunch, don't you?"

"Uh-huh. Looking for a woman with a voice only heard over a telephone is a he said-she said situation and we wouldn't have a chance of prosecuting with success. I have a feeling there is a guy behind the kidnapping and he used his wife or girlfriend to make the call to West-Com. A woman from the bank is too obvious, don't you think?"

"I suppose. Unfortunately, I can't think like a woman. Are those pancakes ready? I'm starting to salivate."

"Come and get it. You supply the syrup and the appetite." Toni paused, "And you do the dishes."

"It's a deal." Scott drowned a stack of pancakes in butter and syrup and dug in. Toni poured some coffee, joined Scott at the little table and said, "I'll give you and Spectrum a ride to the vet."

"Thanks. I was about to ask." They both laughed.

Toni dropped Scott and Spectrum off at the shelter and drove to the bank parking lot in back. She sat in the car and waited for Mr. Isaacs to arrive to open the bank for business. She called to him when he locked his car and started for the back-door of the two story brick building.

"Mr. Isaacs!"

He flinched, turned to see where the voice had originated, then relaxed when he recognized Toni.

"Good morning, Ms. Thornton. How might I help you?"

"I wanted to warn you that two of our boys are coming to the bank this morning to see if we can trigger a reaction that will lead us to the persons responsible for the kidnapping. I'll be waiting outside to follow anyone that leaves early."

"Thanks for the warning. I'll keep it quiet."

"How many employees do you have and do they all park here?"

"Besides me, five people: four women and one man. They're supposed to park here and leave street parking for our customers."

"Okay, that's good to know. Have a good day."

"You too, agent Thornton."

Toni followed Isaacs with her eyes until she heard the lock on the door click. She then walked around to the front entrance and waited for Manietta and Kalber to appear. She could see the clock inside the bank and wondered why time seemed to pass so slowly when she waited for someone. She leaned against the marble wall next to the heavy glass doors and closed her eyes for a moment until someone inside the bank unlocked the front doors. The bank was ready for business but she continued to wait outside the transparent entrance.

Several people had entered, conducted their business and left the bank before the two henchmen arrived in their black pickup. They parked at the curb and were laughing as they approached the bank.

"Been waitin' for us?" Manietta asked.

"No, I've been waiting for bank robbers. I'll follow you in and watch as you mingle."

"Mingle?"

"She means talk to the people inside, Manny."

"Oh, yeah—I knew that." He pushed the thick glass door open and stepped into the lobby. Kalber and Toni followed him inside. Manny held the door open for an elderly woman that was exiting the bank.

"Thank you, young man." Manny nodded and let go of the heavy door.

Kalber headed for the closest teller behind the main counter and began a conversation, and in a few seconds, turned to Toni and shook his head that the woman wasn't a candidate. Manietta approached the adjacent clerk and talked for nearly a minute before he walked over to Toni and said, "It's not that one, she's from Australia—has an accent." Two other possibilities remained, Mr. Isaac's secretary, and another woman that Toni had not yet seen.

Kalber joined Toni and said, "I could hear one of them coin counters in the back. Somebody's in that room." He pointed to a closed door not far from the president's office. As they watched and waited, the door opened and a mature woman with gray hair stepped out looking at a slip of paper.

Kalber snickered, "Looks like my mom. We can forget about her. The voice we heard has to be from a young chick."

"There's only one other woman at work here, Mr. Isaacs' secretary. I'll get her so you can hear her voice."

Toni approached the closest teller, flashed her FBI identification, and asked to see the president.

The teller said, "Please follow me."

Toni motioned for Kalber to join her and they went into the president's office.

Mr. Isaacs looked up from his computer monitor and said, "How can I help you Agent Thornton?"

"I'd like to have a few words with your secretary. This is Agent Kalber." Kalber nodded to Isaacs and his secretary and stood back. Toni read the secretary's ID badge. "What can you tell us about the kidnapping, Sharon?"

Sharon related what Isaacs had told her and that the danger was now over. Toni glanced at Kalber and he shook his head.

"Thank you, Sharon. That's all we needed to know. You can get back to work. Thank you Mr. Isaacs." Toni nudged Kalber and they left the office. When they reached to counter, Toni noticed the male teller was gone. She asked, "Where is the fellow that was here a few minutes ago?"

"Kevin? He said he wasn't feeling well and went to get his car." The teller pointed toward the back door. "He's only been gone about a minute."

Toni ran out the door and saw a red Ford Ranger pickup leaving the parking area and turning north. She ran to the Cherokee and spun the tires leaving a rubber streak on the pavement as she entered the road and began following the pickup. She was two cars behind, but her eyes were laser focused on the small pickup. Two minutes later, she watched the truck pull into a driveway and honk. Kevin ran to the front door of the cottage and knocked.

Toni parked across the street where she could watch the front of the cottage and the red pickup, shut off the engine, and saw a young woman appear at the door and let Kevin inside. Toni sat and waited. Five minutes later, Kevin reappeared, got in his Ranger and drove away. Toni decided not to follow the pickup, she was going to get Kalber and Manietta and bring them back to the cottage.

When she returned to the bank, Kalber and Manietta were waiting in their truck parked at the front curb.

"Hop in guys, I'm taking you for a short ride."

As she drove back to the cottage, she told the men what she wanted them to do. She parked where she had been previously, shut off the engine and crouched down out of sight. Kalber and Manietta crossed the street and knocked on the front door of the little house. Toni heard the knocks, raised her head just enough to see the men, and waited for the door to open.

Kalber knocked again, much louder than before and after another wait, maybe thirty seconds, the door opened very slowly.

Manietta gave Toni the prearranged signal, clasping his hands behind his back, indicating the woman was the one they had talked to before. Toni watched as Kalber and Manietta went inside. Toni's plan was working.

She moved into the passenger seat but kept crouched low and watched the cottage front door for nearly five minutes before the men exited the house. Toni heard the front door slam shut; probably rattling the windows. When the men were near enough to the Cherokee so Toni didn't have to yell, she said, "Kalber, you drive."

They drove back to the bank and the men transferred to their truck. Toni said, "Meet me over at the Drums' house. We need to talk."

Back at the Drums', Toni and Scott met with Kalber and Manietta. Toni asked, "What did you tell the woman in the cottage?"

Kalber answered with a big grin, "We told her she owed us fifteen grand for our expenses. She has to pay us tonight or it doubles tomorrow. Each day late adds another five grand."

Manietta added, "And we told her to bring the money to tower seventeen—just like you told us, and come alone."

Scott knew how Toni thought, so he finished. "Okay. You guys move your things to tower twenty, it's unoccupied. Agent Thornton and I will take tower seventeen and wait for the payoff money."

Manietta said, "Where the hell is tower twenty?"

Scott smiled, "I'll draw you a map. You'll need an ATV to get there; you have to cross through three shallow creeks. I'll rent you a vehicle that will fit in your truck."

Kalber observed, "Seems damn complicated to me."

Toni looked at Kalber, "Can you drive an ATV?"

"Christ, I can drive anything with wheels."

Scott had to get Kalber and Manietta out of the way so he said, "You guys follow me down to Harley's. It's a rental place on Main Street. I'll get you an ATV. The food in tower twenty is yours; the owners are in jail." He glanced at Toni, "Get our things ready and feed the dogs. I'll be back in about forty-five minutes. Then we'll go to tower seventeen and wait."

Toni went to the apartment and packed two suitcases, one for each of them. She made sure to include handguns and plenty of ammunition, although she hoped the guns wouldn't be necessary. She imagined the banker's girlfriend, Carrie Sawyer, would not be armed, according to Kalber, she seemed a bit naïve. But Toni didn't know about Kevin Knox, and there wasn't time enough left in the day to investigate his background.

She made four sandwiches, tossed in a couple of apples, two cans of Pepsi, and a Zip-Lock full of coffee. She had no idea what Kalber and Manietta had for food except for peanut butter she had seen in the back of their pickup days ago. Her last thought was first-aid equipment, which she placed in Scott's shaving kit. She closed and latched the suitcases and set them next to the apartment door. She sat down for a minute, reviewed what she had packed, and suddenly realized she was hungry; that reminded her to feed the dogs.

After three quarters of an hour had elapsed, she began to listen for the sounds of the Cherokee, and she finally relaxed when

Scott pulled into the driveway after an hour had passed. He climbed the stairs and announced, "I got them located, and picked up some burgers for us.

Aren't you hungry, or have you had something already?"

"I was wondering why you were taking so long; you're usually very punctual."

"Yeah, my stomach was gnawing on my spinal column so I stopped at McDonald's. There were three people ahead of me. Sorry."

"Do you want to leave a message for Julie and the boys? I don't think we want them in our way if anything goes wrong."

"Yeah. I thought of that when I was with Kalber and Manietta. They won't bother us, that's for sure. How are the pooches?"

"They're fine. I took them out in the backyard for a few minutes and they took care of business. Are we taking Spectrum with us?"

"I don't think so. He should stay here with Suzy so she doesn't get frightened. She hasn't met Danny and David yet."

"You've named her Suzy?"

Scott chuckled, "It's only temporary. I'll let the boys decide on a name."

"Does Julie want a dog?"

"I don't know. If she doesn't want the boys to have a dog, I guess I'll have two."

"Uh-huh, and then some puppies will come along."

"That could happen. Did you pack the guns?"

Toni looked at Scott in disbelief and said, "No, we'll shoot rubber bands if necessary."

"Sorry, Toni. That was a stupid question."

CHAPTER 35

Scott sat down on a bar stool at the kitchen counter, took a bite from his hamburger, and started writing a message to Julie and the boys. It was a simple note, he just wanted to warn them to stay away from tower seventeen; he would explain why later in the evening. He folded the note, stuck it in his pocket and stood up.

"I've changed my mind about taking the dogs with us. They'll be our early warning system. If you'll get them in the car, I'll bring the bags, and tape the note to Julie's front door where the boys will see it if she doesn't."

Toni stuffed most of her burger in her mouth and started down the stairs. Scott grabbed a roll of tape, the two suitcases, swallowed the remainder of his burger, and locked the apartment door. When Scott reached the car, the dogs were on a blanket in back, and Toni ready to drive. The suitcases were loaded and they headed to tower seventeen. It was 3:07 p.m.

Scott glanced at Toni as she watched the speed limit in town, but when she got to the dirt and gravel road leading to the tower, her lead foot took over, and Scott grabbed the handhold on the door. He wanted to say slow down, but held back. Toni wouldn't put them in danger. When they reached the tower, both dogs wanted out of the car. That's when Scott decided he would drive on their return trip.

Toni had parked the Cherokee as close to the bottom of the tower as possible to leave parking space for whomever was bringing the payoff money. She hoped it would be the woman she had seen at the cottage. She didn't relish the thought of fighting with a man at a height of sixty feet above the ground, but with Scott present, the chances of that occurring were very small.

Suzy balked at going up the steps at first, but when she watched Spectrum ascend the first flight, she followed. Scott and Toni took their time going up the seventy-five steps, pausing every so often to look through and over the trees. When they reached the top of the tower, they placed their suitcases inside the cabin, and made a 360 degree survey of the forest.

As the agents circled the deck around the cabin, Toni observed, "I'm beginning to see why people love the wild-wild-west; it is breathtaking beautiful from here."

"Yes, and you can imagine what a disastrous impact forest fires can have."

"Look, Scott! Is that an eagle?" She pointed at a bird circling a rise of trees several hundred yards away.

"Hard to tell. Could be a hawk looking for an evening meal." He turned away and went in the cabin. "I'm going to unpack and check my weapon."

Toni said, "I'll be there in a few minutes. I want to watch the movement of the shadows and the change in color of the forest as the sun drops toward the horizon."

Scott opened his suitcase and noticed his shaving kit tucked under his Kevlar vest and holster. He asked himself why Toni had packed it, they hadn't planned to stay overnight. He smiled after sliding the zipper and looking inside. Then he wondered if she had thought of absolutely everything they might need. He set the opened kit on the counter for easy access, just in case he burned his finger on the stove, and started some coffee.

It was 4:35 when Toni entered the cabin and poured herself a cup of Scott's coffee. She made a face, added some sugar and found some milk in the refrigerator. She sat beside her suitcase, extracted her forty caliber handgun and sipped from her mug of tan liquid. The tower was in full shadow and yet the sky was still bright blue. She looked at Scott and commented, "The coffee is tolerable, but let me make the next pot."

"Be my guest." Scott wondered what Kalber and Manietta were doing more than six and a half miles away in safety at tower twenty.

Toni seemed to have read his mind. "Do Kalber and Manietta know about the superstitions at Shadow Valley?"

Scott thought for a few seconds, "Don't know, but it wouldn't bother them. Well, Manietta might wonder a bit, fewer brains to work with."

"Yeah, I've noticed. Want anything to eat?" Toni was looking through the cupboards and she let the second cupboard door slam shut. Spectrum raised his head off the floor and looked at Toni. Suzy was sound asleep. "Lots of peanut butter—not much else. Couple of cans of tomato soup and some crackers. Our boys didn't experience eating at fine restaurants."

"I'm not hungry, thanks. They were here for the money, a couple of days of sandwiches was not a big deal. Now they're headed for jail."

"You don't think they'll try to run? They've got that truck and an ATV"

"Nope. They know we have a chopper and know who they are. They'd get added time if they try to run."

"You should have gotten some fries. I'm going to make some soup."

Scott laughed, "Geez, Toni, we probably won't be here for more than a few hours."

"Want to hear my stomach growl?"

"Hey, don't scare the dogs. You'd better fix the soup." He went outside and Spectrum followed. "I'm gonna walk the deck." He made one revolution, sat down at the top of the steps and glanced down at the Cherokee. Spectrum came up behind him and stuck his nose between Scott's right arm and chest. Scott swung his arm back and scratched his dog and said, "Good boy. We'll be back in the air before long." Spectrum whined and lay down.

With the sun going down, the temperature in the forests began to drop and Scott went back into the cabin to get his jacket and see if any soup was still available. Toni was snoozing on the cheap sofa, but became alert when she heard Scott's footsteps.

"Any action out there?" she asked, as she sat up.

"Nah, no movement at all. The birds are in their nests."

"I left you some soup."

"Thanks. I'm warming it up."

The agents exchanged small talk for about fifteen minutes before Toni suddenly said, "Shh. Did you hear that?"

"What?"

"Sounded like one of the steps creaked." Toni drew her gun and stepped to the door, which was still open, and cautiously looked out and down the stairs.

Scott suggested, "Maybe it was shrinkage of the wood; the apartment ceiling does that all the time at night."

"The dogs didn't react; I guess it was nothing." She stood at the door and looked into the darkness. "Should we kill the lights?" She holstered her weapon.

"I was just thinking the same thing." Scott reached up and turned out the lamp by the sofa. Toni flipped the switch by the door and extinguished the ceiling lights.

They sat in darkness for about a half hour before they heard a vehicle drive up and park at the bottom of the tower. Toni crept to the edge of the deck and looked down to see what had arrived.

"A red pickup."

"The banker?"

"Probably."

They heard a voice call out, "Anybody up there? I've got the money."

Scott yelled back, "Yah, we're up here. C'mon up."

"You come down!"

"That's not the way it works, kid. Bring it up."

"I can't see where I'm going!"

"Following the railing! We'll light the doorway for you."

Scott picked up the floor lamp, plugged the cord into the socket inside the doorway and set the lamp on the deck. Toni reached out, turned on the bulb, then backed into the cabin behind the wall, crouched, and drew her handgun.

"Toni, move back and get behind the fridge."

The footsteps were getting louder and Spectrum began to growl. Suzy moved over beside Toni and lay down. Scott had to see what was coming, so he crouched below the window and cautiously peered out. He saw a man's head, then chest, rising into view. Five steps to go. A shot rang out and the lamp was extinguished.

"Damn!"

Another outside shot and Scott rolled backward on the floor with a bullet in his chest.

"Shit!" screamed Toni. She emptied her forty caliber in a few seconds, shooting through the door, window, and wall. The empty clip dropped to the floor and she was reloaded in seconds. She heard a commotion as the man either fell or ran down the steps to the landing ten feet below. She stepped over Scott's body and looked at his face. He was in pain, but took a deep breath and said, "I'm all right, got the wind knocked out of me, and I twisted my leg—hurts like hell. Watch yourself out there, his girl might have a gun, too."

Toni kept close to the deck and glanced down the stairs to the landing below; the shooter was down, motionless, and his gun was on the second step above him. Toni crept down the steps, eyes sweeping in all directions, looking for signs of another shooter, until she reached the body. He had a pulse. Blood was coming from his right shoulder and left thigh, soaking into his clothing. She rolled him over and his eyes focused on her.

"Y-You were in the bank."

"That's right. Agent Thornton, FBI."

"Not a kidnapper?"

"Hardly. Girlfriend with you?"

"Y-yeah, don't shoot her. She's got a thirty-eight."

"Spectrum!" Toni called out and the dog came down the steps, stood on all fours, and growled. "Stay, Spectrum!"

Toni cautiously worked her way down four flights and then stopped, crouched and looked below. No one was there. Scott called out, "Under the pickup, Toni. I can cover you from here. Light tan parka and jeans." Scott had his high intensity flashlight illuminating the truck.

Toni reached the ground and kept the wheels of the vehicles as cover as she approached the pickup. "As soon as you toss out your gun, we'll get your boyfriend to the hospital. He's got two bullets in him. You want to die underneath the pickup?"

"Okay. I'm coming out."

"Toss the gun first."

Toni heard a noise, but it could have been from a rock, so she moved behind the Cherokee and chanced a peek at the ground between the vehicles. She moved quickly, kicked the gun under the Cherokee, and said, "Okay, slither out from under the pickup, but stay on the ground on your belly."

As soon as the woman was out from under the truck, Toni handcuffed her and helped her to her feet.

"What's your name?"

"Darci Yates. Who are you?"

"Agent Thornton—FBI. Where are the keys to the truck?"

"Kevin has them, I don't drive."

"All right, climb in the back of the pickup. My partner and I will get your boyfriend and we'll take him to the hospital. He's lost quite a bit of blood."

Toni climbed the steps to where the body was and saw Scott wrapping Kevin's thigh with a compress and tape to quell the blood flow. The shoulder wound had already been treated. Suzy and Spectrum were watching as Scott bound Kevin's thigh.

"How are we going to get him down?"

Scott replied, "We could just drop him over the side, or If we had a rope, we could put it around his neck and lower him."

Kevin said, "Real funny."

"Well, since I've got a bum leg and can't carry you down, we've got to lower you somehow. Any bright ideas?" Kevin didn't respond, but Toni said, "I'll see if I can find some rope in the cabin."

Toni hopped over the two men and entered the cabin. They could hear noises as if someone were ransacking the cabin. About a minute passed before Toni called out, "Found some rope, but it's only about fifty feet long."

"That should do. We'll drop him in two stages. We'll tie him to that kitchen chair."

They ended up lowing Kevin in three stages after using about half the rope to secure him to the chair. Following the first drop, Toni said, "We're going to need more muscle. You and I can barely do this. Darci is going to have to help."

After Kevin was on the ground, they loaded him into the back of the pickup, and Toni drove with Kevin and Darci handcuffed together. Scott met them at the hospital. The hospital called Sheriff Howell, and the sheriff called Julie.

"Julie?"

"Yes, sheriff, what is it?"

"Scott's here in the hospital. He was shot in the chest, but he is only bruised."

When Julie heard the word shot, she hung up the phone, and rushed to the hospital. She ran down the hall to the emergency room and found Scott sitting on a gurney; his chest being wrapped with tape as he held his arms above his head. She took several steps toward him and said, "What the hell did you do? Did you try to get killed?"

Scott laughed and Julie got even more excited. "I think you'd better become a ranger so I can look after you. The animals don't have guns."

"But I thought you didn't like the notion I had of becoming a ranger."

Julie's excitement hadn't diminished much, and she said, "Well, I've changed my mind. I like the idea of you being around."

"I like the idea of being around, too. So does Spectrum."

Toni entered the emergency room escorting Darci and handcuffed the young woman to a chair.

She joined Scott and Julie and said, "Guess what this kidnapping caper was all about."

Scott said, "Jealousy?"

"Nope. Darci needs eye surgery and doesn't have insurance, and Kevin has minimal insurance through the bank. They wanted enough money to get Darci's eyes fixed so she could have a more normal life."

Scott shook his head and said, "They sure went around getting the money in the wrong way."

Julie went over to Darci and commented, "I have an idea how you can get your operation. You come see me when you get out of jail."

Darci was wiping her tears and looked up at Julie, "Oh, thank you."

Chapter 36

Julie helped Scott put on his shirt and asked if he had also been shot in the shoulder when she noticed the small bandage.

"No, some wood splinters poked through my shirt. I didn't need a bandage, but I let that young nurse fuss over me. I think she likes my hairy chest and muscles."

"Oh, pooh. She was just doing her job."

Scott grinned, "With that smile? I think she likes me."

Julie shook her head, "Will you ever get serious?" She scanned the emergency room and said, "Where's Toni? Was she injured, too?"

"No. She's taking the girl, Darci, to jail. Kevin, her boyfriend, is having surgery to remove two bullets."

"You shot him?"

"Uh-uh. Toni did. I was on the floor trying to catch my wind." He slid off the gurney and planted his feet on the vinyl tile, wincing when he put weight on his left leg.

"What happened to your leg?"

"Twisted it when I fell. It'll be all right tomorrow. How's your ankle?"

"Doc said I can take off the cast in two weeks; I'm counting the days." Julie took Scott's arm to support him and looked into his eyes, "Ready to go home?"

They had taken a few steps when a voice from behind them said, "Hold it! You are required to use a wheelchair until you get out of the hospital." Scott and Julie hesitated, turned around, and saw Nurse Berg pushing a wheelchair, rapidly converging on them. After Scott was seated, Julie pushed him to the front door, and he walked gingerly to Julie's pickup.

When they arrived at the Drums' they found David and Megan talking with Toni in the living room. Scott dropped onto the sofa and rested his left leg on the cushions. David had moved to give Scott room to spread out. Julie went into the kitchen to get dinner started.

Toni addressed Scott, "Megan's got a problem. We don't know what to tell her."

Scott saw the grim look on Megan's face and David's appearance of frustration. "What's this all about? Do you need a doctor?"

David grinned and answered, "No. It's nothing like that. Megan just found out Rick is coming home, confined to a wheel-chair, and she doesn't know how to tell him she doesn't want to be his girlfriend any longer."

Scott reacted by looking into the kitchen and calling, "Julie, I need your help."

Julie came rushing into the room asking, "Are you in pain?"

"No. I have a mental task that I can't handle."

"I don't think that's unusual." She walked over beside Scott and David got up to give her room to sit down. David sat on the floor beside Megan, and she started over from the beginning.

After a couple of minutes of explaining the situation, Megan said, "I don't want Rick to think I don't want to be with him any longer because of his injuries, but it's about having friends with other girls and boys, and being accepted by the students. When I was with Rick, I was abandoned and felt isolated—no friends at all, except David, of course." She rested her hand on his shoulder.

Julie raised one eyebrow, and said, "When will you see Rick?"

"Tomorrow. David's going with me. Mom has a bridge game she has to attend—it's part of a duplicate tournament."

Danny cleared his throat and said, "If we all go, we'd have them outnumbered."

Everyone laughed, and Julie commented, "Okay, Danny. Don't you have some schoolwork?"

"Yeah. But I want to hear the details." He stood up and Julie motioned for him to leave the room.

Julie announced, "I can go with you and David, Megan. Actually, I can meet you at Rick's. When do you want me there?"

Megan smiled, "Oh, thank you, Mrs. Drum. We were going out to see Rick at three o'clock."

"I have some work near there tomorrow, so I'll see you at three o'clock. Megan, would you like to stay for dinner?"

Megan didn't hesitate, "Sure, Mrs. Drum, thank you. I need to find out some more about my biological father. He's injured so he can't get away." She glanced at Scott, grinned, and everyone else laughed.

In the morning, Scott's strained leg had recovered, so he and Toni went to Harley's and rented an all-terrain vehicle, and traded the Cherokee for a pickup. After loading the ATV, they drove to the parking area near tower twenty where Kalber and Manietta had left their black pickup. Toni took the wheel and Scott strapped himself in tightly to prevent too much chest pain, and they began crossing through the timber and streams to tower twenty. Toni drove deliberately, so slowly that Scott at times thought he could move faster if he were walking, be he was thankful Toni was considering his chest injury.

When they arrived at the tower, they found Kalber and Manietta's ATV parked about ten feet from the tower's stairway.

Scott called out, "Kalber, you up there?" The agents listened, but there was no response.

"I'm going up. Cover me." Toni started up the first of four stairways. When she arrived on the top deck, she cautiously approached the cabin door and looked in. Kalber and Manietta weren't there. "Scott! Nobody's home! Come on up."

When Scott entered the cabin, Toni held out a piece of paper, stepped out into the sun and looked at the impressions. "I need a pencil, Scott." She found a pen on the kitchen counter and a pencil in the silver-ware drawer.

Scott circled the cabin on the deck, but saw nothing of interest. He entered the cabin and saw two plates of food on the table, but it appeared that nothing had been eaten. The utensils were spotless. The two men had vanished.

Toni was shading the indentations in the paper and finally said, "The paper says help us in capital letters. What do you think it means? This is creepy, Scott. What do you think happened to them?"

Scott didn't answer immediately, but combed through all the men's belongings. It looked like they hadn't unpacked their things before something had happened. "Jesus, Toni, how are we going to explain this? Where the hell did those guys go?"

"Should we check around outside? We can each take an ATV and motor around the area—see if we can find anything." Toni stood there shaking her head. "I don't believe there's anything in the manual for handling a disappearance like this."

"Okay, let's drive around for thirty minutes. See if we can spot anything. Keep your weapon handy."

Scott said, "All right, I'll go east and north, you go west and south, but don't be gone for more than a half-hour. I don't want to search for you."

They roared off in opposite directions and returned as planned. Nothing was found so they left a message that they would be back in twenty-four hours to see if the men had returned. They left Kalber and Manietta's ATV at the tower, and drove their rented ATV back to the pickup that had been rented a couple of hours earlier.

The agents stopped at the police station and informed Sheriff Howell what they had found at tower twenty.

Sheriff Howell commented, "That doesn't surprise me. Some strange things have been reported out there in the past. Some people have blamed it on Bigfoot, and others on voodoo. I don't go out there unarmed or alone; Deputy Doureline will tell you that. He gets the willies every time someone mentions Shadow Valley."

Scott grinned, "You actually believe that stuff, sheriff?"

"Well, if you two are going out there again tomorrow, I'll go with you, otherwise, I'll be busy here in town." He nodded, "Three of us will have enough firepower to knock anything down. I'll be takin' my rifle."

"We'll pick you up at nine o'clock. This afternoon, we're going to take the chopper out there and look around. If we don't find them today or tomorrow, we'll call off the search, and report them missing."

Sheriff Howell said, "Keep me informed."

When Megan and David finished classes, they drove to the Hadleys' in Mr. Isaac's jeep, and they parked next to a large van about ten yards from the Hadleys' residence. They had arrived about fifteen seconds ahead of David's mother at 3:10 p.m. The young people were getting out of the jeep when Julie drove up in her pickup.

"Have you been waiting long?" she asked.

David replied, "Hi, Mom. Nope. We just got here."

They rang the doorbell and were met at the entrance by Vivian Hadley. "Oh, come in, Julie. I'm happy you brought Megan and David to come visit with Rick. He's outside in the fresh air—out in back." The visitors followed Mrs. Hadley through the living room, dining room, and out through French doors onto a large covered patio.

Megan was first through the open French doors and saw Rick in a wheel chair sitting at a card table next to another wheel chair at right angles to him, occupied by a pretty girl with long blonde hair. They were playing cribbage. Megan moved next to Rick and grabbed his left hand. "Rick, it's so good to see you," she exclaimed.

Rick looked up and said, "Hello, Megan. I'd like you to meet my girlfriend, Donna Givens. We're convalescing together." He smiled and Donna said, "It's nice to meet you, Megan. Rick has told me all about you."

David sensed the awkward moment and moved beside Megan and grabbed her hand.

He looked at Donna and said, "I'm David Drum. Megan and I are best friends—we're next-door neighbors. This is my mom, Julie, she's a forest ranger."

Megan smiled and added, "Yes, David and I are going to the prom together. How did you and Rick meet, Donna?"

"I was riding on a motorcycle with a boy on the way to a horse show and we were hit by a truck. Broke both legs—similar to Rick's accident. We came out of anesthesia about the same time, and the nurses told us we were both talking kinda goofy. The nurses thought we were boyfriend and girlfriend so they put us in the same recovery room. We got to know each other and fell in love." Rick and Donna were holding hands as she told about her accident.

Megan said, "What happened to the boy you were riding with?"

"He was thrown clear and only had a couple of bruises. He didn't even come to see me at the hospital, the louse."

Julie stepped forward and said, "It sounds like you are both healing well. Best of luck to you."

"Thank you for coming by, Mrs. Drum, and for bringing Megan and David. It's nice to see kids from school again." Rick looked a David and said, "Take care of Megan, David. She's a special girl."

"I know, Rick. Good luck with your rehab. Hope you both have a full and speedy recovery."

"Thanks. I'll miss graduation exercises, but I'll come by in the fall and watch football practice. We should be able to walk by then."

As they left the Hadleys' residence, Julie commented, "That was a real surprise—something I couldn't have anticipated. How do you feel, Megan?"

"Relieved, Mrs. D. I didn't have to tell him I was dumping him. I didn't know how I was going to do that. But the accident hasn't changed him much. I just hope Donna knows what she's in for."

David observed, "Maybe things will work out for them; they've got months to figure out directions for the future."

"That's another thing I like about you, David—your optimism." Megan clasped David's hand, led him to the jeep, and with her hip, bumped him into the driver's seat. "Let's go home!"

As they pulled into the Isaacs' driveway, David asked, "What are you going to wear to the prom?"

"Will you really go with me? I'm sorry I volunteered you like that without asking."

"Megan, I was going to ask you anyway. You'll be the prettiest girl there. All the guys are going to be jealous. I'm going to have to practice some dancing with Mom; she knows how to waltz."

"I can do that, David, besides, hardly anyone waltzes anymore—everyone just freestyles."

"Well, I don't want to embarrass you, Meg."

Megan started giggling, "You can't embarrass me, David—never!" She grabbed his head with both hands, pulled him down to her level, and gave him a kiss that wasn't just a peck on the lips.

CHAPTER 37

While David and Megan were visiting with Rick and Donna, Scott and Toni were warming up Delilah, readying for their aerial view of the Shadow Valley tower area. Scott thought Spectrum would be able to detect motion near the trees much more efficiently than the agents could, so the dog took his usual position, the co-pilot's seat, forcing Toni to sit in back.

Scott flew 200 feet above the trees and started a spiral path a half-mile from the tower.

Scott said, "People, Spectrum," and the dog gave his full attention to watching for movement among the trees below, occasionally glancing at Scott for a second or two before resuming his tenacious watch for motion.

After ten minutes of circling the tower, Toni said, "We can't see much from here, Scott. We've got to be on the ground."

"Yeah, I agree. Let's stop the air search and return with Sheriff Howell in the morning." He discontinued Delilah's circular motion and pointed the chopper toward Suddenly. When back at the Drums', the agents played Frisbee with Suzy and Spectrum in the back yard until David and Megan pulled into the Isaacs' driveway. Megan went in the house, changed to jeans and a sweatshirt, and joined the agents and David at the outdoor table on the Drums' patio.

Megan asked, "Did you find those men you were looking for?"

Scott replied, "Not yet. We're going out there again tomorrow, with the sheriff, and search the grounds. I think we'll take the dogs—Spectrum's a good tracker."

David said, "What about the other one—ah, Suzy?"

Scott thought for a moment before he answered, "We'll take her, too, and find out if she can help us track those guys. I initially thought we'd leave her in the truck, but I've changed my mind. Her nose might be as good as or better than Spectrum's."

Toni's curiosity compelled her to ask Megan, "How did your meeting with Rick go?"

Megan's face lit up in a big grin, "Really great. Rick has a new girlfriend—a cute blonde in a wheelchair. I didn't have to say much of anything. Oh! I told Rick that David and I were going to the prom together, but he didn't seem to care in the least. I spent all those hours worrying about what he would think about me breaking up with him—what a waste of time."

"I've found out over the years, what others think is really not very important in the long run," Toni voiced her opinion as she glanced at Scott.

Scott remarked, "In general, I agree with Toni, but there are certain instances in life when another's opinion is very important, as with love, marriage, and family."

David grinned and said, "I can think of two others; the high school principal and the coach."

"Megan!"

"That's my mom, I've got to go." She slid out of the bench seat and said, "See you tomorrow, David." She waved as she went through the gate to her patio, and yelled back, "Bye, FBI!"

Scott got up and said, "I'd better feed the dogs, they're going to need energy tomorrow."

Julie called out, "Scott, can you help me?"

He looked at Toni and she said, "Oh, all right, I'll feed the dogs. You see what Julie wants."

David followed Toni into the garage saying, "I need to know how much food to give them."

Scott entered the house through the slider and found Julie sitting on the sofa with her hands folded in her lap. He sat beside her, put his hands over hers and said, "Are you all right?"

When he focused on her face, he saw tears running down her cheeks. "What's the matter, Julie?"

Julie leaned into Scott's shoulder, but didn't answer. She began to sob.

"Have you hurt your leg again?"

She wiped the tears from her right cheek with her hand and shook her head.

"Please tell me what's wrong. I want to help."

She straightened up, wiped her eyes, and said, "Do you love me?"

He put both arms around Julie and pulled her close. "I fell in love with you the first time I saw you—that night at the Isaacs' barbeque when Bruce brought me home with him. I hoped you would like me. I think about you all the time—that's one of the reasons I want to leave the FBI and become a ranger—so I can be near you—even if you don't love me."

"I love you, Scott, and so do the boys. We can be a family—the boys need the influence of a man in their lives. Do you want to have some more children?"

Scott hesitated after he heard the words more children, but then he realized Julie was thinking about Megan. "I would love to have children with you, Julie. Will you marry me? I didn't know when to ask the question, but it seems like this is a good time."

"Yes." She looked at his lips and they kissed, and after a few seconds, they heard, "Hey, what's going on in here? Mr. Wilson, you're making out with my mother."

Danny appeared from the kitchen and said, "Do we have to change our name to Wilson?"

Scott and Julie began to laugh, and Scott said, "Only if you want to, boys. I can adopt you."

Danny said, "Nah, I think I'll keep Drum, it's shorter."

Julie stood up saying, "Danny, you are a funny young man. What shall we have for dinner?"

The only thing Scott had remaining to do in Suddenly, before flying to Spokane and turning in his final report before resigning from the agency, was to meet with Sheriff Howell and look for Kalber and Manietta at tower twenty. Toni and Scott loaded the dogs into the pickup and drove to Sheriff Howell's office at eight-thirty the next morning.

The sheriff and Deputy Doureline were waiting beside the deputy's pickup, which had an ATV loaded in back. The two policemen were armed with their handguns, a rifle, and a shotgun.

Each man was drinking coffee.

Scott leaned out the window and said, "Where are the doughnuts, Sheriff Howell?"

"I took your advice, agent—I've got to lose about eighty pounds, or buy bigger under ware."

Scott smiled and said, "Good for you. You want to follow us, or take the lead?"

"You agents go on ahead, we'll be right along."

Scott and Toni were unloading their ATV when the sheriff drove up and parked beside the rented truck. Spectrum and Suzy were watching from the cab windows and were beginning to whine; they wanted out. Scott asked Toni to ride in back with Suzy, and he would drive with Spectrum beside him in front. However, when he let the dogs out of the pickup, they didn't know Scott's plan, and they took off running toward the tower. Toni unbuckled, got in the front seat and said, "Let's try to follow the dogs; maybe they'll find our boys."

Sheriff Howell yelled over the noise from the engines, "Lead the way, we'll cover your ass."

Scott headed down the bank to the first stream and crossed quickly, stirring up the sediment below the slowly moving water. Toni looked back to see the other ATV following in their tracks. It took about ten minutes for the vehicles to reach the tower. Scott was taken by surprise when he glanced up and saw both dogs on the top deck looking down at him and Toni. Spectrum barked and moved out of sight.

Toni unbuckled, stepped out of the ATV, drew her pistol, and started up the steps with Scott about six steps behind. He felt a twinge of pain as he began ascending the third of the four flights of stairs, so he slowed his pace. "Be careful up there, Toni! My leg's acting up."

When he reached the bottom of the fourth flight, Scott looked down and saw the lawmen standing with their guns ready. He started up the last flight and met Toni coming down with the dogs.

"Nothing's changed—same as yesterday. I gave the dogs the scent of the men from their bed sheets. We'll follow the hounds."

The dogs descended the stairs rapidly and took off across the clearing and into the forest. The sheriff and deputy had started after the dogs, but were taking their time. Scott and Toni caught up to them as they entered into the trees.

They had walked about twenty yards into the timber and the undergrowth was getting denser and more difficult to negotiate. Scott stopped, whistled for Spectrum, and held his position so the other lawmen could catch up. Neither dog returned, but the lawmen heard barking. Scott said, "I'm pretty sure that's Spectrum," and he pointed in the direction of the bark.

Toni had veered off to Scott's left and they had lost sight of each other. She called out, "It's easier going over here, gentlemen. Looks like someone's been through here before." The men joined her and continued on in the direction of the bark. They had travelled about fifty yards, climbed over some downed trees, and snagged their clothes on wild berry shrubs before reaching the dogs.

Suzy had dug a groove in the dirt beneath a small noble fir, but was sitting beside the hole and whining when the law officers arrived. Spectrum was lying on the ground beside her and barked when he saw Scott.

"Looks like your dogs have found something, agent." Sheriff Howell picked up part of a dead branch and handed it to the deputy. "See if you can deepen that hole the dogs have started."

Deputy Doureline dropped to his knees and began widening and deepening the furrow Suzy had created. The others watched for nearly a minute before the deputy was a little winded. He stopped digging and said, "There's some clothing—think it's a shirt sleeve." He moved some loose soil away with his gloved hands and said, "Yup. It's attached to an arm. I'll go after a shovel sheriff. We need some diggin' tools."

"I'll go with you, deputy, there's a fold-up shovel in our ATV," said Toni.

Scott added, "See if you can get the vehicles closer. We're going to have two bodies to haul back to the trucks." He looked at Toni and said, "Oh, yeah, better bring some sheets or blankets from the tower."

Toni waved, turned away, and followed the deputy back toward the tower.

Sheriff Howell stood over the hole, looking down at the exposed arm, and said, "I wonder how many more corpses are buried out here." He shook his head and said, "I guess we'll never know."

Scott asked, "Have there been any killings around here before?"

"Not that I can recall, and I've lived here all my life—maybe before the last century. If you're curious, the basement of the library has some old records from the eighteen hundreds. I think the newspaper back then was called *The Suddenly Journal*."

Scott and Sheriff Howell talked for nearly thirty minutes before they heard the engines of the ATVs in the distance then growing louder as the vehicles drew nearer. Spectrum sat up and cocked his head and came over to Scott. Scott reached down and scratched the dog between the ears and said, "It's all right—that's Toni coming back."

It took about twenty minutes to uncover the two bodies, wrap them in sheets and blankets and load them in back of the ATVs. Toni and the sheriff examined the bodies and found each man had been shot in the chest and the back of the head. The bullets had not passed through the bodies, so Doctor Lindsey, the coroner, would recover them for study. Sheriff Howell would send them to the state forensic laboratory.

Deputy Doureline filled in the holes, tamped the earth down, and said, "Let's get out of here. Just thinking about this place makes me jittery."

Sheriff Howell checked the seat belt and ropes on the body in back of his ATV, climbed into the driver's seat, and said, "Get in, Deputy, let's get back to town and give Doc Lindsey something to work on."

Scott made sure the body wrapped in a sheet and blanket was secure and said, "I'm driving, Toni. We don't want to lose a corpse on the way back." Toni stuck her tongue out at Scott, tossed him the key, picked up Suzy, and got into the ATV's passenger seat. Spectrum climbed in and lay down at her feet.

The ride back to the tower and then to the pickup was uneventful and too noisy to carry on a conversation, but Scott didn't want to talk, he was planning his trip to Spokane to turn in his resignation to Del Adams and buy a car. He wasn't relishing the paperwork that he would have to turn in concerning the Suddenly, Montana kidnapping case.

After the four law officers transferred the bodies to the morgue, they met at Joe's Diner for lunch. Scott picked up the tab and the agents said goodbye to the sheriff and his deputy, then they returned the ATV and pickup to Harley's. While they walked back to the Drums' apartment with the dogs Toni asked, "Are you going to marry Julie?"

"Think I should?" He wanted to grin and laugh, but he kept a poker face.

"You'd be crazy if you don't. She's in love with you, big time. And her boys would love to have you as their dad. I heard them talking—they want you to stay."

"Well, Toni, I've already asked her, and we're getting married as soon as I get out of ranger school."

"You snot! If you hadn't planned to get married, I have pressed charges against you."

"What kind of charges?"

Toni laughed, "The worst kind for you, stupidity!"

The next morning after the boys had left for school with Megan, Julie gave Toni and Scott a ride to Delilah after agreeing to take care of the dogs until Scott returned in two weeks.

The agents had cleaned the apartment thoroughly and packed all their belongings the night before. Julie watched from her pickup as the agents put their things in the chopper. Toni got in Delilah and Scott climbed in and started the engine.

Julie's eyes began to water—she hated goodbyes. She had said goodbye to her husband over four years ago and he never returned.

Scott got out of Delilah and ran over to the pickup and said, "I love you Julie, but I'm not saying goodbye—I'll be back in two weeks—in a car." He grabbed her in a bear hug, kissed her, and ran back to Delilah.

Julie watched as the chopper took off and headed west. She cried all the way home.